FRED SABERHAGEN

A MATTER OF TASTE

TOR
fantasy

A TOM DOHERTY ASSOCIATES BOOK
NEW YORK

A MATTER OF TASTE

Copyright © 1990 by Fred Saberhagen

A Tor Book
Published by Tom Doherty Associates, Inc.
49 West 24th Street
New York, N.Y. 10010

Tor® is a registered trademark of Tom Doherty Associates, Inc.

Cover art by Jim Thiesen

ISBN: 0-812-52575-2

First edition: July 1990
First mass market printing: January 1992

Printed in the United States of America

0 9 8 7 6 5 4 3 2 1

"I will not die — " I told him, choking on my fury, and my own blood, and could not find the breath to say the rest.

"Oh, no?" The swordpoint feinted even closer to my eyes, then moved a small handsbreadth away. "Not yet you won't, good Prince Drakulya. Not this moment. But soon. Very soon."

I understood that Bogdan had spared my sight because he wished me to continue to see what was happening. Perhaps he craved also to see in my eyes at last some expression of yielding, of despair, at least of fear. In that hope, at least, he continued to be disappointed.

In the next moment I could feel the cold steel of Bogdan's blade slide inside my left cheek, the sensation transforming itself into the heat of fresh pain as the blade ripped its way out.

"What words of defiance now, Drakulya?"

Tor books by Fred Saberhagen

THE BERSERKER SERIES
 The Berserker Wars
 Berserker Base (with Poul Anderson, Ed Bryant,
   Stephen Donaldson, Larry Niven, Connie Willis,
   and Roger Zelazny)
 Berserker: Blue Death
 The Berserker Throne
 Berserker's Planet
 Berserker Lies
 Berserker Man

THE DRACULA SERIES
 The Dracula Tapes
 The Holmes-Dracula Files
 An Old Friend of the Family
 Thorn
 Dominion
 A Matter of Taste

THE SWORDS SERIES
 The First Book of Swords
 The Second Book of Swords
 The Third Book of Swords
 The First Book of Lost Swords: Woundhealer's Story
 The Second Book of Lost Swords: Sightblinder's Story
 The Third Book of Lost Swords: Stonecutter's Story
 The Fourth Book of Lost Swords: Farslayer's Story
 The Fifth Book of Lost Swords: Coinspinner's Story
 The Sixth Book of Lost Swords: Mindsword's Story

OTHER BOOKS
 A Century of Progress
 Coils (with Roger Zelazny)
 Earth Descended
 The Mask of the Sun
 A Question of Time
 Specimens
 The Veils of Azlaroc
 The Water of Thought

1

Angie Hoban found Valentine Kaiser waiting for her just where he had said he would be, occupying the end booth in a busy street-level coffee shop just off Michigan Avenue, a little south of the Water Tower. From outside she could see through the window that he was watching the entrance, and as soon as she came in through the revolving door he got to his feet, smiling. Tall, youthful, and actually one of the handsomest men she had ever seen. He was pulling a business card out of his vest pocket now, and as soon as she came within reach he handed it to her.

A flashy printing job, she noticed, red on yellow. The message was simple enough:

Valentine Kaiser
Celebrity Publicist

At the bottom were two phone numbers with different area codes, both of them somewhere in California, if Angie could trust her memory on such matters; she'd visited the West Coast a couple of times. There wasn't any address on the card; the implication seemed to be that Valentine Kaiser moved fast, so did his business, and if you had to mail him a message or travel to his office, you weren't going to reach him in time anyway.

She dropped the card into her purse, thinking that she could always throw it away later.

"And you're Angelina Hoban. Even prettier than you sounded on the phone." He spoke in a low voice, as if musing to himself, and didn't wait for her reaction; any way she wanted to take it was quite all right with him.

In another moment she was sitting opposite him in the booth, and ordering coffee. In front of her companion stood another cup, almost untouched, or perhaps it had been diligently refilled by the hurrying waitress. Outside the plate-glass windows, faintly steamy with October chill, Chicagoans were hurrying past as Chicagoans generally did. Inside the coffee shop things were comparatively slack, the weekday lunch-hour rush having abated hours ago.

"So, what's this all about, Mr. Kaiser? You said something about a talk being to our mutual advantage?"

"Call me Val," the man across the table said, smiling. Then he paused, as if he were trying to plan his answer carefully. His behavior in the flesh reinforced an impression she'd formed during their brief phone conversation. Certainly this was not a man who'd try to drown her in a gush of salesman's or press agent's babble. The sincere type. Angie suspected that he was some kind of salesman, though, and that he could be very convincing if he did lie. The scar of some old injury, or blemish, spread over a large part of his right cheek, but too faintly to destroy his looks. Dark, Mediterranean type, though not tanned—she'd heard somewhere that tan had been out for a couple of years now among Hollywood people, among celebrities in general, she supposed. And what exactly did a Celebrity Publicist do?

Sizable shoulders, and a lean waist under the vest of his three-piece, blue-gray suit. Most likely a college athlete somewhere, only a few years ago, and still in very good condition. Red tie, white shirt, all in all a sharp dresser, though a little more conservative than she would have expected from California, which she sometimes tended to identify with Hollywood.

"I understand," said Kaiser, evidently having completed his mental preparations, "that you're going to have the pleasure of paying a visit to Mr. Matthew Maule this evening."

"Who told you about that?"

"And, you may well ask, what business is it of mine? You're quite right, I can't argue." Valentine Kaiser smiled engagingly, displaying excellent teeth, probably not capped. "I'd love to tell you who told me, but the fact is I promised I wouldn't, and I keep my promises. I do happen to know you're engaged to John Southerland—right? And the Southerland family, as you know, has a connection with Mr. Maule. And—let me just put it this way—certain members of the family would like to see that Mr. Maule finally gets credit for a lot of the great things he's done over the years."

"Gets credit?"

The self-proclaimed publicist spread his hands. "There's the hospital for burn victims he endowed in California—I could show you pictures. There's the Retired Stage and Screen Actors' Fund; there's—well, I could go on all day. The thing is, I'd like to be able to get in to interview him." Having revealed that much, Valentine Kaiser shut up suddenly, as if reminding himself not to babble like a salesman.

As if, thought Angie, he were trying to mold himself into a brash extrovert, but it didn't come naturally to him. She felt a growing sympathy. "So you want to—write an article about him?"

"That's about it. Yes." Kaiser looked relieved.

3

Still an element of suspicion persisted. "If you want to interview this man, have you tried just asking?"

"Angelina—what do your friends call you? Angie? Angie, if it was only that easy." The man sitting across from her shook his head. "A lot of people have tried just asking Mr. Matthew Maule, over the years. Let me tell you right up front why I invited you to have a talk with me. What I really hope to have you do is, eventually, put in a word for me so I can get an interview."

"Wait a minute, wait a minute. I don't even know him."

"But you're going to know him. Right? All I say now is *if*, having met me, and having met Mr. Maule and talked to him, you think you can put in a word for me with a clear conscience. See, we think this man deserves to get his proper recognition."

Angie's coffee had arrived. She added a little nondairy creamer, picked up the heavy cup, and sipped at it absently. Not as bad as you got in a lot of these places.

She was intrigued by the man across from her, but had the feeling that she wasn't close to understanding him. She said: "You know . . . some people might say you have a hell of a lot of nerve."

"I know." Kaiser let his gaze slide over her shoulder. His forehead wrinkled as if the mild accusation pained him. It was hard to tell how much, if any, of the pain was real. "People do say that, all the time. It's one of the hazards of my business, and so far I've managed to live through it." Then suddenly he looked directly at her, grinning. He had an engaging grin.

Angie found herself hesitating between annoyance and laughter. "I tell you, I don't even know the man, this Mr. Maule," she said at last. "How in the world am I supposed to persuade him to give you an interview? Assuming that I wanted to?"

Her companion nodded thoughtfully. He raised his cup to his lips—she noticed now that he was wearing a golden wedding ring on one strong finger—then put it down as if struck by a sudden idea. "If you don't want to risk offending the reclusive Mr. Maule by helping me boost his reputation—then how about just helping me defend it, for a start? You won't have to ask him anything."

"Excuse me?"

Kaiser shook his head and put on the expression of one forced to contemplate something distasteful. "There are a few rumors about him—I don't believe them for a moment. And I wouldn't pass these stories on to anyone I didn't know was going to be his friend. They're ugly things, and I'm not going to repeat them in full even to you. But there's one in particular—it has to do with the way his condo here in Chicago is said to be decorated. Outrageous, sexist, obscene—you get me, I'm not talking about art here. I'm talking exploitation."

"I'm sorry, I don't—"

"I'm not talking artistic nudes. I mean really exploitive pictures of women. Bondage and sadism. Photographs and paintings, even murals painted right on the walls. Let me repeat, I don't believe the truth of such a thing for a minute. But if I can't get in to see the place, how can I deny it authoritatively?"

"Mr. Kaiser, I hope you don't think I'm going to try to sneak you in there. To snoop around his paintings and pictures, I suppose you'd want to take photographs too. Whatever your good intentions. As I keep telling you, I've never even met the man myself, I—"

"Sure, sure." Her companion's tone was soothing, and

he made sideways brushing motions with his large, capable-looking hands. "No, no, I'm not trying to push you into doing anything like that." The way Kaiser made it sound now, that he might talk Angie into sneaking or smuggling him in must have been really the furthest idea from his thoughts. "But let me say this. If you, after having actually been in the apartment, would consent to talk with me once more, very briefly, just to verify that these terrible rumors are all so much crap, excuse me, I'd be very pleased. See, believe it or not, I am very conscientious about what I do. And to kill these rumors I'd like to have the direct testimony of a reliable witness. I'll never quote you directly without your permission, I'll never use your name."

Later, Angie was to wonder what might have happened if she had simply got up at that point, or some point earlier, and walked out. But it didn't matter, because that was not what she did.

She did slide out of the booth and stand up, but she wasn't angry. There was something almost irresistibly attractive about the man, and his story sounded just wild enough to have the possibility of truth.

"You already have my phone number at work, Mr. Kaiser," she said. "However you got it. If you want to call me again, in a few days, I'll tell you then whether I want to talk to you again or not. If my answer is no, then I expect you not to—"

"Great. Excellent." It seemed that the young man was genuinely pleased. He stood up gracefully now to shake her hand. "That's all that I can ask of you now. And when you get into that apartment, just look around. Keep your eyes and your mind open. That's all I ask."

Angie spent most of the next two hours at the Museum of Contemporary Art, which was only a few blocks from the coffee shop, over on Ontario east of Michigan. On her way over to the museum, where she was to meet John Southerland, she several times slowed her walking pace to look up thoughtfully at the gigantic multi-use building in which John's mysterious Uncle Matthew lived—where he maintained a condominium, at least, and spent some of his time. Immensely tall, formed gracefully of bronzed steel and glass, it stood among its twenty-, thirty-, forty-story neighbors like an adult among small children. The Southerlands had plenty of money, and evidently this kinsman, old friend, or whatever he was, did too.

She wondered which of the Southerlands, if any, had really called in a Celebrity Publicist and had given him her phone number at the hospital. John's mother, most likely, if anyone . . . well, she, Angie, wasn't going to say anything about Valentine Kaiser to John just yet. It wouldn't hurt just to wait until she'd seen what Uncle Matthew's apartment really looked like.

She was in the museum, in front of an Andy Warhol, wondering if there might be some deep meaning that she was missing, when her fiancé caught up with her. John was twenty-seven, four or five years older than Angie. They'd met several months ago, at a party, a fundraising kind of thing really, given by some of John's friends. Angie had been present as an administrator, attractive and knowledgeable, if somewhat junior, of St. Thomas More's, the hospital which stood to collect most of the raised funds.

John was a little under six feet, half a foot taller than Angie, strong-jawed, and sturdy, as befitted a former amateur wrestler who'd once made it to the state finals. His light brown hair, cut fairly short, still retained a tendency to curl.

They kissed. The embrace was a bit on the casual side,

appropriate for a couple who'd already been sharing an apartment and a bedroom for a month. He asked her: "How was your day?"

"Interesting, so far." She didn't tell the most interesting part, not yet, but mentioned a couple of incidents having to do with her job. "I'm looking forward to the evening."

John grunted something. It was not precisely an agreement.

Twice, as they walked back toward the looming tower that housed Maule's condominium, it was on the tip of Angie's tongue to tell her fiancé about her encounter with Valentine Kaiser. But each time she bit the impulse back. Later, of course, she'd tell him—and tell Uncle Matthew, too, most likely. Most likely the three of them would have a good laugh about it. That is, they would provided that Uncle Matthew didn't turn out really to be the kind to put up photographs of—but of course he wouldn't. No one who Johnny felt so close to could turn out to be like that. And in any case, Angie wanted to handle the matter of Valentine Kaiser herself, not simply turn him over to the menfolk.

"So," she said instead. "Uncle Matthew is taking us out to dinner?"

"Yeah." John, walking beside her, sounded preoccupied, almost as if he might be developing belated doubts about the evening's plan. "He's not actually my uncle, you know," he added, almost absently.

"Yes, I know that." Angie felt vaguely troubled. "Because you've told me about half a dozen times over the past month."

"I have?"

"Yes. Every time you say he's not really your uncle, and then you get stuck, as if you don't know how to continue. So what is it about Uncle Matthew? Obviously he's important to you, if you're bringing me to meet him."

"Well, he is," said John, and then appeared to get stuck again.

"Do you want to invite him to our wedding?" It was the first time she'd raised the point.

"I do," he said at once, then waffled. "But there's some question . . ."

"Yes, there seems to be. He's some old friend of your father's?"

"Well. Actually, no, he isn't. Dad's met him, but he doesn't even . . . he's an old friend of the family." John seemed pleased at having found that way to express it. "He was a good friend of my grandmother, who died during that episode when I was kidnapped. When I was sixteen."

So then, thought Angie, we are making progress. Non-Uncle Matthew must be quite elderly. She was growing increasingly curious about, and anxious to meet, this man who was not quite an uncle, who had known John's family for many years, but whom nobody in John's family liked to talk to her about, even when it was certain that she and John were getting married.

Matthew Maule. And now, not for the first time, she had the feeling that somewhere, before ever meeting John, she had heard that name, or read it . . . that could easily have happened, she supposed, in the case of a man of wealth and power, no matter how reclusive he tried to be.

The building in which the mystery lived admitted Angie and John somewhat awkwardly at street level. Feet thumping on a temporary wooden sidewalk, they skirted the barricades of a construction area before arriving in a small retail mall of shops. Next came a busy lobby. Presently the two of them were alone in one of the express elevators, beginning a long ascent.

John suddenly raised his hands, drawing her attention to them. On the night they had first met, Angie—feeling then, at the discovery, more than pity, a vague thrill of mystery and romance—had realized that both of John's little fingers were missing. His hands had only three fingers and a thumb apiece, almost as if they might belong to some character in an animated cartoon, where economy in the number of digits to be drawn was of some importance. But it was obvious as soon as you looked closely at John's hands that he hadn't been born that way; dots of old scar tissue, the tidy residue of surgical repair following some much cruder damage, marked each knuckle where a finger should have been.

"I've already told you something about how I lost the fingers," John said, with the air of someone about to take a plunge.

"About how you were kidnapped when you were sixteen. Yes, that must have been so horrible. My poor darling! I was too young then to pay much attention to stories in the news." And since they were alone, Angie reached for his hands, one after the other, and impulsively kissed the scarred knuckles.

John murmured something that was almost a groan. Further exchanges of affection followed, until the young man with an air of urgency disengaged himself. They were passing the sixtieth floor now, and going up faster, feeling the change of pressure in their ears. There was not much time left to talk in privacy.

John said: "I've been putting off trying to explain something. About Uncle Matthew."

"Really? Don't tell me! He's not really your uncle?" Angelina, wide-eyed, was nodding as if in an exaggerated effort to give encouragement.

"You're not making it any easier."

"All right, I'm sorry, darling." She felt contrite. There must be some genuine difficulty. "Start again. Could it be—something about the way he decorates his apartment, maybe?"

"Decorates his apartment?" John was looking at her vacantly. "I don't have any idea what that means. I've never been up here before."

"Oh. *I'm* sorry. Never mind, go on."

John drew a deep breath. "Well, as I was trying to say, one thing you don't know yet, Angie, is that if it weren't for this man you're going to meet, the rest of me would doubtless be in about the same shape as my two missing fingers." He raised his hands again, wriggling the eight digits he still possessed. "I mean I wouldn't be here now."

This was unexpected news; but it did sound vaguely as if it might connect with the image of the eccentric philanthropist. Angie said: "No, you didn't tell me anything like that."

"Now that I've told you, forget I've told you. I mean, it stays within the family, okay?"

"You mean within the small segment of the family in front of whom it's safe to mention Uncle Matthew's name."

"Ah . . . yeah."

She gazed at him hopefully. "Okay. But surely there's nothing shameful about his having somehow saved your life. Why should it be a secret?"

"Nothing shameful. No. Just don't mention this man to my father, okay? Judy is okay to talk to, and Kate and Joe." John leaned back against the elevator wall with his arms folded. The numbers on the floor indicator over the door kept creeping higher.

Suddenly John had a new idea. "By the way, if he doesn't want to eat or drink anything at dinner tonight, don't pester him about it, okay? Often he's on a—special diet."

"Sure." She paused. "John, are you under the impression that you've explained anything to me? Because I think I'm still right in there with your father. I mean, as fitting into the category of those who don't understand at all."

John stared past her, obviously nervous and trying to think. At last he said: "Maybe it'll be better if you meet him first."

"Maybe it will. Meet him and see his apartment."

"Sure," John agreed, looking puzzled, obviously wondering why she kept mentioning the apartment. And now Angie and the man she loved seemed to be on the verge of quarreling.

Angie liked John's two older sisters, Judy and Kate, though she had seen very little of Judy. And she liked Kate's husband, Joe, who used to be a Chicago cop, before he married into the Southerland money, and even for some time afterward. Was there perhaps a trend in the family to marry people who didn't have nearly as much money as they had?

They had passed the eightieth floor and now were slowing to a stop. The door opened. Angie, disembarking from the elevator, caught a glimpse out of a window at the end of a corridor, looking down now on most of the smog and muck of the city's atmosphere, with a startling panorama of Lake Michigan, shoreless as an ocean. She supposed that from up here on a very clear day the Michigan shore, fifty miles away, would be visible.

John found the door number he was looking for, and pressed the button, then without waiting for a response knocked lightly. His left hand came over and took hold of Angie's right, as they stood together in front of the viewer centered in the upper panel.

Fully thirty seconds had passed, and Angelina was about to wonder aloud whether they should ring again, when the door opened.

Whatever tentative, imaginative image of Uncle Matthew Angie had been beginning to form went glimmering. Surely a friend of John's late grandmother ought to be older than this. The man in the doorway was no more than forty at the outside. Lean, a few inches taller than John, putting him a shade over six feet. Straight black hair cut rather short, a chiseled face, high cheekbones, arresting eyes that at once fastened on her expectantly. Even as he opened the door he was still shrugging his solid shoulders into a gray-brown sportcoat.

"Good evening," he said in a low voice, still looking directly at Angie. There was a suggestion of some European accent in his voice, of formality in his manner despite relatively casual dress.

"Good evening," said John, and paused perceptibly, perhaps to swallow. "Uncle Matthew. This is Angelina. We're going to be married."

"Ah. Ah!" Uncle Matthew must have been expecting them, but still gave an impression of genuine surprise. No matter, he was pleased. "Come in, come in! And such a beautiful young woman. Congratulations are certainly in order!"

As soon as she had stepped across his threshold, he reached for both her hands. A moment later she was being embraced and kissed on both cheeks. John and Uncle Matthew were pumping each other's hands. And then she and the two men had all burst into a pleasant babble of phatic utterance, even as Uncle Matthew, with a city-dweller's routine caution, made sure that the door was closed and bolted behind his guests.

"Angelina, John, you must each have a drink to celebrate. But no, later perhaps, dinner reservations have been made on the ninety-fifth floor, and it would be good to be prompt."

There wasn't much time to look around the apartment. But, for the time being, enough. Angie noted with relief that of naked women, exploitive photographs, pornographic paintings, there was no sign, not at least from her vantage point near the entrance.

In fact, at first look, what she could see of the entry and the living room struck her as almost disappointingly ordinary, except for the unusual number of bookshelves, and a crossed pair of wooden spears, or harpoons, serving as wall decorations. She could heartily approve of bookshelves.

The furniture was unobtrusive, generally modern, with the notable exception of an upright piano. Living room, with a half bath off the entryway, small dining area, and a glimpse of what must be the kitchen beyond. Two closed doors were visible down a hallway, before it angled out of sight. Those must lead, Angie supposed, to bedrooms. Maybe the bedroom walls were covered with raunchy pictures, but somehow she doubted it. One thing that struck her as something of an oddity was the art. To judge from the modern furnishings, you might have expected to see contemporary art framed on these walls, but instead, along with the spears, hung mostly reproductions of Renaissance masters. My God, they *were* reproductions, weren't they? Skillful copies? Or might they be . . . but that was silly. These paintings, with the piano and all the books, gave the apartment a vaguely old-fashioned air despite the modern furniture.

In a matter of moments they were all three back out in the corridor, then striding, all arm in arm, toward the elevators again.

They reached the elevator lobby just as an upward-bound car opened its door to discharge a fortyish lady with an elaborate dark coiffure, smartly gowned for indoors, carrying a bag of groceries in one arm. She smiled and nodded to Uncle Matthew, and he returned the smile with a small gentlemanly bow. I bet, thought Angie, there are days when he has to beat them off with a stick.

"Neighbor of yours?" John asked, making conversation, once they were in the car and on their way up to the ninety-fifth floor.

"Yes . . . devoted to the residents' association, in which she persists in trying to interest me. Well meaning, I am sure." Uncle Matthew's expression conveyed a subtle irritation, which soon disappeared.

The ninety-fifth floor was occupied by one of the city's finer restaurants. As far as Angie could tell, no one among the staff recognized Uncle Matthew, but, in some way she could not quite put her finger on, he seemed to convey to them a sense of his status and importance.

Once they were seated, Uncle Matthew conversed cheerfully and urbanely on a variety of subjects. Skillfully he drew out his guests with questions on their work and on their pastimes.

Until Angie seized the opportunity offered by a pleasant pause and cleared her throat. "Look, Uncle Matthew—shall I call you that?"

"You certainly may."

"We'd like you to come to our wedding."

Their host glanced with faint amusement at John, who was awkwardly trying to find words with which to second the invitation. "Thank you, Angelina. But I fear there may be a problem about the date—?"

"Twenty-fifth of next month," John blurted out.

"Ah, almost a Thanksgiving wedding. Too bad, but I shall be unable to attend. So, the three of us must celebrate this evening—we ought to achieve a memorable celebration of some kind."

And soon the two young people were relaxed, eating and drinking heartily. Uncle Matthew, true to John's prediction, but still to Angie's concern, ate nothing and drank almost nothing. He pleaded the requirements of a special diet. "But do not concern yourself, my dear. Enjoy yourself, and I shall feast my eyes upon your beauty."

John reacted to that with a swallow. Angie, feeling Uncle Matthew's gaze, found herself wondering how she would have reacted had she not been recently engaged.

Somewhat to John's relief, the waitress who was serving their table soon began to replace Angie as the object of Uncle Matthew's admiration.

This waitress was a statuesque and impressive redhead, somewhere in her middle or later thirties, Angie estimated. It was obvious that something about this dark-haired, fortyish customer impressed and intrigued her. When he looked at her with interest, the woman was unable to keep her mind entirely on business.

Fortyish? Squinting at Uncle Matthew now, Angie decided she had better add a few years to the estimate of his age she had formed in his apartment. There was a touch of gray in his hair she really hadn't noticed before. Very distinguished.

During the lengthy intervals when the waitress was elsewhere, and Uncle Matthew's attention more or less fully available, Angie pressed him as subtly as she could for information.

"John tells me that you saved his life. I mean that time when he was kidnapped."

"Ah? And how much did he tell you? It must be a painful subject for him to talk about."

"He told me very little, unfortunately. Nothing more than the mere fact. I was hoping that you'd be willing to fill in some of the details."

Uncle Matthew was looking at John, who said uncomfortably: "Well, since Angie's going to be marrying me, well, I thought she ought to know, uh, all about family affairs."

"Apart from certain occasions—of which this evening is one of the more pleasant—I really have little connection with such affairs." Uncle Matthew's fingers, pale in slender muscularity, long-nailed, and somewhat hairy on the backs, toyed with his glass of almost untasted wine. There was a dinner plate before him too, but it had remained smooth and clean. He had unfolded his napkin, but that was about it.

John was stubborn. "I thought she ought to know," he repeated.

"That opinion certainly poses an interesting problem. She is not marrying me, John."

"You thought I ought to know what?" Angie demanded bluntly.

Infuriatingly, the two men continued to ignore her for the moment.

John was still hesitating. "Well . . ."

Uncle Matthew produced a winning smile, which he

could do better than almost anyone Angie had ever met before. He reached across the table and took a hand of each of his young guests. "Come, come, we must not allow such questions to interfere with our evening. My affairs can surely have no crucial bearing on your marriage."

John heaved a sigh, as if a weight had been removed. "I guess you're right."

"Of course I am. Depend upon it." Uncle Matthew patted both hands and released them.

"It's not that I want to push into your affairs, sir, believe me. Far from it. But well, dammit, you saved my life. And I'm not going to forget that. I want you to know that—well, that you're welcome to come to our wedding if you want." The young man raised his head with a look of determination, ready to confront his parents and anyone else who might object.

"Of course you are," Angie agreed warmly. She liked Non-Uncle Matthew, was coming to like him better and better as the evening progressed, and it was her wedding, and if that scandal-mongering liar Valentine Kaiser ever dared to call her again . . .

Uncle Matthew said nothing for a moment. His face hardly changed, but nevertheless Angie had the impression that he was moved.

The dinner moved along. Uncle Matthew entertained his guests with stories of extremely odd people he had known years ago when he had lived in Paris and in London. Unlike many fascinating speakers, he was a good listener too. When Angie ventured an anecdote or two of her own, he seemed genuinely interested in the problems of hospital administration.

The food and wine and coffee were superb, and in Angie's perception time passed with amazing speed. As they were leaving the restaurant Uncle Matthew took the opportunity to return to the table to leave a cash tip, and at the same time to manage a few quiet words alone with the red-haired waitress.

Angie, looking on from a distance, nudged her fiancé. "I wonder if something's developing there."

"I wouldn't be surprised." John's tone was dry.

Neither of them felt inclined to resist Uncle Matthew's invitation to stop in at his apartment for a nightcap.

Reentering the tastefully decorated condo a few floors down, Angie was on the point of starting to tell the two men about Valentine Kaiser. But at once she felt reluctant to mention the man and his ridiculous suspicions—or insinuations—for fear of spoiling the evening.

The party, having developed delightfully during dinner, continued in the same vein. The old piano was a natural conversation piece, and it proved to be in excellent condition when Angie picked out something on the keys.

"Do you play, my dear?"

"Very little. I should say, no, not really. I did have lessons once."

After he had served the drinks Uncle Matthew was not shy at all about sitting down at the piano, where he revealed an impressive talent. Within half an hour, Angie, a glass of amazingly good brandy in her hand, found herself singing what her host assured her were old Balkan folk songs, parroting from his instruction what he said were the words of the original language. John, not usually much of a singer, and somewhat flushed with brandy, was gamely joining in.

Time, in Angie's mind at least, was soon forgotten. Then her concentration on the music was interrupted by a savage slosh and rattle of sleet against the curtained windows, and the building could be felt swaying, minimally, in the wind. Their host, evidently a long-term resident, took no notice. Momentary uneasiness was quickly squelched by an obviously sincere invitation from Uncle Matthew, offering Angie and John one of his spare bedrooms in which to spend the night. During the dinner conversation, enough had been said to make it plain to him that they were already cohabiting.

They both accepted, with relief; and John was reminded of old times. "Remember the big snow we had, sir, about the time we had that—trouble?"

"Yes indeed. No storm like that tonight, fortunately, but plenty of freezing rain and icy streets." Thoughtfully he struck a chord, then began to pick out from memory yet another simple but lovely melody that Angie had never heard before. "Here is a song about winter. Hunters wandering in the snow."

John, his brandy glass in hand, had gone to the window and pulled back a curtain to peer out past its edge. "Yep, looks like rotten weather out there," he announced in the cheerful tone of a man who has already made his arrangements to stay in.

Angie yawned. Not so their host. Despite his years, he seemed to be getting only more wide-awake as the evening —actually for some time now it had been the morning— progressed.

Again she yawned, quite uncontrollably. The old man, she thought, perhaps subliminally noticing that he looked even a trifle older than at dinner, had probably slept till noon. But she'd had a tough day at work, and it was really getting late. And of course she'd been drinking, more than she ought, really, while he never seemed to drink at all.

"I hate to be the one to call it quits—but—" A

helpless yawn preempted the explanation Angie had been about to offer.

There were actually three bedrooms in the apartment, she noted while making her way down the angled hallway to the one her host had specified.

John had lagged behind in the living room, where he was still talking with his energetic non-uncle. Angie groped inside the doorway at the hallway's end; a bedside table lamp came on when she found the wall switch. The bedroom she and John had been assigned was as neatly furnished as the living room, with no signs of recent habitation. A couple of commonplace paintings were on the walls. Certainly the room contained no more sign of disgusting pornography than did the more accessible areas of the apartment. Valentine Kaiser! she thought with disgust. What had that man's real game been? Angie had a notion to tear up his business card and flush it away. No, she was certainly going to tell the men about him. Only—it would have to wait till morning. She wasn't in the best of shape for any serious discussion now.

On second thought—it might be important.

She was on her weary way back to rejoin the men in the living room when the door chime sounded melodiously. Who would that be, at this hour of the morning? Probably some sleepless neighbor with a complaint about their noise, though Uncle Matthew had told them earlier that the building's soundproofing was excellent.

As Angie reentered the living room, her host had just admitted someone from the hallway and was closing and bolting up the door. Angie needed a moment to recognize the waitress from the ninety-fifth floor, whose red hair was now bound up under a scarf, and who naturally had changed out of her uniform. While the newcomer stood looking a shade hesitant and awkward, Uncle Matthew helped her out of her cloth coat as if it had been a mink, and indicated with gracious gestures and murmurs that she ought to come in and make herself comfortable.

Introductions were soon made. John and Angie, one after the other, shook hands with Elizabeth Wiswell. Angie thought she caught the faintest whiff of garlic, barely detectable, from the other woman. Well, if you worked in a restaurant, she supposed, that must be one of the least worrisome of the occupational hazards.

Angie decided that it would be hard to imagine Matthew Maule failing, once he had made up his mind, to put a woman at her ease. Mentally putting herself in the other woman's place, she would have expected to feel a certain embarrassment in this situation. But any tendency Elizabeth might have started to display in that direction had evidently been already overcome. The fair skin of her face was lightly flushed and she was smiling.

"I don't know what's wrong with me," she remarked, giggling.

"Very little, I should think," Uncle Matthew, looking and sounding fresh as a daisy, reassured her. "Please, sit down. Would you care for a spot of brandy?"

John, looking terminally groggy, murmured something, something that was going to have to serve as his good night to the world at large. Now he was tugging gently at Angie's arm. Her head spinning faintly, she allowed herself to be guided back down the hall to their assigned bed and bath. John softly closed the bedroom door behind them.

Five minutes later, Angie was sitting up in the double bed, still wearing her bra and panties, listening to her lover brush his teeth behind the bathroom's half-open door—new toothbrushes in sealed wrappings, along with a few other toiletries, had been provided. And Angie had just made the irritating discovery that she was probably going to have trouble getting to sleep after all.

Not that Uncle Matthew and his new girlfriend out in the living room were noisy; even when Angie listened, she was unable to detect any sounds at all from that direction.

Just out of sight, John ran water in the bathroom sink, spat, rinsed, and spat again. At last he appeared, in his undershorts. He looked tired, but not quite ready to collapse instantly.

He cleared his throat. "Honey?"

"Yes?"

"There's a tape recorder over there." He gestured economically toward a table against the room's far wall.

Angie turned eyes too weary for curiosity in that direction. "Yep, there sure is. Inform me of its relevance."

"Uh, the point is, that Uncle Matthew was saying a while back, while you were out of the room, that the tape in the machine holds a kind of story that he's working on. He suggested that maybe, if you were to listen to the tape, it might answer some questions for you."

"A story. He's working on. Then he's some kind of a writer?"

"Yep. Among other things. At least he's collaborated on some books." John came over and bounced down on the bed, flat on his back. He closed his eyes and sighed. The bed was comfortable.

"Is the one he's working on auto-biograph-ical?" After all that brandy, Angie experienced a momentary pride in what she felt was flawless pronunciation.

"I dunno. I guess, if he thinks it's relevant. Not that you have to listen to it tonight—but if you feel like it in the morning—"

But she was already out of bed and approaching the

machine. Suddenly weariness could be fought off yet a little longer. The temptation to have some questions answered was irresistible.

When she located the proper switch and turned the tape player on, there was a moment of faint, hissing background noise, seeming to provoke a renewed rattle at the snugly sealed windows. And then she found herself listening to what was undeniably Uncle Matthew's voice.

2

And the damnable machine is running now. Recording properly, I trust. At last. The miracles of modern electronics.

(The sound of a deep breath.)

Let me begin the narration of this particular segment of my life upon the day of my assassination. That momentous event took place in early winter, toward the end of the year of Our Lord 1476. The scene was a cold and soggy battlefield not many miles from the city of Bucharest, an arena of snow and mud freshly littered with the bones of brave men—these being in the circumstances indistinguishable from those of some men not so brave.

Wet snow had fallen on that morning, and here and there across the trampled field the whiteness of new snow still persisted on the ground, shreds and untouched spots of purity amid a mire of horse manure, something like a warrior's virtue. The picture was enriched with mud and blood, and speckled with the blackness of crows, that old Corvinus symbol, who were attending in considerable numbers to see that good food was not wasted. Also contributing to the visual composition of the scene were the dun and silver of the scattered bodies of men and horses and their equipment—some of both species had been armored. Here and there the brightness of a fallen

25

banner caught the slowly declining light of a gray winter afternoon.

(Another deep breath, almost a sigh.)

To tell the story that concerns me here, I need describe neither the devices of those banners, nor the causes which they represented. Suffice it to say that the battle in which those men and banners fell had been an honest one, as battles go. It might not be strictly honest for me now to claim victory for the side that I commanded. But many of us had survived, and we had been left in possession of the field.

Against the treachery that followed, however, I was not so successful.

As the scene I intend to describe opens, the forces loyal to me—save for a handful of frightened camp followers, unwilling to do anything but watch—had already been drawn away, by deliberately falsified reports. And three traitorous officers, reinforced by a handful of men-at-arms they had suborned to their cause, had caught me alone, away from my Moldavian bodyguard. With drawn swords those three had surrounded me and set upon me.

At the last moment I was not completely taken by surprise. More than one of the attackers felt the bite of my own blade before I was disabled, and at least one of my chief opponents—his name was Ronay—was rather seriously hurt. Oh, I was good with the sword, yes, but not that good. Much of the credit for my prolonged survival against such odds was due to the reluctance of the common soldiers to attack me. Those men were still almost too much afraid of me to be of any use to traitors.

Alas, at three to one the odds were still too great. Let me name the foul three here: they were Ronay, Basarab, and Bogdan, the last-named the chief instigator and leader of the plot. In my capacity as Prince of Wallachia I had trusted all three of these vile men, had treated them as my comrades on the field of battle. All had been loaded with honors and with material rewards.

Nay, I will go further. Almost, my attitude had been that of a father or an uncle toward them. The traitorous trio were all young, and I was well over forty. But when they came to kill me, they had no easy time of it, for all that.

Even as I fought, grunting and gasping for breath, my feet slipping in snow and mud, I made a silent, mighty vow—nay, it was more than a vow—that I would never die until I had avenged myself upon these three for their treachery.

... and now, more than five hundred years later, trying to tell my story, trying to grapple with my own beginnings, I relive as in a dream that struggle to the death upon that field of fading light. Peering toward those distant figures through the haze of centuries, nay, through the fog of death itself, I am no longer able to say with certainty which of that day's far-off events I observed with my own eyes, and which I have come to know of only through the words of other witnesses.

The first serious wound I suffered on that day was made by Basarab's sword, when his point came into my left side, under my cuirass.

From that moment on the three of them were certain that they had me. Ronay could afford to retreat, nursing his own hurt. Bogdan and Basarab began to play with me, making sure to keep me between them—though at first it was a cautious game they played, knowing me to be still deadly dangerous.

I fought on, though weakening, ignoring their jibes and insults, saving what breath I had for fighting. But I could not face two skilled opponents at once. One of them would stab me, from behind, and then the other. I suffered at least half a dozen additional wounds before I was no longer capable of resistance.

Bah, I have no wish to dwell upon the grisly scene of my own butchery. Yet still it must be told.

When I fell for the last time, going to my knees, unable to rise again, unable any longer even to raise my weapon in defense, someone struck me with a sword hilt from behind and sent me sprawling. Then someone else's boot kicked at my sword, until it had been knocked out of the reach of my weakening fingers.

More kicks and shoves, with booted feet, turned my bleeding body over so that I lay face upward. I was trying to reach the dagger at my belt, but my knife too was yanked away. Then a sharp blade came stabbing into my unprotected groin; the muscles of my lower body spasmed uncontrollably. Pain fashioned a sound, that I suppose must have been almost inhuman, and drove it upward from my throat.

The body on the ground continued to gasp for breath. "Hold his head still." This was the voice of Bogdan, still panting, issuing an order. I could perceive his face, fierce and triumphant, looming over me.

In a moment someone—I thought it was Ronay, come back to savor my last moments—was crouching just behind me, knees vising my head in place. My arms no longer moved; my muscles and my strength were gone; all I had left was nerves and blood.

The point of Bogdan's sword loomed close to my face, approaching my eyes. Elsewhere I have related how my whole life's allotment of fear came to be used up before I was old enough to have a beard. So here, let me say simply that it must have been without fear, with hatred only—say rather hatred glowing with a helpless rage—that I gazed up at him. Perhaps I would not have turned my head had I been able.

"I will not die—" I told him, choking on my fury, and my own blood, and could not find the breath to say the rest.

"Oh, no?" The swordpoint feinted even closer to my eyes, then moved a small handsbreadth away. "Not yet you won't, good Prince Drakulya. Not this moment. But soon. Very soon."

I understood that Bogdan had spared my sight because he wished me to continue to see what was happening. Perhaps he craved also to see in my eyes at last some expression of yielding, of despair, at least of fear. In that hope, at least, he continued to be disappointed.

In the next moment I could feel the cold steel of Bogdan's blade slide inside my left cheek, the sensation transforming itself into the heat of fresh pain as the blade ripped its way out.

"What words of defiance now, Drakulya?"

I would have given him some, had I not been choking, more seriously than before, on my own blood.

"The end of your triumphant smile at last, good prince. How I have longed to see it wiped away! And now, why should I leave you a nose, to carry in the air so arrogantly? Half a one will serve you just as well, for the short time of breathing you have left."

During the course of my next few gasping, gurgling breaths, Bogdan's sword did a fair job of cutting and peeling away a sizable portion of my face. In the background I could hear Basarab laughing.

Suddenly Ronay, speaking in a low voice, pausing at intervals to grunt with the discomfort of his own wound, ventured to suggest that since the Sultan was going to pay them a good price for my head, it might be as well to leave my face at least recognizable.

Bogdan made a sound expressing doubt. The suggestion had come somewhat too late.

I will not die!!

(There is a pause on the tape.)

Ah, the images fade, true memories blending imperceptibly into the knowledge of things that I could only have imagined, heard later from the lips of some other eyewitness, or reconstructed by logic.

Or—is it possible? Possible that, in some way I still cannot understand, my soul—if it is permissible to use the jargon of modern physics—that my soul, I say, quantum-tunneling the barrier of death, I might have observed every detail of my own butchery, my spirit hovering out of the body though not yet fully detached from it?

I WILL NOT DIE!!!

Pain could no longer elicit the smallest outcry from the body, and it had ceased even to twitch under the ministrations of Bogdan's blade. Presently I ceased even to breathe. Shortly after that, some providential distraction, probably a report that my Moldavians were near, drew my enemies' attention away. (Let me add parenthetically that before succumbing to this distraction, Bogdan turned back, suddenly suspicious, taking no chances, and cut entirely through my neck.)

The distraction, I say, was providential, because as soon as my enemies were out of sight some of my loyal though humble friends among the camp followers mentioned above, displaying considerable courage in the midst of their grief, made a brave effort to preserve my poor clay from the further indignities that the traitors and eventually the Sultan would certainly have inflicted upon it.

This effort naturally required that they substitute

some other body for my own—the mere disappearance of my corpse would not have been acceptable to the traitors. (Though now that I think back on it, what a delicious superstitious fear it would have provoked among them!) The near obliteration of my face, to the point where my loyal friends themselves had difficulty in recognizing me, made their task considerably easier.

Also a great help to them was the fact that my corpse lay on a recent battlefield, surrounded by fresh candidates for substitution.

A selection was quickly made from among these, and a partial change of armor and clothing was effected, no easy matter in itself—have you ever tried to dress a corpse? Quick cosmetic surgery was performed upon the face of my replacement—his hair and mustache were already an approximate match. Body build was generally similar. Height is irrelevant among those who have become permanently horizontal. And given the muddy condition of the field, one of its occupants tended to look a great deal like another anyway.

To shorten a somewhat lengthy episode, which I am finding increasingly painful to relate, let me say at once that the replacement was a success. When Bogdan and his two close associates came back, they abandoned with scarcely a glance the hacked-up torso and limbs they thought were mine, picked up by its dirty hair the head of pseudo-Drakulya, and at once packed this grisly object away in a cask of salt to start its journey to the Sultan. There was, I suppose, hardly any point in trying to clean the flayed thing up. Much later I heard that the trophy was indeed exhibited upon some palace gate or wall, the head of the dread Lord Impaler, *Kaziklu Bey,* brought down at last, only to be so elevated among his enemies.

But from that day of my assassination, it was long, long, before the Sultan ever entered into my thoughts again.

Meanwhile my own body, unhappily disjunct, had been conveyed from the field by my friends in greatest secrecy, bundled in its two pieces upon the back of a mule. Darkness had fallen long before the corpse reached a place of sanctuary, where another friend or two appeared to clean it up and lay it out for honorable if secret burial.

This sanctuary where my remains had come to rest temporarily was a farm not far from the battlefield, and also not far from the island monastery of Snagov.

A rough plank table had been constructed, in some outbuilding, for the job that had to be done, and on this my body was laid out supine, head just a little distant from neck stump, a tall candle at my feet and another near my detached head. During the following preparations, these candles took turns in extinguishing themselves, for no good reason that I could see. Perhaps there was more of a draft than I could feel.

Two of the farm women did most of the actual corpse-washing. Meanwhile a handful of other people came and went, to marvel and to grieve.

And, of course, to pray over my dismembered body. The prayers as I recall were for the most part Catholic, for I had been and remained a dutiful convert from the Orthodox faith into which I had been born.

Among the topics of conversation addressed by those preparing me for burial was the fact that my grave would probably be only temporary, that the late unhappy prince would want to be moved someday to a prepared vault hidden beneath a certain castle.

But for the present all concerned would be satisfied,

could I but be laid peacefully to rest in some soldier's grave, unmarked and shallow, humble as most such are, and lonelier than most. Somehow I was to be accorded at least the minor dignity of a plain wooden coffin, the best my friends could manage, and the sounds of its construction resounded through the night.

One at least of my mourners had come from the nearby monastery, where, as he said, only he and one other were aware as yet of the fact that my body had been saved, and my funeral preparations were quietly under way. The two who knew the secret would try to keep it, but the speaker considered it inevitable that eventually the story would spread through their ranks.

He also mentioned that Ronay had sought shelter in the monastery for treatment of his wound. I had richly endowed this establishment, as well as several others, whilst I was still capable of breath, and when I heard this it seemed to me ungrateful of its abbot now to thus comfort and encourage my enemies.

Shortly after the monk had spoken of Ronay, the people in attendance on my corpse had a bad few moments, when both candles inexplicably went out at once. Fortunately for their peace of mind, a fire was available—a small one in a brazier, no one wanted to keep a corpse too warm—and the darkness never became absolute. The tapers were easily relighted.

To begin with, the butchered body was stripped of its begrimed and bloodstained garments, the borrowed ones along with whatever items of its proper clothing it still retained. Most of these being hopelessly damaged, they were taken to another room to be consigned to the fire. Parenthetically I may add that I was oddly touched, later, when I heard that a few scraps of bloodstained cloth had been retained, in the manner of holy relics, by some of the humble folk who had considered themselves happy and fortunate under my rule.

A little later, by chance, all of the attendants were out of the room at the same time, probably getting more water and cloths. As the first two returned, they stopped abruptly, and the more timid one smothered a little outcry.

Somehow my head, detached as it was, had in the interval of their absence rolled or shifted its position slightly. I have no good explanation of how such things can happen. The one dark eye still visible amid the mutilations was wide open, its fiery glare directed into nothingness. The bloody jaw now gaped more widely than before, the tattered lips that no longer really formed a mouth hanging in a bloody fringe around that silent, shouting grin. At least one of the breathing onlookers, to judge by a remark he muttered later, got the impression that those jaws were shouting, a great bellowing of breathless defiance.

In fact there was scarcely a sound in the room, save for the quickened breathing of the attendants and a steady, remote dripping. Water, either inside or outside the shed. Outside rain now fell alternately with sleet, making it a dismal night altogether.

Trembling slightly, but firmly confident in the power of their prayers to protect them against the things of night and evil, the corpse-washers examined the body again to make sure that nothing else had changed, and there was no drip of blood. No, the body of Vlad Drakulya was no longer really bleeding at any point. The raw lips of his many wounds were sealed with clots. When presently, in the continued process of washing, most of these blood clots were dislodged, there appeared beneath them the unmistakable signs of pink, fresh scarring, as if some healing process of near-miraculous rapidity had begun before death supervened. One of the attendants made some muttered comment about this; the other one told her to shut up.

But the first woman was not finished. "Now you can see both of his eyes," she remarked when a gory wrinkle of loosened forehead had been tugged and smoothed back into what was more or less its proper position.

There was some difficulty about getting the eyes to stay shut; in itself this is not uncommon with corpses of a fair degree of freshness. No doubt even the observed movement of the head was not totally without precedent. The traumatized jaw muscles, or what Bogdan's sword had left of them, might well have spasmed once again.

"Ought we not to sew up some of these gashes? Would his face look better with stitches in it, or—"

"No time for sewing now." The face—if the surface they were contemplating was still deserving of the name— was going to look frightful in the extreme, whatever the corpse-tenders did or did not do.

"I suppose you're right. No time. Wash him, clothe him decently, put him into a box and underground." Afraid that my enemies might finally have tumbled to the trick, or that some informer might betray the substitution of another corpse, they were trying to get it all done, including the burial, before dawn.

And now a priest—he was not the first of his calling to do so on this night—came into the presence of the body from which, all onlookers were quite certain, the soul had permanently departed. Again prayers were recited for the repose of the departed spirit. For a man of notably bad reputation, even for a prince, even in this notably wicked time and place, this one seemed to have no lack of friends who wished to help him—as soon as he was gone. Perhaps some of those who prayed for his soul were afraid not to do so. Ah, would that they had all been so brave and industrious in his defense before he ceased to breathe—but perhaps my protests, particularly at this late date, are churlish and unfair.

Meanwhile, as we have mentioned, other hands had been at work in the hasty construction of a coffin. The torso with its limbs, garbed in some crude but decent cerements, was now laid reverently within. The coffin-makers had calculated the length to a nicety, avoiding any need to lay the prince's head in his lap or under his arm like a pumpkin. The severed member fit into its proper place, albeit a trifle snugly, just above the neck.

My dagger had been picked up on the field and brought along, and now, along with some jewels of moderate value and a crucifix, was put into the coffin. Someone quickly and quietly removed the jewels again, at the last moment before the lid was put on. The wrists were crossed upon the breast, the dagger rested near the hands, and it seemed to one of the attendants that the right hand and arm had shifted position slightly, doubtless because of the bumping around and shifting that the box was getting, and that the lifeless fingers were curving, even tightening noticeably, around the hilt.

A man's voice, beginning to grow ragged with strain and tiredness, announced: "His eyes have come open again; the lids popped back as soon as I took the coins away."

"Well, let them be open, then." The elder attendant was more phlegmatic—and not about to send off any real coins for burial. "It will not matter to the soul. Or to the body, either, at the Last Trump. And I tell you we have no time. Bogdan's men may have discovered that they're sending the Sultan the wrong head. It's not impossible they'll come here searching for the right one. We must have the burial completely finished before dawn."

"And I wish we could do something to reattach the head." One of the younger conspirators, quite a worrywart, still fretting, reached to clasp the skull with both hands to readjust its position slightly. He tugged, and blanched, and snatched his hands back. He opened his mouth to remark on what he had discovered, but then changed his mind, closed his lips firmly, and forebore to say a word.

Small wonder he kept silent. It wasn't really possible that head and neck could have knitted themselves together. Instead it was possible, quite possible—in fact it was much more likely—that he was going mad.

No one else repeated his discovery, or shared his mad delusion. In a few more moments, the last loyal farewells were said, the last formal prayers muttered, and the lid nailed more or less adequately onto the coffin. Then the silent burden was hoisted on shoulders, carried outdoors, shoved into a wagon, and borne joltingly away.

The journey in the wagon took much less than an hour, and yet the small clearing in a woods where the coffin was unloaded seemed a completely isolated place, quite out of sight of any road or human habitation.

Two men had been here for some time, digging by the light of a shaded lantern, and the grave by general consent was pronounced deep enough as soon as its intended occupant arrived. The last of the diggers climbed out hastily. The lowering of the box into the grave and the shoveling in of earth were the work of only a few moments; a great deal more time was spent in tamping down the earth, scattering the inevitable remainder of loose soil, and in general concealing the fact that here an interment had taken place. The next snow would hide the remaining traces of disturbance, probably until spring; and doubtless by then the likelihood of a search would be remote.

But the gravediggers, having taken careful note of

certain landmarks, assured themselves that they would have no trouble in finding the grave of their beloved prince again, once things had calmed down and it became feasible to think of moving him to the secret place beneath his castle.

That relocation was eventually to be accomplished. But not by those who planned it on the day I fell.

3

In Angie's dreams the recorded voice of Uncle Matthew continued to hold forth, calmly elegant, just slightly accented, sounding as if it ought to make sense even while it delivered the horrible absurdities of some monstrous and bloody fantasy. When she had turned on the tape in the small hours of the morning she had been in no state to evaluate, to separate fact from fiction. Brandy and weariness had overcome her completely as she listened.

But now the tape machine had somehow been turned off. Perhaps she'd done it herself before collapsing. She was lying in bed, and someone was knocking at her door. Tapping, rather, at the door of the unfamiliar bedroom where she had fallen asleep.

Angie sat up, and there was John in bed beside her, just where he ought to be. But they were in an unfamiliar room—

Her mind cleared somewhat. Yes, this was Uncle Matthew's place. The dimmer component of the bathroom light was still on, indirectly illuminating the bedroom through the partially open door between. On the other side of the bed, the curtained windows were still dark around the edges, showing that the sun wasn't up yet. Still night, and someone knocking persistently on the guest bedroom door. Something must be wrong.

"Just a minute!" Angie called, her voice emerging as an uncertain croak. Climbing groggily to her feet and wrapping a blanket around her, she started for the door. Now, just outside it, a voice—female, low, and anxious— was calling softly, the words impossible to make out.

Halfway to the door, Angie decided that she required reinforcements, mumbled some kind of a reply to the person knocking, and turned back to the bed to wake up John. His wristwatch lay on the bedside table and she glanced at it in passing. Almost five A.M.

John was hard to rouse, but in a few moments he had stumbled to his feet, functional though hardly up to speed, and was pulling on his pants. Angie used the interval to throw on a few garments of her own. Together they went to the bedroom door and opened it slightly. Just outside stood Elizabeth Wiswell. The buttons on her blouse were misaligned, and her clothes in general looked as if they had been hastily pulled on. Down the shadowy hall behind her the apartment was mostly dark; some light was coming from one of the other bedrooms.

The woman looked pale and haggard, appropriately for the hour. Also she was worried. "Something's wrong with him in there," she told them simply.

John opened the bedroom door a little wider. He rubbed his eyes and massaged his day-old growth of beard. "What?"

Elizabeth's voice rose querulously. "I don't know what. He just looks awful. His eyes are partly open but I can't get him to wake up. And there's blood smeared all over his mouth. I'd have thought he was dead, but he moves, a little. Is he subject to fits or something?"

Angie saw that John was staring at the waitress's neck. He blinked his eyes and stared again. Angie could feel her own flesh creep. There was a tiny, fresh blood spot visible on Elizabeth's throat—no, two tiny spots, a couple of inches apart, and around them some dried smears as if the little wounds had been oozing for some time. But the woman seemed completely unaware of the fact.

John muttered something, pushed past her, and led the way down the hall, to the room in which Uncle Matthew and the waitress must have retired not more than a couple of hours ago. After giving a token rap on the slightly open door, John pushed it open and led the others in. A moment later he had reached for a wall switch and turned on an additional light.

The single figure now occupying the queen-sized bed was sprawled across it diagonally and concealed up to the armpits by a sheet. The rumpled cover left bare the pale and wiry arms, the muscle-rounded shoulders. Uncle Matthew's head lifted slightly when the light came on. He turned his face away from the brighter light and toward the visitors.

Or—was this really Uncle Matthew? Angie, coming closer to the bed, paused suddenly, for a moment doubting whether she was looking at the same man. This face looked altogether too young, and at the same time too unhealthy. The pallor of this face was intense, the features somehow altered. The glossy dark hair, now entirely free of gray, was wildly tousled. Angie saw that Uncle Matthew's gaze, pointed in the general direction of his visitors, was unresponsive, his eyes glassy, hardly more than half open. If she hadn't just seen the body move, she might well have thought the face before her now was dead.

And Elizabeth was right, those certainly looked like bloodstains on his lips and chin and cheeks. As if he had been drinking clumsily, or sucking blood—Angie giggled suddenly, a strained and awkward sound.

No one took any notice.

"Uncle Matthew?" There was horror in John's voice. He was wide awake now. As he leaned forward, closer to the bed, something crackled faintly beneath his hand pressing down the sheets. Puzzled, John shifted his weight and pushed again, testing. The effort produced a renewed crunching sound. "Oh," he said then, as if he had just remembered something.

The man who was lying across the bed suddenly rolled over on his back, an abrupt, almost convulsive movement. His eyes opened a little wider, and then sought those of the younger man. The gory lips twitched, revealing stark white, pointed teeth. It looked as if he were trying, so far without success, to communicate something to John.

"Sir? What is it?"

A straining, an evident attempt to answer, but no speech, hardly any sound.

Angie chimed in, pleading, "Uncle Matthew?"

The man in the bed gurgled, gasped for air, and murmured something. It was at last a response, but far from intelligible. He made an abortive effort to raise himself, but could get his head no more than a couple of inches from the pillow before falling back.

Elizabeth the waitress had followed John and Angie into the bedroom and had been hovering uneasily in the background. Now she said: "At first I thought he was just drunk, but—I don't remember that he even had a drink. We'd better call a doctor. If he's bleeding like that around his mouth." She giggled inappropriately. Unlike Angie's nervous laughter earlier, Elizabeth's went on for some time.

But John was shaking his head emphatically before Elizabeth had even finished speaking. "No," he said decisively. "No doctors."

Angie looked at him with a questioning frown, but said nothing for the moment.

"Well, he's your relative. Me, I don't like the way he looks. In fact I think I'm getting out of here. Where'd he put my coat? In the front closet, I suppose." The woman was obviously growing more and more upset every time she looked at Uncle Matthew in the bright light.

"I'll help you find your coat," said Angie, turning away from the bed. Meanwhile she was wondering whether she ought to try to break it gently to Elizabeth that her throat was bleeding slightly, but before she could decide the doorbell chimed.

"Who could that be?" asked Elizabeth automatically. Angie thought that after several hours of quiet it wasn't likely to be the neighbors complaining about noise.

All three of Uncle Matthew's guests moved into the living room, approaching the front door and its closed-circuit color video.

John turned on the viewer beside the door, and all three looked at the little wall-mounted screen. Angie started to speak, then bit her tongue. From the corner of her eye, she saw Elizabeth raise her fingers to her mouth; then the women looked at each other in puzzlement at their shared reaction.

Before either of them could decide what to say, John made his own comment. "Some young guy," he muttered. "Whoever it is, I never saw him before."

"I think I have," said Angie timidly.

Valentine Kaiser, wearing a trench coat, was standing there front and center, posing accommodatingly right in front of the electronic eye so anyone inside could get a look at him. Somewhat vague in the background was the figure of another man, who appeared just about tall enough to look over Kaiser's shoulder. Angie couldn't be sure, but she didn't think the second man was anyone she'd ever seen.

Despite the hour the celebrity publicist appeared cheerful, clean-shaven, and wide awake, swinging his arms a little, shifting his weight restlessly as he waited. As she watched, Kaiser extended his arm and pressed the chime again.

John was looking at her now, and she turned slowly away from the viewer, trying to think of how to explain to him who Kaiser was. "I think I—" Angie began, and then was distracted by Liz.

The waitress had already retrieved her coat from the front closet and put it on. In the act of adjusting a scarf she paused, dabbed with her hand at her shapely neck, then looked at her fingers. "Oh, my God, I'm bleeding too," she murmured. Eyeing her companions she giggled once more, and Angie wondered suddenly if Liz might be drunk or high on some other drug.

"Angie," John was asking, an edge in his voice, "do you know who this guy is out in the hall?"

Elizabeth, with coat and scarf now firmly on, was holding her right hand stiffly out in front of her. For the moment, as she regarded the fingers marked with pinhead red spots from her throat, she looked completely sober. "I don't want to meet him," she muttered. "Is there a back door?" she asked distractedly. "A service door? I'm going to just slip out that way, if . . ."

"Wait," said John sharply. He looked from one to the other with a hard gaze that puzzled Angie, then concentrated on her: "Were you going to say you know him?"

"I recognize him," she admitted in annoyance. If he would only give her the time to explain properly . . .

"You do? Who is he, then?"

"Tell you in a minute." Angie, her anger suddenly

flaming because of being barked at, stepped quickly to the door and started to open the locks while keeping the security fasteners in place. Two of these, designed to allow the door to open no more than about six inches, guarded the front portal of Uncle Matthew's residence. Both were made of thicker steel, were more elaborate in design, and looked much stronger than the usual door chains that served as household protectors in the city.

John at first moved as if he would prevent her from opening the door, but then stepped back. "All right," he muttered. "I want to get a look at him directly."

In another moment, confronting Valentine Kaiser face-to-face through a six-inch gap, Angie tried to summon up her best skill at vituperation, but found that any talent she might ordinarily possess along that line had deserted her. "What in the world do you want?" was the nearest thing to scathing words that she could think of. "At this hour?" She did her best to make her tone compensate for the deficiency.

Seen directly, Kaiser looked worried, or at least concerned, rather than jaunty. Not that he was lacking confidence. Sounding almost cheerful, he answered her question with one of his own. "How's Mr. Maule doing?"

"What do you want?"

Their visitor looked grave. "I had an impression that he might be ill. One gets these feelings sometimes, you know, when one has known someone for a very long time. May I talk to him, please?"

"No. Go away." Angie paused. "You say you know him?"

"For a very long time, as I say." As if in afterthought he pointed behind him with a thumb. "Forgive me, this is my associate, Mr. Stewart." The trench-coated figure nodded. Kaiser gave Angie a reassuring smile. "Now, may we come in?"

"No!" This from John, standing close behind her. Angie, who had been able to feel herself wavering, felt grateful for the support.

Kaiser did not look grateful at the refusal. "So? Then he is ill. I was afraid of that. Sorry to disturb you now but it can't be helped." His tone was not exactly repentant. "Believe me, it can't. Let us in and we'll talk about it." He made a little movement forward, stopping just short of the doorway.

Valentine Kaiser . . . who was he? A young man, yes, but still definitely one you could turn to with a problem. Almost, Angie found herself willing, hoping, to be convinced that he might after all have some good reason . . .

"You're not coming in," said John firmly, from just behind her.

That stiffened her backbone. "Who are you, really?" she demanded. "What was all that story about publicity?"

Kaiser shook his head. Then somewhat plaintively, making an awkward gesture with both arms, he appealed: "Do we have to talk out in the corridor?"

Angie turned to look at John, but he was not softening. "Who are these people, Angie? We're not letting anyone in."

Kaiser ignored him. He craned his neck, trying to look in past both of them, as if trying to spot someone else. The waitress had retreated around an angle of wall, but that didn't let her escape. Kaiser raised his voice slightly. "I see another young lady in the background. How about you, miss? You think we ought to come in?"

Elizabeth Wiswell, looking dazed and not exactly young, took a few steps forward, as if unwillingly. She moved until she could peer through the doorway at the young man in the hall, and then she stared at him as if in the grip of some terrible fascination. The blood spots showed dark upon her pale throat. Her mouth opened, but what she might have said was never heard.

John suddenly let out an inarticulate cry and hurled himself against the door, slamming it shut. One of the men outside—Angie had a blurred impression that it was Stewart—reacted, lunging forward and trying to hold the door open, but that effort came too late. The heavy, dull slam the barrier made in closing suggested to Angie the thickness of the wood.

In the next instant Liz screamed loudly and put her hands up over her face.

At the same moment Angie shouted: "John!" She had recoiled against the wall; startled by the violence of what she perceived as John's overreaction, she stared at him in wonder.

John didn't answer. With his shoulder still braced against the wood, his face pale, his fingers working with desperate haste, he was turning the heavy bolts on each of the four separate locks and latches that held the door shut tight.

The expression he turned to Angie stilled her startled questions in her throat.

"Angie, we can't let them in," he was beginning, in a frightened voice. Then he stopped, looking wildly about. "Where's Liz?" he demanded, a sudden edge of panic in his voice.

For a moment Angie only continued to stare at her fiancé in astonishment. She had never seen him look like this—he was pale to the lips and absolutely terrified.

But in the next moment she turned her gaze around the living room and entryway. The other woman was gone. "She said something about going out the service entrance. I guess there must be one . . ."

"Oh, my God!" John's words were quiet, but desperately urgent. Already he was running at top speed for the back door, or for the place where Angie supposed the back door would have to be if it existed.

"What is it?" But he wouldn't delay in his headlong flight, wouldn't pause to answer. Angie followed, helplessly infected by his fear.

Running on bare feet, they pounded through the apartment to the kitchen. There, set in one wall of the tiny adjacent laundry room, the back door stood open as far as its security devices, similar to those on the front door, would allow. Elizabeth was standing just inside, talking to someone through the gap. When John shouted at her she turned, as if with great difficulty, to present a face of helpless horror to John and Angie.

Knocking her out of the way, not pausing to see who might be outside, John leaped at this door as he had the other. Again a heavy barrier slammed shut. Again Angie had the impression that whoever was outside might have made an abortive effort to hold it open.

In another moment John had the locks on this door fastened.

Then he turned, leaning his back against the door, fixing the trembling waitress with a baleful stare. "Don't call out. Don't ask any of them in. I'm warning you."

Elizabeth, shivering despite coat and scarf, had retreated to sit in a chair at the kitchen table. She shook her red curls. "I didn't," she said in a tiny, helpless voice. "I won't."

Angie, scowling at the man she was planning to marry, moved to stand beside Elizabeth, silently stroking the woman's hair with her right hand. Meanwhile Elizabeth had seized Angie's left hand and was clinging to it, almost as if she needed help from drowning. Liz was still trembling. Angie was silent now, but her anger was going to burst out at John in about fifteen seconds, unless he came up with some very good explanations.

The video panel beside the back door was identical with the one in the front room. John, having made sure the door was sealed—and having terrorized everyone in the process, Angie thought—had switched on the video and was studying the screen intently. He muttered: "Not a real hallway at this end, just service stairs. There's a landing, and the back door of someone else's apartment. He's still there. Know this guy, Angie?"

Angie looked at the viewer, and beheld another male figure, not Mr. Stewart, also unfamiliar. How many people were with Kaiser, and why would he send someone to the back door, when he came to the front? Was he some kind of a policeman? Or—

The buzzer on the back door sounded, and simultaneously the door chime from the front.

John ignored the nearer summons. Moving at a reluctant walk, almost a sleepwalker's groping stumble, he was halfway back to the living room when Angie gave up calling his name—he couldn't seem to hear her—and ran to stop him with a hard pull on his arm.

Once she had his attention, she said, calmly and firmly: "I don't know what it is about the people out there that upsets you so. If they're so scary, don't you think it's about time we called the police?"

"No!" It was anything but a sleepwalker's answer. "Don't you see? That's just what they want us to do."

"What?" The two of them were arguing on the threshold of the living room, with the front door in sight, its adjacent video screen showing that Valentine Kaiser was out there still. Elizabeth Wiswell, moving like a lost soul, still in coat and scarf, came wandering past John and Angie and sank down in a chair at some distance from the door.

John must have seen his fiancée's fear and confusion. He made a conscious, visible effort to speak to her calmly. "If we call the cops, those people out in the hall will disappear. For the time being. And if the cops get a call saying there are mysterious people in the hall threatening us, they'll insist on coming in and looking the place over. Just to make sure we're not lying when we meet them at the door and say everything is fine now. The cops will want to make sure there's no one being held hostage in here."

"All right! So, let them come in and—"

He overrode her. "No! Once the cops see Uncle Matthew, in the shape he's in, nothing will stop them calling an ambulance and having him carried out."

"Frankly I think we ought to call one ourselves. John, he really looks like—"

"I know what he looks like. The trouble is, once they move him outside the walls of his own house—well, there'll be no way we or the police can protect him, if your acquaintance who came to the door means to do him harm."

Angie blinked. "Protect him?"

"It looks to me like someone's poisoned him. Then those—strangers show up out in the corridor and want to see him. I don't like it."

"You mean—you're saying the police couldn't protect him from Valentine Kaiser and his—"

"Do you know what Kaiser is?"

"What he is? He gave me a card that said he was a 'publicist,' whatever that is. I don't—"

John, shaking his head hopelessly, switched his attention to Elizabeth, who was sitting huddled in one of the living room's soft chairs. "Liz?" He had to call her name several times to get her attention.

At last she raised green, frightened eyes.

"They sent you, didn't they? That man out in the hall? They told you to come in here and then call one of them in?"

She nodded. Her eyes were dreamy. "The big young fella there, he talked about that, telling me I ought to invite them in if they asked me to. I don't know why he wanted that. I never expected *he*"—her eyes moved in the direction of the bedroom where their host still lay—"was going to—to—" She raised her fingers to her throat. And giggled, faintly, once again.

"You see," said John to Angie, "this is someone's home. They can't get in here unless they're invited. I don't know why it works that way, but it really does." His voice sounded reasonable, even if what he was saying made no sense at all.

Angie hesitated. "'They'? Who're 'they'?"

"Kaiser and his buddies out there. His friend Stewart wasn't, he was a normal man." John's voice was growing ragged again. "But *they* can't just push a door in, not a door to someone's house. They can't stop me from shutting them out, though God knows they're strong enough."

"John? I think you better get hold of yourself. If you—"

"Who is this Kaiser, anyway?"

"I don't really know."

"Angie, that guy in the hall is working every trick he can to get someone to invite him through that door. But once he's in the apartment—we're dead, if he wants us dead. And when I look at him I'm scared shitless. It's like eleven years ago."

"I want to go home," said Elizabeth Wiswell suddenly. "I don't feel good." Her slight body made convulsive nodding motions; in a moment, hand to her mouth, she had leaped from her chair and was hurrying down the bedroom hallway. In another moment, sounds of retching came from that direction.

The other two paid her little attention. Something, Angie suddenly understood, in this situation is taking John back to when he lost his fingers. She had a question ready, but before she could ask it, John pushed past her and went to stand beside the viewscreen, just as the door chime rang yet again.

Putting his hand on Kaiser's miniature image, in an urgent whisper he turned his head to Angie and ordered: "Whatever you say, whatever you do, don't invite any of those people in. Okay? I'll do my best to explain the rest of this to you later."

She was angry, perhaps because she knew she had once been on the brink of issuing such an invitation. "Do you need to keep saying that? Do you think I'm crazy? Or are you?" Then she wished she hadn't asked the question.

"No, I'm not." He paused. "That's the least of my worries." Suddenly he held up his four-fingered hands, wiggling the digits briefly like someone miming quotation marks. "This experience," he said, "taught me something."

The door chime sounded yet again. John turned swiftly and pushed the button, beside the video panel, that allowed voice communication.

"What is it?" he demanded.

Kaiser's voice, distorted by the system's third-rate audio, came through. "I said, would you open the door, please?"

"No!"

The man in the hall did not sound discouraged.

"John? Angie? Let me talk with the young woman who's with you, please. I want to satisfy myself that she's free to leave this apartment if she wants to. Then I'll go away, if you insist."

"How did you know my name?" John demanded.

"Angie called you by name. Don't you remember?"

John looked doubtful, of his memory if not his purpose. And Liz, emerging feebly from the bedroom hallway, looking almost as pale as Uncle Matthew, shook her head silently and shivered.

Angie said to the intercom: "She doesn't want to talk to you. Go away."

John turned off the sound again. He was looking at her fiercely, but his voice was so low that she had to strain to hear him. "Angie, you really know that man?"

"I told you, or I've been trying to tell you, I've met him once. That's all."

"Where'd you meet him? *When?"*

"Yesterday afternoon. I was going to tell you all about it, but—I've got his business card in my purse." She looked about. The purse would be back in the bedroom. "His name's Valentine Kaiser, and he's a 'celebrity publicist,' whatever that is, or he claims to be."

That provoked from John a burst of near-hysterical laughter. "I haven't met him. I've never seen him before. But, I told you, I know *what* he is."

"So? What are we doing now, just letting him stand around out there, and his friend, and harass us all night? I say call the police. Maybe Uncle Matthew really needs an ambulance." And she too laughed. It was a foolish, panicky sound and she hated herself for making it.

He was shaking his head emphatically. "No ambulance and no police. Uncle Matthew's not like other people.

Believe me, honey, I know what I'm doing. I'm calling Joe."

That made her pause, with its sheer apparent irrelevance. "Joe Keogh?"

"Yes." He was already picking up the phone, in a little alcove off the living room.

"Why? What's Joe Keogh got to do with this?" Then Angie turned to look at the silent video screen. Valentine Kaiser was waving his arm in an unmistakable gesture of farewell.

"Look, John. I think he's leaving."

Receiver at his ear, John came far enough out of the alcove to look. Now Kaiser, with the smaller figure of Mr. Stewart staying shadowlike behind him, had definitely turned and was moving away. Almost at once they were gone out of the camera's limited range.

"They're going," Angie said doubtfully.

"Let's hope so." John didn't sound as if he even considered it a possibility. In another moment he was addressing the phone, in the careful voice of one confronted with an answering machine. "Joe, this is John. We're at Uncle Matthew's, and I'm afraid we've got an emergency. Uncle's sick, passed out, I don't know what. And we've got *nosferatu* in the hallway, trying to talk their way in. Three of 'em at least. I don't like their looks. Give me a call back here as soon as you can."

With a look at Angie, as if to say: *That's all we can do at the moment,* he hung up the phone.

Angie asked him: "What was that word you said? The name you called them?"

"Oh. *Nosferatu?* It's an old word from some European language, I forget which. It means vampires."

"Vampires."

John was looking at the viewer again, listening at the door. "Honey, I don't think they're really gone."

When she went into the bedroom to look at Uncle Matthew again, the translation of *nosferatu* didn't sound so crazy.

Time passed. When John made his first attempt to reach Joe Keogh, it was five-thirty. Now it was six and still dark outside, the long autumnal night persisting. Angie and John monitored the video panels almost continuously, but the presences that had haunted the front hall, and the rear-service landing and stairs, failed to reappear.

Everything outside the apartment looked and sounded absolutely peaceful.

Liz still sat in her living-room chair, looking as if she were numbed, or stunned. John tried to question her once more, but found it difficult to provoke a response.

Angie, heavy-lidded, told herself that she would hang on until daylight. Then it might be possible to get some sleep. If Uncle Matthew, who looked as hideous as ever, didn't die in the meantime. And John remained adamant on what not to do for him. "We can't call a doctor for him, Angie. We just can't. If we do, whatever else happens, Uncle Matthew is going to be carried out of here on a stretcher. And believe me he's not going to survive that. Especially with those—people—waiting to get at him."

Angie looked at her lover's four-fingered hands, and Uncle Matthew's face, and didn't know what to think.

At some point after the curtains began to show light around the edges, Liz departed. She went out the back way, after John, with the air of a man performing an heroic act, had first unlocked the door and stuck his head out and looked around. Then Liz went out, waved once, and went on down the stairs; they could hear her feet on the concrete for a couple of flights before the sound disappeared.

With the back door locked and bolted up again, John went to one window after another in the apartment to confirm the reality of daybreak. Since all of the windows looked out on the north side of the building, all the daylight they could gather, at this season of the year in particular, was indirect. The fog had largely dispersed; in early morning light the city below looked as mundane and busy, the lake as calm and mysterious, as ever.

The last room they entered on this tour was their host's bedroom, and here John, without offering any explanation, insisted that the curtains should remain tightly closed. In this room they were really special room-darkening draperies, Angie noted.

The condition of the patient, as seen by artificial light, was little changed.

As they were adjusting the bedclothes, something under the bottom sheet again made a faint, peculiar crackling sound.

Angie prodded at the bed, calling forth the noise yet once more. "What's this crunchy stuff under the bottom sheet?"

John, as if he already knew, didn't bother to look. "I'd say it's a garment bag, or something very like one. Plastic, filled with dried earth."

"And why's it there?"

"Because. *He* needs it, if he's going to sleep."

Angie thought it over. She'd known a good many people with stranger health quirks than that. Well, one or two anyway. Then she paused, looking at Uncle Matthew's corpselike face. Something else was not so innocently explained. "Seriously, it looks like he's been drinking blood."

John, on the other side of the bed, paused for a full ten seconds before answering. "I'm sure he has been," he said at last in a dull voice. "Blood is what he lives on."

"John, I said I'm serious."

"And I'm very serious too. He does live on blood. In fact it isn't always human blood, but blood is all he drinks. The only nourishment he needs."

Angie couldn't think of anything to say.

John was gazing at her sadly. "You saw Liz's throat."

"I . . ." Angie was about to protest this outrageous, unbelievable line of argument when a new observation drove even blood-drinking momentarily from her thoughts. Looking back at the man on the bed, she stared for a few moments and then whispered: "John? I think he's dead."

John hardly bothered to glance at the man whose nature he was trying to explain. "No, he isn't."

"I'm *serious*. I don't think he's breathing. I—"

"He's not supposed to breathe."

Everything Angie's lover was telling her, in this new, numbed voice of his, struck with an impact against her sanity. Every time her mind rejected what he was saying, she had to draw new energy from somewhere to try again. "What?"

John spoke slowly and carefully, though now with a little more animation. "He doesn't need to breathe except when he wants to talk. That's the only time he needs the air. His chest doesn't move up and down when he sleeps. But ordinarily you don't notice that unless you look for it."

Angie looked. The figure in the bed remained as immobile as a corpse. The rumpled sheet above its chest stood absolutely still, as if it were covering a statue. "But you can't be serious."

"I wish you'd stop telling me how serious you are, and that I can't be serious."

Her eyes fell again to the man in the bed. The deadly immobility, the pallor of the skin. The predatory teeth, partially visible through parted lips. The blood.

She said, involuntarily: "He looks like . . . like . . ."

John went on in the same tired, careful monotone. "I know what he looks like. He looks like a vampire. *Nosferatu,* remember? Because that's what he is."

"A vampire? You're trying to tell me that this man is actually—that he's a vampire."

Her fiancé's numbed lethargy began to crack. "Not trying anymore, honey. I've given up trying to break it to you gently. I'm telling you, because that's what he is. And so is Kaiser. Angie, whatever you do, never say a word of invitation to any of those people who were out in the hall. *They can't come into someone's house if they're not asked."* John, for the moment looking totally insane, leaned toward her as he uttered the last sentence.

But this time Angie didn't think that he was crazy. Crazy would have been easier to deal with, somehow. She could only wish for some answer as manageable as that.

"Thanks," Angie said vaguely. "I wasn't going to do that."

Recovering somewhat, John seemed ready to talk plainly and sanely once again. He gestured toward the window. "The sun's up now. They may have to lie low for a while."

"That's great—if they have to hide from sunlight."

"They sure don't care for sunlight much. A large direct dose can even kill them. But that doesn't mean they can't come out at all in the daytime. They love our Chicago climate. You met Kaiser in the daytime, right?"

"Right. I met him indoors. And the day was cloudy."

"Sure. And he looked just about normal?"

"You saw him in the hall. Sure he looks normal."

"But he isn't. I've had experience. Honey? I know how this must sound, but it's real. This isn't like the movies."

"No," she said. "It isn't anything like that."

John looked at his wristwatch and moved toward the bedside phone. "I'm going to try Joe again."

"Joe? Joe Keogh? Why is it important to call him?"

But John didn't answer. He had already picked up the phone and was punching numbers.

Angie looked once more at Uncle Matthew, shuddered, and started to move out of the room. At that moment the front door chime sounded.

John put down the phone and came with her to the door. The color images of two people showed on the little screen. One was Valentine Kaiser. The second, standing beside him and locked in the circle of his arm that came around her neck and shoulder, was a woman with red hair, wearing a cloth coat.

John switched on the sound.

The switch caught Elizabeth Wiswell's voice, softly desperate, in the middle of a sentence. "—me in, please, you've got to let me in. He'll let me go if you do. If you don't, he's going to drink my blood. All of it. He says that and I'm sure he means it."

Kaiser's arm moved slightly and her voice fell silent. Another image hurried across the screen, someone on the way to work most likely. When Liz and Kaiser had the corridor to themselves again, her pleas resumed, low, quavering, and sometimes hard to understand.

"He means it. They all do. Please, you've got to let him in now. He won't hurt you. If you don't, they're going to—" John hit the speaker switch, and a moment later the switch that turned off the video. The little screen went blank.

Now someone had begun pounding, though feebly, on

the door. If Elizabeth was still trying to talk to them, from out there in the hall, it was impossible to hear her through the soundproofing of the walls and the door's thick wood.

John and Angie looked at each other. He said: "There's a chance they won't hurt her. I think a better chance than if we let them in. And it won't do any good to call the cops. It won't do any good at all. Do you believe me, Angie? Do you understand me?"

She made a gesture between a nod and a shrug.

John hurried back to the phone in the nearby alcove.

Someone was still thumping weakly on the door.

Aimlessly, moving in shock, Angie turned away and wandered back down the hallway, into the guest bedroom where she had had about two hours' sleep before the vampires—the bad, dangerous vampires, not the one that wasn't quite John's uncle—came on the scene.

Sinking down into a chair, she stared at the tape machine. In a moment she began to cry.

4

The return of full awareness, the reestablishment of the full presence of the soul within the mangled but mysteriously healing flesh, was a long, gradual, and parlous process. I need not discuss here what trials and journeys my soul, my self, was required to undertake before that process was complete. Nor will I detail here all the twists and turns through which that evolution progressed, before restoring my spirit to my transformed body. Suffice it to say that at length, however tardily, full consciousness returned, was localized in altered flesh.

In drastically altered flesh indeed. More on that subject later.

To begin with I understood little more than that I was alive, though garbed in the cerements of the grave. I was out-of-doors, where bright moonlight—oh, it was undoubtedly only the moon, however fantastically bright it seemed to me—showed me that I was alone, occupying a small glade in a woodland setting. When I came to myself I was crouched on all fours upon the earth, like some beast about to spring. The cold of the winter night meant nothing to me. My limbs were free of any restraint, and by this I knew that I must have somehow escaped my murderers, whose last efforts to torment me filled what were almost my last clear memories.

Almost, I say. For it seemed to me that I could remember listening and watching in some disembodied fashion, even as others prepared my corpse for the grave.

And the newly refrozen snow around me still showed the dirty traces of excavation and burial.

Slowly I stood erect, trying to recognize the sylvan spot in which I found myself. Had it been only a dream of death, that seeming memory of falling to the swords of my treacherous lieutenants, of inhabiting a coffin, of riding in it through the night aboard a jolting wagon?

But now I was not dreaming. I was as certain on this point as the reader is of being wide awake and reading now . . . and just at this critical juncture of metaphysics I was distracted by a peculiar physical sensation.

Something, besides the obvious damage caused by recent wounds, seemed to be gravely amiss with the muscles of my chest. The truth was that I no longer breathed. But this lack was more than compensated for by the discovery, which followed swiftly, that I no longer felt any need to do so.

Pain I still experienced in plenty; sharp pangs, radiating from my many injuries, shot through my body whenever I moved. But I had known worse torment. I was a soldier, and wounds and suffering were part of my natural state.

For the time being I could ignore the pain. And if I were in any danger of bleeding to death, I thought, I would have done so long ere now. The fact was that I did not even feel weak; indeed, quite the opposite. And a quick inspection of my wounds satisfied me that I was no longer bleeding at all.

Strange. But, even stranger, the mere thought of blood evoked neither fear nor disgust, but instead a rich, red thirst, a craving of such intensity that for the moment I forgot all about my pain and injuries and stood there growling like a hungry beast.

That red thirst could not entirely distract me from an even stronger lust. This was a great and all-encompassing drive for vengeance, without which, perhaps, my will might have failed, and I would never have found the power to come out of my grave. This craving was centered primarily upon the traitor Bogdan, and to a lesser extent on his two chief companions, Ronay and Basarab. As for the common soldiers who had taken part in the attack on me, I scarcely thought of them; they had done me no real harm, and besides they were mere hirelings, only obeying orders.

At the moment none of the three men I wanted were in sight, nor did I have the least idea where I might lay hands upon two of them. But as for the third, Ronay, a part of my recent and most strange dream had concerned him. It seemed to me that I could remember someone's voice, saying that Ronay, wounded, unable to ride far, had sought shelter within the nearby monastery of Snagov.

Walking slowly, I was halfway across the clearing, looking for some landmark by which to orient myself, when I heard a small animal scuttling in dead leaves nearby. Acting upon a new instinct, as strange to me as it was irresistible, I pounced on, caught, and killed a rabbit that had innocently chosen to wander nocturnally near my grave.

Aching in the roots of my canines, indifferent to the sensation of furry skin against my mouth, I drank greedily from the torn veins of the little creature. New energy, supremely welcome, flowed into my tormented body. But an access of mental and physical strength only sharpened my craving for revenge.

Casting aside the small, drained body—I cared not for the flesh, the blood was all—I began to consider with new clarity the all-encompassing strangeness of my new mode of existence. The sharpness of my senses with which I had detected the rabbit's exact location, the speed and precision with which I had been able to seize the creature before it could spring away—these augured well for my ability to accomplish whatever vengeance I might decide upon.

But now, newly fed, I was able to think beyond the needs and cravings of the moment. Where was I? Certainly not upon the field where I had fallen. And how, really, had I come here? I could not doubt the reality of the scene on the battlefield. But to credit my memory, to think that I had somehow witnessed my own death and burial, seemed a great absurdity.

Though I had not yet begun to realize the fact, I had of course awakened standing on my own grave, my transformed body having risen like so much smoke up through my coffin's wooden lid and all the earth that held it down. Stalking to and fro about the little clearing, moving in effortless silence, I knew only that I experienced a strong attraction to one particular spot of bare earth, in the center of the disturbed ground.

Snarling with impatience, I at last broke free—for the moment—of this tender psychic bond between myself and my grave. The Snagov monastery was somewhere nearby, it must be, and Ronay might be in it.

In a moment I had passed beyond the borders of the clearing. The thousand little sounds of the winter countryside at night came to my ears, whose powers seemed preternaturally acute. The subtle moonlight, even in the shadows of the trees, seemed to my eyes as bright as day. Pain wracked me with each stride I took, yet I could continue to ignore it. I scarcely noticed that the snow made little sound or none beneath my feet, or that my skin, so lightly clothed in a mere winding-sheet, was and remained impervious to winter cold.

Certain subliminal clues that I had absorbed during my supposed dream, or derived from the general shape of the landscape around me, eventually combined to give me a firm idea of where I was. I altered my course, striding briskly over dormant winter fields, passing like a shadow through leafless groves. Indeed, it was no trouble to increase my pace to a wolflike if still two-legged lope.

Minutes later, from a treeless hilltop, I had my confirmation. Snagov on its island was clearly visible before me in the moonlight, and in the next moment I was loping toward it.

Snow and rain had entirely ceased to fall. I did not know it then, but almost twenty-four hours had passed since my interment. The sky was quite clear enough to allow me to get my directions from stars and moon. I realized now that I must have awakened at a considerable distance from the battlefield. Everything in this new and strange reality seemed to confirm the truth of the experience that I still in some sense regarded as a dream.

As I descended from the hill the lake vanished from sight behind trees, only to reappear as I drew near it. There, as plainly visible to me as in the noonday sun, was the island, with the main buildings of the monastery on it. One light only was visible, in the highest window of a low tower. The ice that sheathed the lake was too dull to offer any reflection of this spark.

If what the dream-voices had told me was correct, Ronay was there, somewhere, sheltered in one of those dark buildings. With scarcely a pause for thought, I stepped out upon the ice. It was no colder beneath my soles than the frozen earth and snow had been.

The weather, as I may perhaps have mentioned, had been somewhat unseasonably mild in recent days, and the ice was thin. When there came a sudden crack beneath my feet, I found that a new instinct took over, shaping my reaction. My body changed form almost instantly. Hearing and vision blurred; I sensed, somehow, that a human observer would have seen nothing but a cloud of mist where my form had been. Continuing to advance by the power of my will alone, I drifted wraithlike over the watery gap.

The change to mist-form and back again was accomplished smoothly and almost unconsciously. I had almost ceased to be aware at all of my own condition, with the thought that Ronay, at least, was now nearly within my grasp.

Arriving on the island in solid human shape, I stepped lightly up the snowy slope of its south shore and paused to listen carefully just outside the monastery walls. Inside approximately a hundred human beings were asleep, some fretfully, some peacefully. The wall was twice my height, too high for a man to leap and catch the top of it. But a moment later, obeying the prompting of another instinct, I had done just that.

Then I was crouching atop the monastery's outer wall, surveying the scene within.

There was the tall church, there the cloister, and there a block of monastic cells, with barns and other outbuildings clustered beyond, all as clearly visible to me as if in broad daylight.

I drifted rather than jumped down on the inside of the wall. No one, as far as I could tell, had observed my arrival. Next I tried to decide where my prey, if he was indeed within these walls, was most likely to be found. With increasing impatience I walked among the courtyards and cloisters, having no idea in which of them Ronay might be sheltered.

Observing that a light burned in the church, and that the front door was partly open, I moved in that direction. I experienced no difficulty crossing the threshold onto consecrated ground. The sanctuary lamp burned on the altar, and close before it two hooded figures, their backs to me, knelt in prayer. I took the opportunity to launch a paternoster myself, but made no sound, and neither of the monks turned around. I could hear them breathing and mumbling, and I was sure, on hearing even that much of their voices, that neither was the man I sought.

Outside the church again, I drifted once more, almost at random, in the form of mist. On my right hand were the stables, and some of the animals sensed my presence, but it did not alarm them. On my left hand were the latrines. Since Ronay was wounded, I thought, he would most likely be in the infirmary, wherever that might be.

Again I took my search indoors. At some doorways, leading to the actual cells, I experienced a mystifying inability to enter, as if invisible glass of immense strength were there to hold me back. I growled, and prowled on, perforce exploring only where I was permitted.

Eventually, exhausting the possibilities, I managed to locate the right building. It was not a proper habitation, but only a temporary shelter, and I experienced no barrier to my uninvited presence.

The interior consisted mainly of one large room, containing four simple beds set moderately close together against one wall. Three of the beds were empty. In the fourth lay the man I had come seeking.

In those days of deadly ignorance regarding matters medical, fever after a wound was as common as not, and

Ronay's had set in on him already. His face was bathed in sweat, and I observed that in his restless tossing he had kicked back the blanket with which some tender monk had covered him. I could also see that bandages, now bloody and past due to be changed, had been skillfully bound to his right side. Those bandages, along with the clusters of dried herbs and jars of salve upon his bedside table, showed that some considerable amount of time and care had been devoted to the traitor's treatment. Well, it had all been in vain.

No attendant was currently on duty. An empty chair stood close beside Ronay's bed, and another chair, with his clothing, armor, and weapons piled on it, was placed against the wall a few paces distant, under a carven wooden crucifix, about half life-size.

My old associate's eyes were closed at the moment of my entry into the room, but his febrile tossing showed that he was not asleep. Despite my silence as I came in, he promptly opened his eyes, raised his head, and stared at me. The small light of a wall icon and that of a single additional candle on a table near the middle of the room sufficed to show him my figure. I took on solid human shape once more as I came walking toward him—gaunt, horribly scarred with sword cuts, corpse-pale, and doubtless (I really never noticed at the time) carrying traces of grave-soil clinging to my cerements.

My victim gasped—at least he made a most extraordinary sound, for which I can find no better name—and I thought for a moment that he was going to scream. But after that one gasp he was stricken silent, as if from sudden lack of breath. His countenance distorted itself into that indescribable expression that appears only when nightmares come true. In the centuries that have passed since that night, I have grown familiar with the variations of that look.

Then, galvanized, Ronay abruptly moved, displaying more energy than I had thought his fevered, weakened body likely to possess. Trying his best to push himself up out of bed, and finding his strength unequal to the task, he clawed about him with both hands, as if he hoped to find a weapon. His anguished gaze turned toward his sword and dagger, which lay piled on the chair with his other property, and in a moment he had fallen out of bed in a futile effort to extend his reaching arm that far.

The floor was stone. Ronay fell hard and lay still for a moment, but he did not lose consciousness. As a result of the fall and his exertion, the wound in his right side had opened again, and I saw the red come welling swiftly from beneath the bandages. My old associate's face was pale, as pale no doubt as my own, and I experienced some concern that he might even die before I came within reach of him.

Ronay, keeping his face turned toward me as I continued to advance, tried awkwardly to get away, dragging himself backward on his elbows.

His lips were livid, his voice was thin and gasping. "Drakulya—no. You are not here. You are a vision, a vision sent by the Fiend!"

Crying out thus, he failed to realize how far he had moved in his surprisingly rapid backward progress. The chair, top-heavy with his arms and armor, tipped easily when he bumped into it, spilling its burden that crashed with a great noise on the stone floor.

Moaning, scrambling, Ronay turned his back upon me for a moment, clawing for his dagger. Not that he hoped to stab me yet again. No, he understood that matters had gone beyond that in my case. Rather, when he had grasped the weapon, he turned back toward me, holding the hilt up, making a cross of hilt and blade above his hands.

"Get thee back to hell!" my former lieutenant shrieked at me. Or, rather, so he tried to shriek. The sound was more like a sob. His voice was failing now, in his extreme weakness.

I paused, a couple of strides away, considering the fevered wreck before me. Actually, as a result of my own somewhat befuddled state, I had come this far with no firm plan of revenge in mind. Perhaps chief among my mixed feelings at the moment was disappointment. I had naturally wanted to catch Ronay in full possession of his faculties. Now, on the contrary, I was sure that the fool must be totally delirious to imagine that I had come from anywhere but solid earth. I was no evil spirit, but Drakulya, a man. Though slain, a live man still, because I had refused to die.

I, of course, was conscious of no effect upon myself from all of Ronay's terrified onslaught of commands and curses. Certainly it would have been hard to find anyone less qualified than he as a spiritual authority. The dagger he brandished was only a crude cross, a sacred symbol held by an evil man. I could have lunged forward and snatched it away from him. But I did not. Nor did I speak. I only resumed my advance—very slowly.

"Come not to me! You don't want me!" Now the wretch was almost sobbing. He had no energy remaining to drag himself away. "It was Bogdan who planned your death. He who tortured you, not I! Seek Bogdan! I am innocent!"

I spoke at last, quite naturally, as I thought. "Oh, Bogdan's turn is coming, I assure you. And Basarab's. But yours has come already." And at this pleasant thought I smiled.

This coward who had conspired to murder me was

gasping continuously now, trying and almost failing to draw breath. And now he threw down his useless dagger and, like a child, tried to hide his eyes. To make the bad dream go away. Standing over him, filled with disgust, I reached down and snatched him up. To me he felt even lighter than a child. I tried what I might do with my grip upon his shoulder and could feel the bones there begin to snap, quite satisfactorily, beneath the pressure of my fingers.

Of course with all the noise of falling arms and armor he had made, we were bound to be interrupted. Having just completed the mangling of one of my victim's shoulders, I was about to begin upon another joint when I heard behind me a shout of mingled rage and horror. Turning, I beheld a robed monk, who gazed back at me with astonishment, fear, and fury mingled in his countenance.

Before anything else could happen, several more monks came running in and, on finding their patient in the grasp of such an apparition, added their voices to the shouts of the first.

If they were going to do no more than shout, I could ignore these intruders for the moment. I turned my attention back to the subject of my justice. Ronay in my grip looked corpselike, his eyes half-open, breath suspended. I was gazing at him closely to determine whether or not he was already dead when to my surprise I felt my arm seized from behind. The monk who had run in first, a small man foolhardy in his bravery, was interfering. I shook him off with irritation, and he flew back to sprawl across an empty bed.

To my great disappointment, close inspection confirmed that Ronay was dead. No doubt about it. Loss of blood and shock combined had done the job, and what good were all my nascent plans for vengeance now? I hurled the corpse away, and was just growling my irritation at this development when a great blow smote me from behind. Such was the savage impact that I imagined for a moment I had been hit with a mace; fortunately the force was mainly distributed across my upper back and left shoulder, falling only slightly on my head.

Recoiling, I spun around to face this new challenge. It came from the courageous little monk, and the weapon he had swung at me, and was preparing to swing again, was the great wooden crucifix that a few moments ago had been hanging on the infirmary wall.

Hissing and growling, I wasted no time in beating a retreat. My object in invading the monastery had been accomplished—insofar as it ever could be—and I judged it would be blasphemous to treat either monk or crucifix as my first impulse had suggested when one struck me with the other.

Even as I passed out of doors, it crossed my mind to wonder what stories, of my monstrously transformed existence, the monks would now begin to tell. But for the moment I felt little concern over what stories might be told. Ronay had now paid for his treachery, as much as he would ever be made to pay for it in this world. It was time for me to seek out his two villainous companions.

But first, new instincts urged me; there was something else that I *must* do.

What was it?

The answer came to me with an inner certainty, beyond all questioning: Time now for me to go—home.

As I was climbing the outer wall of the monastery, somewhere not far away a rooster crowed. The sky in the east was turning gray as the dark surface of the lake passed softly and swiftly under me again. First the water gurgled and chuckled beneath the softened ice I trod upon. And then the open water drifted beneath my feet as I passed on my way home.

Presently, with the gray eastern sky now brightening almost unbearably, I found myself once more in the glade where I had awakened. Stretching my suddenly weary body out to rest, upon the surface—as I then thought—of that most attractively disturbed patch of earth, I surrendered to dreamless and innocent slumber. Only dimly was I aware, without any particular concern, that I was sinking like so much gentle rain into the earth. I was fast asleep long before the first direct rays of the sun appeared above to touch the barren tops of winter trees.

This time my slumbers were prolonged. My second post-mortem awakening did not take place, as I now believe, until sometime in the early spring of the year of Our Lord 1477. Again I found myself standing, at night, in the clearing above my secret grave. Again I fed, quite ravenously, upon the blood of the first mammalian creature I encountered—it chanced to be a sheep this time.

I understood, vaguely and without knowing how, that a considerable period of time had passed, and that doubtless my surviving enemies were still beyond my reach. Again I slept. Other periods of lucidity and mobility followed, at seemingly random intervals of a few days, weeks, or months.

Among the many aspects of my episodic new life that puzzled me intensely was the fact that I never saw the sun. Actually I could no longer even imagine myself directly confronting the intensity of that solar fire. Could I have feared anything, it would have been the sun. Also more than I could understand were the recurrent, lengthy periods of deathlike torpor in the comforting darkness underground, and the fact that blood—only animal blood, so far—was all the sustenance I craved.

As more time passed the pain of my wounds steadily diminished, until they ceased to hurt at all. Healing progressed, and even the scars, at least the ones that I could see, began to fade.

Even in the face of all these oddities, even with the memory of my own burial to contemplate, the idea never seriously crossed my mind that I had died a true death, that I might now be really dead. Gradually, however, I was forced to admit that neither was I alive, at least according to my old, mundane way of looking at things. This mode of existence, for which I still lacked a name, or was unwilling to assign one, was indeed something new.

There came an awakening different from all that had gone before. Someone, in the middle of a spring night, had discovered my grave. And now the unknown, rhythmic spade, working with benefit of a full-throated nightingale accompaniment, was industriously digging up my coffin.

5

Angie, retreating into the guest bedroom to get away from that soft terrible sound at the front door, turned on the tape machine again. For one thing, she was terrified at the idea of falling asleep; and for another, she had an urge to hear more of the fantastic story on the tape. Her urge was perhaps illogical, but really it was not as crazy as the nightmare into which she and John had fallen during the past few hours. She had a feeling, strong though impossible to justify, that the tape might tell her something that would be useful in getting out of the bad dream again.

Some fifteen minutes later she turned the tape player off again. Unable to resist a horrified fascination with what might be happening at the front door, she returned to the living room.

Here all was silent. No one beat at the front door or pushed the bell. The viewer was still turned off. John, sitting in one of the armchairs, looked up, hollow-eyed, when Angie appeared. Clutching the arms of his chair, he said: "The pounding stopped a few minutes ago."

Feeling compelled to look, Angie went to the viewer near the door and turned it on.

The screen showed that the hallway outside was deserted.

John had got up to stand behind her, staring over her shoulder at the viewer. Now he let out pent-up breath in an exhausted sigh. "They may have let her go," he said.

Angie didn't answer.

"We couldn't have helped her, Angie. With you in here I couldn't take a chance on letting them get in." Then he paused. "Hell, I wouldn't have let them in anyway. I couldn't."

She sighed. "Did you ever get through to Joe?"

"I left a message on his phone. That's all I could do. I know Joe and Kate sometimes turn off the ringer on the extension in their room at night."

A wise move, Angie thought silently, for someone like Joe Keogh, who counts a vampire among his friends, and has married into a family where they call a vampire uncle. Who would be insane enough to do a thing like that?

Angie raised her hands, spread her fingers out, and looked at them. Suddenly she found herself wondering what it would do to you, inside, to have a couple of those little parts of yourself hacked off or torn off or whatever. She was going to have to get the story from John, someday, in detail.

At least her hands weren't shaking. But there had been moments during these last few hours when she'd had trouble deciding whether she was awake or asleep. Or simply losing her mind.

The phone in the alcove rang. John hesitated, gave her a look as if warning her to be on guard, and answered.

"It's Joe," he said a moment later, and she saw his shoulders slump with relief.

Angie at the moment was too tired, too seriously disconnected from events, to feel much of anything. Sitting down on the sofa, she listened to John relating, in the manner of one who expected to be believed, the events of the night just ended. Then, marvelously, what Angie could deduce of Joe's responses to this story suggested strongly that Joe did not think they were crazy. Joe was evidently not demanding to know why the police had not been summoned. It even sounded as if he were ready to give them some kind of help.

At this point Angie began to come out of her dazed state.

Presently John hung up the phone. Obviously he had found his talk with Joe enormously reassuring. Now he announced in an almost normal voice that Joe had promised to come around as soon as possible, probably within a couple of hours. Angie began to be comforted; even if Joe thought he was only humoring a couple of lunatics, something would be resolved now, decisive action would be taken.

While they were waiting for Joe Keogh to arrive, John stalked from room to room of the locked and sealed apartment. He paused frequently to listen at the front and back doors, flicking the viewers on and off. Only once was there someone in the hall, an innocent passerby apparently. He paused also to look out of the windows. Outside there continued to be nothing but grim Chicago weather, once more turning foul enough to hide most of the city even in broad daylight. Several times in the course of his restless prowling John went into the one room where the curtains were still drawn against the daylight, where Uncle Matthew still lay in silence. Twice Angie followed him.

On the third of these visits they paused beside the bed. Now she thought, and John agreed, that the patient's color was a little better. But his lips still looked very dry.

"Shouldn't we get him a drink of water? Or—"

"No. He only drinks one thing."

Angie was about to ask John again whether he was

serious, but bit back the question just in time. Then she suddenly remembered something. "John?"

"What?"

"I've been thinking all along that I've heard the name 'Matthew Maule' somewhere before. I just remembered where. It's in Hawthorne."

John looked at her, uncomprehending.

"Nathaniel Hawthorne, *The House of the Seven Gables*. Matthew Maule is the old wizard who's burned at the beginning of the book. What was the curse he called down on the Pyncheons, the people who'd destroyed him? 'God has—'" She suddenly bit her lip.

"What?"

"'God has given him blood to drink.' That was it."

The two of them stood looking down at Uncle Matthew.

Angie said: "I think he definitely looks a little more— normal."

"Yes, I think you're right. Despite the fact that it's daytime, which ordinarily makes him weaker. God, I hope he's starting to come out of it." The last sentence had the sound of a fervent prayer.

Taking Uncle Matthew by his limp right hand, speaking clearly and distinctly, John did his best to pass along the good news that help, in the person of Joe Keogh, was on the way. But the dried lips would not speak in response, the glassy eyes remained unfocused.

At last John dropped the pale hand and straightened up. "I don't have any idea if he hears me or not. I hope he understands."

"At least he does look a little better. And Joe's coming."

They retreated to the kitchen, where Angie on an impulse began looking into the refrigerator and cupboards.

Somewhat to her surprise she discovered clean dishes and silverware, unopened containers of untouched food, including a fresh carton of milk. Sink and dishwasher were empty. It looked to Angie as if the apartment had just been cleaned up and stocked with supplies in anticipation of guests. The coffeemaker sitting on the counter was new, and as far as Angie could tell still entirely unused. She decided to brew a pot in an effort to stay awake. She still wasn't hungry, but once the smell of coffee hit the air, John decided that he was starving. He found a melon in the refrigerator's vegetable bin and cut it up, then started to open a package of bacon and a carton of eggs. Bread came out of the freezer. Morning daylight, food, and domesticity could hold nightmares at arm's length.

Angie joined in the breakfast preparations, moving about the kitchen chores mechanically, her mind still trying to fight free of terror and shock. Coffee didn't help very much. When she'd had two cups and had eaten something without really being aware of what she swallowed, she sat in the living room and tried to rest while John methodically took care of the dirty dishes. But every time her body started to relax, her eyelids began to sag, an onrush of unreasoning terror came to jerk her wide awake again. The memory of Elizabeth Wiswell's face, her blood-stained throat, her voice, her feeble pounding on the door, would not be exorcised.

Not only was Angie's exhaustion growing, but anger swelled up in her too, making room for itself by forcing layers of fear aside. Several times she asked John: "But what did they want with him?"

"All I know is somehow they managed to—poison him. Drug him. And then while he's knocked out they come around and try to get at him. So what they want can't be anything good."

"How did they poison him, do you suppose?"

John only shook his head.

Giving up for the moment on her attempt to rest, Angie walked to a window and looked out past the wide-open curtains. There was the lake, three or four blocks away horizontally and a comparable distance below. At such a remove, in a momentary patch of sunlight, the water looked tranquil.

She said again, more hopefully this time: "Maybe they've really gone away."

John snorted. "Maybe they want us to think so. I wouldn't bet on it. I wouldn't bet on it at all. Maybe they hope we'll run out on the old man while we have the chance. But I think they'll be back, when the sun goes down if not before."

"And Liz?"

"I don't know what happened to her. I just don't know. But we couldn't have helped her last night. There was nothing we could have done."

"Anyway, you think we're safe in here for the time being?"

"If they couldn't break in last night, I don't think they can do it now." John turned his gaze toward her and his shoulders slumped. He looked exhausted. "I'm sorry, honey."

"Not your fault." Though deep inside, justly or unjustly, she felt angry at him for getting her into this. And for not trying somehow to help the waitress.

John started thinking aloud. "One thing that worries me is that not all of them are vampires. That Stewart wasn't."

"You said that before."

"Yes. That means some of them will be as active as we are during the daytime."

"We're going to have to sleep sometime!"

"Take it easy, honey." He looked at her in a kind of critical horror. "You're moving around like a sleepwalker and your eyelids are falling shut. You get some sleep now, before Joe gets here. It's as good a time as any."

Angie tried, taking off her shoes and stretching out on the sofa in the day-bright living room. But she still kept waking up with a start of terror every time she started to doze off. Between them they decided that John had better take the first nap.

At a little before nine o'clock, a brisk tap came at the door. Angie, slumped in an armchair in a state between sleep and waking, jumped up, but she couldn't make herself go to the viewer. She hastened to wake John, who was lying on the sofa fully clothed, snoring heavily.

The tap was repeated, urgently, even as he awoke and hurried to switch on the viewer. In a moment his shoulders slumped with relief, and he was opening the door. "It's Joe," he said.

In another moment Joe Keogh, wearing a topcoat, was in the room. Angie had met him a couple of times, briefly, over the last few months. Joe was about forty, his fair hair beginning to be streaked almost invisibly with gray. Of average size and sparely muscular, he couldn't have put on more than a few pounds since his days as a Chicago cop. Today his tough-looking face was set in a grim expression.

John did not waste a second in barring and chaining the door again behind him.

Joe looked quickly around, while in the process of pulling off his topcoat and tossing it on a chair. He was wearing a sportcoat now and an open-collared shirt. He nodded to Angie and gave her a smile calculated to be reassuring. "How you doing?"

She was sitting in a chair, feeling weak in the knees.

"Better, now that you're here. You must think we're crazy, but—"

"Oh, no. I know better than that. John and I have both been through this kind of thing before. How's the old man doing?"

"No change," said John. "Still the way I described him to you on the phone."

"Let me see him."

In Uncle Matthew's bedroom Joe, frowning, bent over the bed and inspected the patient without touching him. He could only shake his head afterward. Angie observed that he looked more worried now than when he'd entered the apartment. "Damned if I know. I've never seen anything like it." He studied Angie. "I suppose Johnny's been explaining a few things to you?"

"I don't know if I can make myself believe what he's told me. I keep thinking we ought to call the police."

The ex-cop shook his head. "No, John's right, that wouldn't be a good idea."

Johnny interrupted to ask their visitor: "Was anyone watching the place when you came in?"

"No. But that doesn't mean they're not around. Angie, tell me more about this guy who calls himself— what? Valentine Kaiser?"

Angie repeated in more detail the story of her phone call from Kaiser, and her coffee-shop meeting with him. Joe, who hadn't heard any of this before, listened with intense concentration.

When she'd finished, John contributed his own description of the man, as he had seen him briefly standing in the hall. He added: "No doubt about *what* he is."

Joe was nodding slowly. "I think I could tell. Hell, I know I could. And you should be able to tell better than me."

"After what I went through eleven years ago, there was no doubt in my mind. I don't have any trouble recognizing one of them when I see one."

Joe was suddenly sounding like a cop. "Is this Kaiser one of that bunch who were involved in your kidnapping?"

"No. I'm sure he's not. I never saw him before. But I can tell what he is."

Something else was beginning to bother Angie, bother her more and more, and she decided that she was going to take care of it. Maybe she couldn't do much for the old man, as Joe called him, but at least she would wipe the blood off his face. While the men talked, she went into the adjoining bathroom to wet a towel.

While in the process of doing this she discovered that in this bathroom there was no mirror over the sink. A flat, glassy screen of the proper size and shape was there. But it reflected only dully.

The screen was built right into the wall, and wouldn't open when Angie tugged at a corner—no medicine chest behind it. And just above the screen, angled down to aim directly at her, was the glassy end of a dark cylinder, recognizable as the eye of a video camera.

Wondering, Angie observed and touched a switch beside the screen. Extra vanity lights came on, and in a moment her own image had appeared, in color and close-up, on the screen that took the place of a mirror. The picture had something odd about it, and Angie needed a moment to realize that this was not the reversed image that an ordinary mirror always presented. When Angie raised her right hand, the right hand of the young woman in the electronic picture, not the left, went up.

Leaving the video turned on, she finished wetting her towel and came back out into the bedroom. "John? Did you see this?"

Following her gesture, he went into the bathroom and looked at the camera and screen. Joe, who tagged along, grinned faintly and shook his head as if in admiration. "Kind of unusual, huh?" But in fact neither of the men seemed especially surprised.

Back in the bedroom, Angie bent over the man in the bed and gently wiped the dried gore from around his mouth, his chin, and his bare chest. His eyes blinked once. Despite everything, she found much that was attractive about his face. Then, shuddering just perceptibly, she threw the towel into a laundry basket.

Speaking about the video arrangement, she said: "I've never seen anything like it. But I can see there are advantages. You see yourself the way you are, I mean not reversed."

The men looked at each other. John drew a deep breath. "Honey? The real point is that Uncle Matthew doesn't care for mirrors."

"He doesn't—?"

"No. And they don't do him any good anyway. I'm only surprised that some of the other rooms, like the one we slept in, do have them. No, I guess I'm not surprised. He likes to be courteous to his guests."

Angie was thinking aloud. "It's almost like he's— disfigured, somehow. Though of course he isn't, he's very handsome. I mean, about the mirrors, and being a re-cluse—" But no, she wasn't thinking straight at all. If you wanted to avoid seeing your own disfigurement, how would a video camera be any better than a mirror? Of course you could leave it turned off—

Joe cut in. "Angie, you haven't got it yet."

"I haven't?"

Joe looked around the room. "Have you got a small

mirror? In your purse, maybe?" He sounded calm and deadly serious.

Without asking any questions Angie went out of the room and came back in a moment with her purse, from which she extracted a small mirror, holding it out to Joe.

"Don't give it to me, hold it yourself. And take a good look at him. In your mirror." Joe gestured toward the man on the bed.

She tried, and blinked, and rubbed the compact glass. She tried again, from several angles, and in several intensities of light. There were the upper bedclothes, cleanly visible, but they were mounded up over nothing but hollow invisibility. And there was the lower sheet, with its crackling plastic envelope of earth beneath it, pressed down as if under the weight of a solid body. But if there was a body there, the mirror was letting her look right through it. She needed a minute to convince herself that the image of the being she had been calling Uncle Matthew was not going to appear as a reflection.

Once having achieved this understanding, she turned a helpless face to Joe.

"Don't ask me why or how," he said. "I've heard of the laws of optics and all that. Maybe there's really an image there in your mirror, but the human brain just won't see it."

And that of course was no help at all.

Angie still had had no sleep to speak of, and in her present state of exhaustion she was turning abnormally suggestible, likely to accept almost anything without an argument. Now she began to fear hallucinations. But reason and fear were both losing the struggle against sleep. At last, on a sofa, in the security of as much daylight as the apartment afforded, she succumbed. Her slumbers were beset by dreams, dreams of pale anonymous faces that came drifting in the night outside the windows of the apartment, mouthing pleas and threats. In her dreams she thought she could hear the creatures through the thick and otherwise inviolable glass, but their voices had no power to awaken her.

When Angie did wake up she felt rested, and more herself than she had for a long time. It was almost as if she had slept for many hours, though the time was only a little after noon. The day was cloudy as before, but the light was still comfortingly full. Angie, now starting to feel hungry, stretched, wondered if she should take a shower, and instead went first into the kitchen where the men were seated at the table with coffee mugs in front of them. Abstractedly she gathered materials and made herself a cheese sandwich. There was mustard in the refrigerator. She poured herself coffee, and prepared to make a second pot.

Then, chewing her first bite of sandwich, she turned to the men. Her voice was deadly serious. "I've had some sleep and I think I'm in my right mind. And now, you are going to tell me what it's all about. Starting from the beginning. The truth and the whole truth. Or else, I swear to both of you, I am going to run out into the hall and scream and scream until the cops come."

Joe was not impressed. He shook his head. "I wouldn't bet it'll be the cops who reach you first if you do that," he said. "Anyway, John told you right. We don't want the cops in here. Not now. They'll come in and see the old man and call an ambulance—"

Angie interrupted. "I know! I know. And we can't afford to let him be taken out of his dwelling place. I just

86

hate to believe I don't have running out and screaming to fall back on as a last resort."

"I think among the three of us we can come up with some better ideas than that."

She pulled up a chair to the table and said to Joe: "Let's hear yours."

"All right. First of all, the people who are trying to force their way in here are vampires, or at least their leader is." He looked at her searchingly. "It's important that you believe that."

"If you and John both—yes. I can believe it."

"Good. Next, there's something they want from"— Joe jerked his head in the direction of the bedroom— "him. From what you tell me they did last night, and what they said, all too probably it's his life. Most likely it's a matter of revenge. But John and I both owe him our lives, or the equivalent. So, we're standing by him."

Angie tossed her hair back. "I wouldn't want you to do anything else. So if I'm going to be a part of this crazy family I stand by him too."

"Good." Joe's expression relaxed a trifle. "But you're in a somewhat different position, Angie. You had no idea what you were getting into here. I'd like to be able to offer you a way out, but that's not possible. It's too late. You're in it now, hell or high water, and all we can do is fight it out together."

In the silence that followed all three people at the table distinctly heard a faint groan from the direction of the bedrooms. After exchanging startled glances they were pushing back chairs, bumping into one another, rushing to get a look at their host.

The one they called the old man had raised himself on one elbow in the bed. He groaned again as the three breathing folk rushed into his room, and he seemed to be trying to speak. Angie, with a rush of relief, thought that he looked much more human than he had for many hours.

The three clustered around him, all talking at once, then all falling silent as they concentrated on trying to understand what he was trying to say. Their efforts were still in vain.

Then Uncle Matthew collapsed, groaning, flat on his back once more. He gave up trying to talk. Still, he looked better, more alive, than he had for many hours.

Joe went to the bedroom windows, making sure that the special curtains were tightly drawn. The old man now looked as if he were sleeping peacefully. Except that there was no sign of breathing. But Angie noted a faint pulse visible in his temple; when she put her fingers on the wiry arm she could feel it in his wrist as well.

Joe, leading the others back to the living room, looked almost elated. "He's starting to come out of it, and that's great. Especially in daytime. His vitality's usually down once the sun's up. I'd say if he makes it through the day there's a good chance he'll really snap out of this tonight."

John expressed agreement. "Then he can tell us what happened."

"God, I hope so. He just doesn't get sick, in my experience. Actually he looks like he's been drugged. But I never heard of any drug that would take effect on one of them . . . tell me again about this woman who was with him last night."

Angie and John obliged. Shortly after Joe had heard that episode in greater detail, he put on his topcoat and got ready to depart. On the verge of leaving, he delivered a few hearty comments obviously meant to boost their morale, capped by his firm promise to return. He also advised against their leaving the apartment for any reason.

"But right now I'd better move along. There're things

I can do better from outside, and I'm going to start doing 'em." He looked at Angie. "I'm not going to offer to escort you away from here. I honestly don't know if you'd be safer staying here or coming with me, but I suspect that staying here is best."

"If John's staying here, I'm staying too. What would I do, go home and wait alone for them to catch up with me there?"

Joe, looking gloomy, thought about it and shrugged. "I don't know if they'd try to do that or not. I just don't know."

"What're you going to do?" John asked him.

"Try to contact Mina, for one thing." He looked at Angie, groping for some quick way to explain. "An old friend of an old friend. She might be a big help." John nodded.

In another moment Joe was gone, out the front door. The viewing screen gave no sign that anyone had observed his departure.

"I feel a lot better with Joe on the job," said John after the door was bolted up securely after him.

"I do too. At least I certainly did when he was here. Johnny, I wish you'd tell me more about this mess we're in."

John led the way back into the kitchen, where he started to make himself a sandwich. "I'll tell you what I can," he said. Then he nodded in the direction of the bedrooms. "He could tell his own story much better than I can. I guess he thought that listening to the tape would break it to you gradually—I don't know. I've been trying to figure out how to tell you about him for about a month now, and I'm still trying."

"Go ahead." Now her voice was subdued; John had his sandwich made, and she was starting mechanically to clean up the coffee cups, the paper towels, the knife with cheese on it.

John sat at the table, munching between sentences. "All right. He's not really my uncle, and his name isn't really Matthew Maule. At least that's only one of a number of names he uses. When I was kidnapped, at the age of sixteen, he was calling himself Dr. Emile Corday. Just an old friend of the family, visiting from London. The Chicago cops are probably still looking for Dr. Corday. Not that he did anything to be ashamed of then. The people he hurt were all kidnappers."

"Oh."

"So I'll tell you what I can. But I can't tell it the way he would. I can't even find the right place to begin."

6

Out in the corridor, heading directly for the elevators, Joe Keogh got as far as the door of the next apartment down the hall before his brisk passage was interrupted.

She came out into the hallway smiling in his direction, making eye contact as if she was determined to intercept him and was not going to be too subtle about it. She might easily have seen him coming, for the door that she emerged from was strategically placed at a bend in the passage, so anyone looking through a wide-angle viewer from inside would command the stretch of hallway in front of the Maule apartment. She was a fortyish lady, average height, overweight but trying to carry it well, with skillfully if showily dyed hair, rich black streaked with silver. Subtle things about her face suggested that battles had been and were still being fought across that territory, again with skill, to prevent or wipe out jowls as well as wrinkles. What he could deduce about her body, swathed in a kind of robe or housecoat—Joe could never remember all the exact classifications for the things that women wore—suggested that it was well maintained, if not exactly shapely.

She opened her door quickly and came out, light on her feet despite her heft, bumping into Joe as he moved to step around her.

"Excuse me, I'm sorry!" Her voice was soft and pleasant, her smile a real charmer. "Were you by any chance in Mr. Maule's apartment?"

No, she's not. That was all that Joe could think of in the first moment, looking the woman over carefully. He mumbled some kind of an apology for bumping into her.

"I'm Mrs. Hassler?" As if she felt rebuffed by his failure to answer her question, the lady now seemed to be asking him if her name was quite acceptable. "It's really none of my business, but I know Mr. Maule slightly. Through the Residents' Association. And I was wondering if he's all right."

Getting too rude with the neighbors could be a bad mistake; if none of them had called in the cops yet, after a night of strange disturbances in the corridor, one of them might easily be on the brink of doing so.

"Mrs.—ah, Hassler, did you say?" Joe wondered fleetingly whether to introduce himself, and if so what name to use. He put off the decision. "Yes, I just came from Maule's place. He's okay. Was there something that alarmed you?"

"Well . . ." Now the lady was going to be reluctant to commit herself. From his police days Joe could recognize the type, desperately curious but not wanting to be involved. She went on: "There were some people in the hallway last night, in front of his door. I don't know who they were . . . I don't know if you could really call it a disturbance, but it was unusual."

Joe shrugged lightly. "I wasn't here last night. Actually, yes, he's a little under the weather today, in fact he's asleep right now. But he's going to be all right."

"He's a *nice* gentleman," she said softly, fixing him with a dark-eyed, liquid stare. "It's none of my business, but I wondered."

"Yes. Well. He's quite all right."

Still Mrs. Hassler was not ready to be reassured and take herself away. "In the city it seems you never know your neighbors. At least rarely. You'd think that in this building we'd be a community. Or at least here on this floor. But it doesn't seem to work that way."

"It would be nice if it did." Joe gave the lady his best, most reassuring smile and a little nod. Then he turned away and moved on. He could hear her door close softly before he'd gone a dozen steps. She thought the old man was a nice gentleman. The way she said it meant she didn't know him all that well—which was no surprise. A much less experienced seducer than the old man would know enough to keep his affairs at a reasonable distance from where he lived.

Before Joe had gone twenty more steps he passed a man and a woman walking in the other direction. Their goal, at this point, could have been any of half a dozen apartments, including Maule's or Mrs. Hassler's. As the couple drew to one side of the corridor to pass him, Joe gave each of them brief but intense scrutiny. He'd be willing to bet his right arm that both these people were breathers. He didn't think he could be fooled, not after knowing the old man so many years, and after certain other encounters less benign. Of course these two innocent-looking breathers still might be agents of the enemy. But Joe didn't think so.

There were about fifty elevators in the building altogether, distributed in several banks, and his wait in this lobby for a descending car was mercifully brief. In another moment he was on his way down. But he hadn't started to relax yet, and it was just as well, because the elevator stopped at the next floor below, and another well-dressed couple got aboard. The woman was on the small side, age hard to guess, hair blond, eyes gray, face strikingly attractive if not conventionally pretty. The man was big, a little taller than Joe, and perfectly matched Angie's description of Valentine Kaiser. Even if the match hadn't been so good, Joe thought he would have known these two at once for what they were. Not that there was anything gross or overt in their appearance to differentiate them from the common run of humanity; with vampires there very seldom was. Corpselike complexions and needle fangs could be considered racial stereotypes, the exception and not the rule.

Broad daylight or not, being cooped up with two of them in the little space, spending long, long seconds well out of public view, was enough to make Joe sweat. No one said anything, but the couple both looked at Joe, and he was sure they knew he knew what they were.

Valentine Kaiser turned away from Joe as soon as the doors closed. Somehow in the next moment he had snapped open the maintenance panel beside the elevator's long row of buttons. Reaching inside, he did something. The elevator stopped right where it was between floors, then, smoothly, with scarcely a pause, it was going up again.

Only when they were ascending did Kaiser break the silence. "We ought to have a talk," he said, smiling at Joe.

"Okay."

"I am Valentine Kaiser. And you—?"

"Joe Keogh."

The other nodded, as if that was the answer he had been expecting. "I've heard the name." He moved his head slightly in the direction of his companion. "This is Lila," he said. Lila stood by smiling at Joe. There were moments when her smile looked kindly, and others when it seemed utterly vacant.

Presently Kaiser reached inside the open panel to manipulate the wiring again. The elevator slowed smoothly to a stop on the ninety-seventh floor. As soon as the door opened Joe's fellow passengers gestured him out. He gave them no argument. They emerged into what looked like some kind of service corridor. Then, with Lila walking ahead at a brisk pace, gesturing for Joe to follow, and Kaiser bringing up the rear, they rounded a corner and passed through an unlocked fire door. Joe, glancing at the door's lock while it was open, decided that the bolts weren't working, having been induced somehow to stay retracted.

The door closed behind them. Now the three people, marching steadily, were treading the concrete steps of a fire stair, going up. Joe wondered how many floors there were above this, but he got no farther than ninety-eight.

Emerging through another fire door, onto the ninety-eighth floor, Joe found himself surrounded by a muted roar of machinery, in a brightly lit, low-ceilinged cavern. One room, he decided, must occupy all or most of the entire level. The view of its more distant portions was blocked by row after row of metal-paneled cabinets, and by bends and straightaways of massive ductwork. The level of noise was high, compounded from fan blades, rushing air, occasional electronic beeps, and other indistinguishable components of the machinery needed to keep the thousands of occupants comfortable in their stores and offices and dwelling units.

No other people were in sight. Valentine Kaiser now led the way, in the manner of a man who knew just where he was going.

Presently, around the corner of an aisle that throbbed

with noise, another vampire met Joe and his escort. This one was a young-looking woman, dressed in jeans and sweater like a college student. She acknowledged Kaiser's arrival with an odd gesture, a nod that was almost a bow, followed by a curious look at Joe.

"Anything yet?" Kaiser demanded of her.

The lookout shook her head, looking disgusted. Kaiser muttered words that sounded like swearing, in a language that reminded Joe of Latin, and moved on.

Lila followed, making sure that Joe came along, as Kaiser led them around another corner. Here some panels had been removed from a bank of metal cabinets, and a figure in coveralls, this one a man and a breather, was at work, with screwdriver, pliers, and some kind of electronic meter.

Looking over the workman's shoulder into the exposed machinery, Joe decided from the number of wires visible that this might be the central tie-up for the building's phone lines.

Kaiser paused just behind the workman. "Any success?"

The man turned his face back over his shoulder, looked scared, and mumbled something.

"You might as well admit it loud and clear, I can hear you anyway. I'm beginning to suspect you're not as much an expert as you've claimed to be."

"Sorry," the workman muttered, not turning around.

"Are you? I'm not sure you know what the word means." Kaiser appeared to be considering how best to explain it.

The man raised his head for a quick look at Joe, as if wondering whether Joe was someone he had to be afraid of too. Then he quickly averted his eyes again.

Joe, leaning back against another paneled unit with his hands in his coat pockets, was observing other features of the surroundings, near and far. These included a power substation, a large part of the building's elevator machinery, and provisions for heating and air-conditioning. Also somewhere nearby, he supposed, would be water tanks and pumps, and of course the phone equipment.

Kaiser gave up staring at his trembling workman and turned to Joe: "I hope you're more useful than he is." He grinned. "You're willing to talk with me, aren't you? Tell me things? Or are you determined to keep secrets?"

"Fine, we can have a talk. Anytime. Would you like to make an appointment?"

Kaiser only grinned. "Maybe we should have our talk sooner rather than later." He ruminated. "Yes, let's do that. But I have a few things to do up here, I'll have to ask you to wait downstairs for me for a few minutes. Lila will walk you down."

Joe didn't ask downstairs where. He was sure that all was going to be made clear to him. Before he and Lila were allowed to depart, Kaiser muttered something privately to the gray-eyed woman, as if giving her special instructions of some kind.

Once she'd received her orders, the woman turned to Joe, put out a hand, and exerted effortless inhuman strength, turning Joe around with a grip on his shoulder as if he were no bigger than a small child. She smiled up at him as she turned him around. Joe knew better than to take it personally. With Lila just behind him, he was marched back to the otherwise still-deserted service stairway and down nine flights of concrete steps to eighty-nine, a residential level.

The corridor here looked just like the one on Uncle Matthew's floor. They encountered no one in the hall. Joe's escort stopped him suddenly, with an effortless tug on his arm, in front of an apartment door. Then Lila took out a key and opened the door and gestured Joe inside.

The place was laid out a little differently from the apartment of Matthew Maule, and was sparsely and plainly furnished. One other person was in the living room, a young woman wearing an army surplus field jacket, open over a dirty-looking shirt. Her jeans were worn, her bare feet grimy. She looked up sharply as Joe and his escort entered, and then relaxed. She was a breather.

"I'll be staying here for a while, dear," Lila said to her in a surprisingly sweet voice. "If you've got anything to do elsewhere, go right ahead."

The young woman seemed about to get up from her seat on the sofa, then changed her mind. "I'm waiting for Val," she said. "You can go ahead, whatever you want."

Lila nodded, apparently satisfied. Joe looked around. He wasn't being invited to sit down. There seemed to be no one else in the apartment, though of course he couldn't see all the rooms.

Casually he started strolling. He liked very much the idea of putting at least a little distance between himself and Lila. His guardian was just standing in the living room, in that untiring way they had. Might as well look the place over a little, if possible, and then—

His stroll had brought him partway down a hall, to a spot from which he could look in through an open bedroom door, past a bed with rumpled sheets and blankets, to an open bathroom door beyond. And in the bathroom was what looked like—

Joe stopped, his mouth suddenly dry. He turned to look back at Lila. Lila, leaning against the front door in a somewhat masculine pose, arms folded, was smiling pleasantly at Joe.

Loosening his topcoat, Joe moved on into the untenanted bedroom and into the bathroom beyond.

It was the waitress, he had no doubt of that from

Angie's and John's description. Red hair, shapely body, naked now. It was hard to tell, under present conditions, about her age. Her limbs were bound with twine, all tied up compactly close to her body in a kind of tumbler's knot, her body suspended head downward over the green-tiled bathtub. Plaster and tile had been knocked in patches from the walls and ceiling, to find a solid purchase for the heavy bolts that had been driven in to give solid support for the chains that held a human body's weight.

Joe was almost sure with his first good look at the discolored face, the half-open eyes, the needle bite wounds on the throat and elsewhere that she was already dead, though a very faint trail of saliva still drooled from the distended lips of her open mouth. The string of clear saliva went trailing down into an indescribable puddle in the tub, where the stopper of the drain was closed, so that the tub had caught and preserved the considerable volume of vomit, blood, and perhaps other fluids that had drained from the woman's body since she was hung up like this.

Joe put out his left hand, and had just time to feel the coldness of Elizabeth Wiswell's shoulder, before a warning voice sounded just behind him.

"Don't touch!"

He turned to see Lila, who had moved a couple of rooms closer, almost twinkling at him. Joe leaned against the doorframe, fighting down a sudden urge to vomit. Briefly he allowed himself to close his eyes.

"And don't throw up in the tub. That would ruin things. We have a kind of experiment going there," the vampire said behind him.

"Who is she?" asked Joe, though he was certain that he knew.

"Just a little thing. A thing that wouldn't do what we wanted it to do."

Joe thought he heard a tiny sound, a faint choking too inhuman to be called a moan, from the body over the tub.

Vaguely disbelieving, he turned his head in that direction. "Elizabeth?"

The tiny sound was not repeated.

"Come out of there," ordered Lila. Joe looked at her, standing five feet away in the bathroom doorway. She added: "I want to show you something, little man-thing. I may even let you have some fun."

Joe stayed where he was. He reached inside his sportcoat and drew a .38 from under his left arm. It was an old-fashioned–looking weapon, dull metal that had been around for some years. On the few occasions when he'd needed it, it had always been dependable.

Lila smiled tolerantly. Of course none of them had even bothered to search him.

"You have a lot to learn," she murmured, smiling prettily, "if you think that bullets are going to hurt us. Now you're not going to have any fun. Pain instead. Pain such as you've never—"

Joe gritted his teeth and shot the vampire twice, aiming as best he could for a button on her blouse that lay just between her breasts.

He imagined that he could see how one of the lead-cored wooden slugs nicked the little button before it went on to tear splintering into the exotic bone and flesh behind it. The double impact lifted the solid body of the woman from her feet and hurled her back. Her gray-eyed, attractive face registering a look of intense surprise, she fell onto the rumpled bed.

Joe took a step forward, revolver ready. He stood for a long moment in the bathroom doorway, watching the sprawled body beginning to undergo grotesque alterations.

The young woman, the breather, from the living room,

was standing in the bedroom doorway looking in. "What is it? I heard—" Then she stopped, staring at the bed.

Her paralyzed pause gave Joe time to reach her before she could turn and run. He grabbed her by the arms and shoulders, and she tried to bite him. He slugged her ruthlessly, revolver barrel across the back of the head.

In another moment he was dragging the stunned breather into a closet, closing the door, and bringing a chair to wedge it shut.

Then he looked back at the bed. In much less than a minute, the true death had overtaken Lila. Her face was shriveling, collapsing on the collapsing skull behind it, like a time-lapse sequence of a Halloween pumpkin in decay. The well-dressed woman's corpse was diminishing rapidly in size, and now even as Joe watched, it disappeared completely. Last to go was the clothing, but at last it went, and then everything, everything that had been directly attached to the form, was gone. He'd seen it happen that way before, to one of *them,* but even so Joe's hands were shaking and a fresh wave of nausea passed over him.

Moving quickly back into the bathroom, he looked once more at the woman suspended above the tub. With the fingers of his left hand he rolled back an eyelid and touched the ball beneath. No doubt about it now, she was as dead as anyone he'd ever seen.

Wasting not a second, but moving with extreme care, Joe moved to the front door of the apartment. He eased it open, then, revolver still in hand, held ready under his folded topcoat, he tiptoed out into the corridor, closing the door softly behind him.

He took the opposite direction from the one by which he'd been brought here. He wasn't going to try to take the rest of them, not now, not alone; that would be crazy. At least two of them were on the maintenance floor upstairs, and he had only four shots left. Even in daylight two vampires together were at least one too many. He wouldn't have tried to take one if he'd been given any choice about it.

Walking briskly, he came to another bank of elevators almost immediately, just around a corner. When he got to a phone, he could leave an anonymous tip for the police, have them check out Valentine's apartment. But he wasn't sure that would be a good idea. Elizabeth Wiswell was dead now and couldn't be helped. Better not have cops swarming around the building until the old man had died or had recovered enough to face them.

A couple of innocent breathers, talking loudly, joined him, waiting for an elevator. He stood waiting as quietly as he could, neither facing them directly nor making a point of turning his face away. He was still holding the pistol ready under his folded topcoat.

He was going down to street level, not back to the old man's apartment; if the people trapped there were going to have a chance, someone was going to have to help them from the outside.

7

The digging, and the nightingale's song, went on above my head. Presently, as I continued to struggle my way toward full consciousness, I could hear with great distinctness the harsh scraping of some iron tool, a shovel doubtless, upon the wooden barrier only a handbreadth above my face. A dusting of powdery earth, along with a few small insects, came sifting down through the cracks between boards. Already, after no more than a mere two years or so in the grave, my coffin was beginning to shrink and warp and fall asunder, even if I was not.

Having reached that stage of vampirish revival in which the mind begins to be competently active, even though the body as yet remains all but completely paralyzed, I considered drawing in a lungful of dusty air and frightening away the intruder with a bellow. Now I could tell that but a single person labored to unearth me. I decided to make no noise. A face-to-face welcome would be more appropriate.

The digging stopped, eventually, to be replaced by a futile tugging, directed first at the head of my container, then the foot. I could hear the intruder gasping with the effort, but neither end could be lifted very far. Evidently to drag my coffin up out of the shallow pit that had once been a secret grave was going to be beyond the lone invader's strength. Instead, there came a new tool-noise. My coffin lid was going to be pried off.

Being already somewhat warped and rotted, as I have mentioned, it came loose readily enough, but only one plank at a time.

Suddenly there was moonlight on my face, reflected and unpainful sunlight in my eyes, enough to make a bright halo of the digger's hair.

I could see at once that my uninvited guest was a woman, young and lithe. Strong, from the way she handled her tools, though not very large; and I could tell by her clothing, garbed as she was in the traditional dress of her people, that she was a gypsy. Bright earrings, forged I am sure of real silver, drew sparks from the moon.

By now I had regained the power of movement. But for the time being I chose to remain still and silent.

Unexpectedly she spoke. "And there you are, my handsome *moroi!* As I thought, a power of magic here. More than a year beneath the sod, and your flesh still uncorrupted." The right hand of the gypsy, who was hardly more than a girl, prodded an exposed bicep with a sharp fingernail and then moved on. "And here is a nice dagger. Well, that will be of some use." But the reaching hand made no move to extract the weapon from my coffin yet.

Still I did not move. My eyes were open, but I held them still and dull as those of a corpse; it is a thing that we can do.

The young woman crouched with clasped hands beside my coffin, speaking to me at greater length, almost but not quite as if she thought I could hear her. The tenor of her speech was rejoicing that her surmise had proven correct and that she found my body still uncorrupted.

Next she untied a small cloth bundle she had brought

with her and began to go through various magical rituals, blowing foul powder in my face and chanting stupid spells. All totally useless, as most such efforts are. As I surmised at the time and later was able to confirm, they constituted an effort to keep me quiet while she hacked off various parts of my anatomy. I waited, joyfully anticipating what was going to happen when I finally moved, and waiting to see if my visitor had any more preliminaries in mind before she began to use her knife.

But there were no more. When the despoiler of my grave raised my right arm, took firm hold of the forefinger, and drew her own small dagger, I judged that the time had come to act.

I had long since left behind me many of the common susceptibilities of breathing flesh, and my assailant would have faced a most difficult task in trying to hack me to pieces with any implement of metal. But I did not allow her to make the attempt. As she held up my arm, tugging hard against a certain inherent stiffness—more appropriate to a day-old than a year-old corpse—I suddenly returned her handclasp. My own grasp was gentle, but still sufficiently firm to insure that the digit she was attempting to isolate should not be left undefended.

The young woman's first reaction was disappointingly restrained; she only gasped, and would have pulled away, but my grip was vastly too strong to allow that. Courageous as she was, I think that in the next moment she might have fainted. But now I had shifted the direction of my gaze, and with my eyes locked on hers I willed her to retain consciousness.

Her next move was a wise one, to throw down the knife she had been holding in her free hand. Then she began to mutter, and presently declaimed aloud, first prayers and then more abominations of witchcraft.

I spoke to her for the first time. "I command you, girl, cease this shameful, wicked way of speaking. If you are going to pray, pray properly!"

Her response surprised me: "And who are you, *moroi,* to call me wicked? Or to give me instructions in prayer?" And she tossed her head in a gesture of defiance.

She had again used the term for undead, and for some reason that gave me pause. Despite all my recent experience I had never yet thought of myself in such a way. "Well," I said at last. "I am undead indeed. But when you come right down to it, what does that mean, except that I am, thanks to the good God, still alive?"

My captive uttered a little yelp of shock and astonishment, an almost endearing sound. "You dare to speak the good Lord's name? He'll strike you down!"

Again it was my turn to be surprised. "Indeed? And why should He do that?"

She was shivering, though the night was not that cold, and seemed unable to answer. "I am Vlad Drakulya," I told her after a pause. "Once Prince of Wallachia. But I suppose you knew that, woman. If not, whose grave did you think you were violating? And what is your name?"

"I am called Constantia." She was shivering more and more with fear by this time, though somehow managing to keep her voice almost under control. Courage has always fascinated and impressed me.

I squeezed her hand—still almost gently. "And on what task, good Constantia, were you about to employ your dagger? Did you think my fingernails might be in need of trimming, after so long in the grave? Is that what brought you here tonight?"

She stared at me, and then produced a tremulous little smile. If my grip was causing her pain she gave no sign. Her spoken answers remained evasive. But of course I understood perfectly well that what must have brought her to my grave was the practice of witchcraft—doubtless she had meant to excise more than one portion of my anatomy to aid her in her spells. Dead men's eyes, fingers, testicles— the witch's shopping list is long—were and are considered of great value. Most in demand are the parts of executed criminals, followed by those of men of spiritual power. Looking back, I can believe that I was considered as belonging to both categories.

How, by what means of bribery or divination, this little apprentice witch had learned the location of my grave I was never to discover. She must have assumed that the body of Prince Drakulya would possess some special efficacy to aid her in her work. But as the situation actually worked out, she was, I believe, content to leave my bones intact, forgetting her original purpose in the dazzling light of her discovery that I was not dead after all. Yes, I know she had expected to find an undead, or thought she had; but to actually observe the fact was something else. Gypsy witches of the time, and Constantia in particular, were not known for the fine precision of their logic.

"Why do you call me *moroi?*" I asked her more than once on that first night as I helped her to fill in my grave above the empty coffin. Of course I knew what the name meant, but to me it was no more than a superstitious word applied by foolish peasants to some of their more unsettling nightmares.

Sometimes, when I asked her this, she must have thought that I was angry, for in answer she would only shake her head and maintain silence. On other occasions, a few minutes earlier or later, she must have considered me to be in a good mood, for she tried to argue that I did indeed fit that category. Not that she had ever known anyone else who was *moroi.*

Our acquaintance prospered from the start, though for some weeks after our first encounter I refrained from sleeping in my proper grave, half expecting that Constantia might come back when I was deep in one of my stupors and renew her efforts to carve me up.

But now to return to those first minutes of her first visit to my grave. Letting go her hand at last, and then clasping her with both arms around the waist, I stepped up out of my newly reexcavated pit, lifting her with me. Her strength was, of course, no match for mine. But no sooner had we demonstrated this than our struggle, that had begun as a tentative combat, began to assume quite other aspects.

Sex, for a vampire, is almost inextricably confused with taking nourishment, and both of course involve almost exclusively the drinking of the blood.

Whatever expectations of sensual delight might have been aroused in either Constantia or myself on our first night together were more than fully realized, though not in the way that I, at least, until the moment of our embrace, had expected.

In my transformed mode of existence, the blood is indeed the life. It is everything, the single physical craving and the single physical requirement. Before embracing my passionate little witch I had scarcely begun to understand that fact; but before our first coupling was concluded, both of us were very firmly convinced.

Ah, Constantia, the first love of my second life! Surely your maidenhood, in the breathing, mundane sense, had been lost long before that night; but on that night you were still as virginal as I was myself in the delights of vampirism. Constantia, where are you now?

In that infancy, dawn-time, childhood of my second life, other women, of course, soon began to appear. Folk who consider that keeping score in such matters is of great importance might say that there were a great many such women, of diverse social classes. My new sensuality having been awakened, I began actively, on subsequent evenings, to seek them out. Yet during the months following my introduction to the little gypsy, with maddening effect upon all my plans both serious and erotic, the great bulk of my time was consumed, wasted, in those lengthy periods when I could only lie stuporous in the earth.

Slowly, very slowly, as those first months of my reborn and transformed sexuality stretched imperceptibly into years, I accustomed myself to the joys and difficulties, peculiar powers and strange limitations of my new existence. With regular feeding, upon both animal and human blood, the wounds that had sent me to my grave healed entirely, even the visible scars disappearing in good time. Mine could have been a heartily enjoyable existence, all in all. But I was prevented from making any philosophical evaluation of my condition, as much by my obsessive craving for revenge as by the lethargy that tended to set in whenever the blood-craving had been temporarily sated.

My two surviving enemies, Basarab and Bogdan, for whom my hatred was as fresh and deep as ever, were seldom absent from my thoughts. But they were not to be found anywhere in the nearby countryside—someone had told me they were gone to Bucharest. It was obvious that if I was ever to come within reach of them, I must find a way of breaking free of my dusk-to-dawn existence, that constrained me to remain always within a few hours' travel of my grave. I seemed to remember, from talk I had overheard on the night of my burial, that there had been a plan to move me to another grave, in a hidden spot under one of my castles. But for whatever reason, no one ever appeared to try to put such a scheme into effect.

Constantia and I continued for a time to see each other frequently. Slowly, gradually, as I say, I grew accustomed to my new mode of existence. Up until this time—despite all the talk of *moroi* in the countryside—I had had no contact at all with other vampires, knew no master of this mode of life to guide me through my apprenticeship, no local community of my race to bid me welcome. Still, as my first affair with the young would-be witch had demonstrated, the state of being which I had now entered was not entirely unknown to the local populace. And I began to understand more fully, from one after another of the young women who became my lovers, how my condition was regarded by their people and the various names by which they thought it should be called. Then, I thought, there must have been others like me, in the past. Where were they now?

The superstitious awe in which I was held was sometimes amusing, sometimes useful, sometimes maddening. I do believe that every single one of my lovers, during that distant epoch, were certain that I must be somehow in alliance with the Evil One; and more than one of them earnestly sought my help in establishing such a connection for herself, as if no greater boon could be imagined.

It was with great difficulty that I convinced these girls and women that they misjudged me, and perhaps the Evil One as well. No doubt one or more of them managed somehow to achieve her wicked aim, without my help. As for my own alleged dealings with the devil, I had long ago taken solemn oaths of fealty to his great Opponent; and for a Drakulya such pledges are not to be set aside.

Despite, or perhaps because of, the stubborn convictions of my breathing acquaintances regarding my spiritual condition, I became ever more firmly convinced that what had happened to me had no connection with the supernatural. Thanks to my own supremely stubborn will—and to the permissive will, at least, of God—the death by sword cuts that I had undergone was no true death. My abode was neither heaven nor hell nor purgatory. Rather it was the grave I slept in daily, my body capable of passing up out of it and back again like so much smoke during the hours of darkness. And this, my earthen sanctuary, was dug out of nothing more or less than the soil of my homeland, in which I had been born.

My lovers were not the only ones who observed me during this period. Certain other peasants of the region accidentally caught glimpses of my mysterious form, near dawn or dusk, and mostly at a distance. These were beginning to whisper that I still lived, or at any rate still walked. So began my local reputation as a revenant, which was to grow gradually over the centuries.

But what the bulk of the population might know about me, or what superstitious nonsense they might imagine, concerned me little, particularly in the first year or two after my conversion. Very little had meaning for me beyond my own affairs. The women who were my lovers, and one or two other peasants who became my loyal if somewhat demented servants—who but a madman would have served a vampire then?—were always bringing me more news than I cared to hear concerning current events.

I listened, more than once, to the story of how my half-brother Radu, called the Handsome, had been confirmed as Prince of Wallachia in my stead. And I heard what I thought was reliable confirmation of what had happened to other members of my family. I was perfectly certain that the only ones I cared about were dead.

What might be the current state of the realm that I

had ruled, and exactly what had befallen the few human beings that I loved—these questions seemed hardly relevant to me then. The monolithic concentration of willpower necessary to achieve what I had achieved in the way of exceptional survival, and the rage for revenge that was its corollary, had left me almost unable to think of anything else. My attempt to revenge myself upon Ronay had been essentially a failure, despite the fact that he was dead. He might very well have died anyway, of his infected wound. Perhaps all I had accomplished on my invasion of the monastery was to hasten his end and lessen his suffering.

During this period I was myself quite mad by ordinary standards—of course observers were not lacking who would have pronounced me thoroughly insane long before the day on which I fell with fatal sword wounds. But now, in the midst of a slow mental and physical recovery, the fever of combat was still on me, the heat of that brief savage struggle in which my flesh had died and been reborn. My sense of time, along with much else, was still awry.

The only news reports to which I paid the least attention were those concerning the two surviving scoundrels of the three who had struck me down. Well before I was able to exercise sufficient control over my new powers and limitations to have a chance of going after them, I heard to my dismay that they had both departed for Italy, there to hire out as mercenaries.

Perhaps, I thought, the traitors had experienced some difficulty in collecting their blood-price from the Sultan and had failed to establish themselves in positions of power at home. Whatever their reasons, a sojourn in Italy was a common enough interlude in the careers of European soldiers of the time. Indeed, I had once visited that chronically troubled land myself, on a secret mission for the King of Hungary.

The news of my enemies' departure hit me hard, and of course there was no question in my mind that I must contrive some way to follow them. But if their townhouses in Bucharest had been too far away for me to reach, in my present state of dependence on my grave, how in the name of Heaven was I ever going to lay my hands on them beyond the Alps?

I need not dwell on my first abortive attempts to extend my effective radius of travel. I soon found that I could rest without reentering my actual grave at every dawn. Any dark, secluded spot, where I could lie in contact with the earth, would do. But having passed the border of my homeland, it became necessary for me to turn back each night as dawn approached. I was unable to obtain my necessary daytime rest in any soil but that of my native country.

Forcing my unabated frenzy for revenge to yield to cold calculation, I took thought on the matter. At first the restriction, like several others to which I now was subject, seemed absurd. If by my iron will I had been able to fight off death itself, then why should I not, by a lesser effort, overcome this seeming triviality of dependence on my home earth? Absurd or not, that was how the matter stood, and so it would remain. How very human, I think now, what excellent proof of the vampire's persistent humanity: Our race can accomplish prodigies, but stumbles nonetheless on many matters that seem small.

There was no way around the obstacle, except in patience and solid, persistent planning. Some fragments of ancient lore, twisted in the telling and retelling, yet gave me the hint I needed: Travel anywhere was indeed possible for the vampire, provided only that he or she carried along, or shipped ahead, some earth of the true homeland on which to sleep. What can the soil, much less the soul, comprehend of the boundaries of politics? Yet so the situation was, and so it still remains.

To help me I recruited a small handful of such breathing followers as I could muster. Not only insanity but dimwittedness was epidemic among them, I fear, and some were continually disappointed that I would have no commerce with the devil. Such tools as I could find, I used as best I could. Still, years passed before I could arrange for systematic shipments of Wallachian earth to Italy, and for my dirt's concealment there in certain carefully chosen places. And my long sleeps, some lasting many months, in my grave or near it, continued also. Years more were wasted—as I then thought—in helpless stupor.

During my periods of wakefulness, word reached me again and again, at discouragingly long intervals, that the two men I sought were still alive, and still in Italy, where they appeared to have found the finest arena on earth in which to display and profit by their skills of treachery and violence. Bogdan in particular had grown eminently successful in his new profession of condottiere, and I felt confident of being able to locate him, at least, with little difficulty.

Such an undertaking as that of my international earth shipments, carried out with a maximum of secrecy, would be far from trivial in any time, including this modern era in which I write. Take my word for it that in the late fifteenth century, with the multitude of political and economic uncertainties obtaining then, the problems were truly formidable.

Yet I persevered, and refused to be hurried. Many

military campaigns had taught me the importance of proper preparation. Despite my unabated lust for vengeance, and the risk of having my adversaries escape, I would not move until I was ready. Decades had passed since the traitors cut me down, and the last years of the century were at hand before I felt ready and able to proceed.

8

Joe had departed Uncle Matthew's apartment around twelve-thirty. For the two breathing people inside the apartment the next forty-five minutes or so passed uneventfully, tempting them to hope that the siege was really over. Then the phone rang, distracting Angie from another episode of the fantastic tale on the tape. There was no extension in the guest bedroom. Shutting off one machine, she ran toward the kitchen to answer the other.

John had reached the instrument before she did, and once again she could see the relief on his face at the first sounds he heard from the receiver.

"It's Joe," he told her in a quick aside.

Angie hurried on into the living room and picked up the extension there, slumping into a chair to listen.

"—the line might be tapped" were the first words she heard Joe Keogh pronounce. He sounded tired and worn.

"The phone line here?" John's voice asked in puzzlement.

"Yes. This one we're using. Today I got a good look at other parts of that building you're in. Up on the ninety-eighth floor, and elsewhere."

John sounded bewildered. "How'd that happen?"

"I don't want to go into a lot of detail on exactly what I did, because the phone might be tapped, as I say. But I did

116

have some trouble getting away from the building." Joe paused to let them consider that. "I'm okay now, and I'll get back to you, don't worry. I promise you help is on the way, but I can't promise when it's going to get there.

"One thing you have to know. Elizabeth, the woman who was in there with you, is dead."

His listeners started incoherent questions. He brushed them aside. "We can talk it over later. The point is, you're in real serious trouble there. Deadly trouble. Stay inside the apartment, no matter who or what comes to the door. Don't try to leave. Don't even think about opening the doors, or talking to visitors except on the intercom. Have you had any more visitors, by the way?"

"No. We won't stick our noses out if you say we shouldn't."

"You definitely shouldn't."

"Joe?" This was Angie. "How did she die?"

"It wasn't of old age, but never mind that now. Just do what I'm telling you. I won't ask how your host there is doing, and be careful what you say about him over the phone."

"All right." John sounded subdued to the point of collapse.

Angie, on an impulse, hung up her phone, got to her feet, and walked softly into the master bedroom. The man who lay there opened his eyes as she entered, and— pleasant surprise!—focused them on her. For a moment his gaze was a hard, probing stare, then recognition came, and he smiled faintly. His lips moved as if he were trying to speak, but no sound came. He shook his head slowly and smiled once more before his eyelids closed again.

"Uncle Matthew?" She advanced quickly to the bed and touched him on the arm, but there was no response.

Still, she had a strong impression that progress was being made.

Hurrying back to the living room, Angie picked up the phone again and heard Joe Keogh still talking. "—what I'm going to do is, try to arrange a meeting between myself and these people. You and Angie won't be involved directly, and it won't take place in that building. I'll try to meet one of them, preferably their boss, alone. Broad daylight, very public place."

John was doubtful. "Joe, isn't that . . ."

"I know what I'm doing. I think maybe they understand now that I do, after some things that happened this morning. So maybe I can talk to them. What we still don't know is what they're really after, and why."

Angie considered, decided to take a chance, and cut into the conversation. "Joe? I just checked on that problem that was mentioned earlier. I'd say that there's a definite improvement."

There was a pause. Then: "Good," said Joe. "I'd like to hear details, but don't give me any on the phone. Not now, anyway, okay?"

"Okay."

There wasn't much more to say on either side. Joe soon concluded his phone call. Angie fought down an impulse to warn him to be careful. If she couldn't think of anything constructive to say at this point, she was going to keep quiet.

Hardly had she put down the receiver, and started toward the kitchen to meet John, when there sounded a kind of wooden pounding from the old man's room.

She hurried that way, encountering John in the hall, and they rushed into the bedroom together. Uncle Matthew had dragged himself out of bed and was lying on the floor naked, except for the sheet in which his body was half entangled. He had somehow managed to pull a dresser partially away from the wall, and was thumping with his open hand on the wooden panel that formed its back.

He quieted when John and Angie rushed in, and allowed them to try to help. In a few moments they had their host propped up in a sitting position on the floor, his back against the bed—he refused to cooperate in being put back in bed, and he was too heavy and too strong to be simply handled against his will. He was grunting now, moaning, pointing urgently at the panel he had been beating on.

"What does he want? What is it, Uncle Matthew?"

John began to feel around the panel. "There must be something there—does it open? Is it a door?"

He moved the dresser out farther from the wall, and Angie went to help. Eventually they located the catch, and the panel proved to be a door indeed. Inside was a secret compartment, broad and high though only a few inches deep. The cavity contained some small jars of dark glass, tightly capped, and a few pounds of earth packed snugly in plastic bags.

Uncle Matthew was grunting in satisfaction, pointing at the bags. Angie opened one, and then stared blankly at the dry, crumbled soil that leaked out on the carpet. "What on earth—?"

"Earth of his homeland," John explained tersely. "I suppose he still needs it, from time to time at least."

The old man growled at them, impatient and inarticulate. He made swift gestures. It took them a few moments to understand that he wanted them to open the bags of earth, pour out the dirt and scatter it over him, spread it on the carpet so he could roll his body in the stuff.

They did this, and it seemed to bring him genuine relief.

Not knowing what else to do, Angie reached into the hidden place for one of the little jars, brought it out, and examined it. Both the jar and its pressed-on metal cap had the slightly irregular look of handmade things. The glass was too dark to let her see what was inside, but the jar was too heavy to be empty. "And what's this?"

"I have no idea." John shook his head.

The old man saw what she was doing, smiled faintly, shook his head, and made a pushing motion with his hand. Carefully she set the jar back on its shelf.

Joe Keogh hung up the receiver of the public phone and stepped out of the downtown booth. He hadn't called from home, nor was he anywhere near Uncle Matthew's condo. Joe Keogh's first effort on completing his morning getaway had been to complete the process already begun of getting Kate and the kids as much out of the way of this horrible situation as possible, into a position of such safety as could be managed under the circumstances.

Fortunately for Joe's current relative peace of mind, he'd made preparations for such an emergency a long time ago. It was something you had to take into account when the extended family included a vampire. Like having wooden bullets ready.

It was late in the lunch hour by now, and the sidewalks were jammed as he started walking back toward north Michigan. He hadn't thought it wise to discuss plans on the phone, but assuming the crisis wasn't resolved by evening, he wasn't sure he ought to go back to Uncle Matthew's condo to spend the night. Whatever the enemy were up to, he thought he might be able to pose them more problems by staying away. For overnight shelter he had in mind another condominium, in another part of the city. A hotel wouldn't quite do, or at least Joe wasn't at all confident about hotels. He wasn't sure that a room occupied by a succession of uprooted strangers would qualify, when the chips were down, as a genuine dwelling place.

What Angie had said on the phone strongly suggested that the old man was at least starting to recover. So it was even possible that this evening after sunset, when his powers waxed, Matthew Maule might recover more or less completely from whatever kind of attack had struck him down. Of course the powers of his vampire enemies would also be at their strongest between sunset and dawn.

Joe kept hiking the crowded Loop sidewalks, moving steadily north and east. He was carrying a briefcase, packed hastily at home, that held a few essentials. Thinking back to his adventures of the late morning, Joe wondered if the enemy were still occupying the apartment with the dead woman in it. Or if they'd managed somehow to get rid of her.

The dead vampire was already gone, of course, but the gunfire could possibly have left some traces on the scene. And the modifications in the bathroom were bizarre. Still, if the woman was gone, there wouldn't be a whole lot for cops to look at there. Once the old man had snapped out of it, the cops could be called in—of course, once he recovered, cops might not be necessary.

Joe, as he had announced on the phone, was going to try to arrange a meeting with Valentine Kaiser. The purpose of the meeting was mainly to stall for time, though he hadn't wanted to say that on the phone.

Joe had left Uncle Matthew's condo around half-past twelve, and his escape from Valentine's apartment had brought him out on the pavement a little after one. The days were short this time of year; he meant to do his best to set up the meeting he wanted this afternoon, but it might

well have to be postponed until tomorrow. He wasn't going
to risk being caught out after sunset.

The other condominium, the one he had in mind to
stay in, was owned by the wealthy Southerlands. Andrew
Southerland, father of John and Kate, sometimes used the
place when for business reasons he had to stay in town
overnight; or when some visiting VIP needed to be housed
for a day or two. Joe, who now spent most of his ordinary
working hours as a private contractor in the security field,
did a lot of business with his father-in-law's corporation,
and he always had a key to the condo too.

In a little while Joe had worked his way east to
Michigan Avenue. Shortly after that he was standing on
the plaza in front of the gigantic structure housing Uncle
Matthew's dwelling. His plan was to hang around here in
plain sight, being overtly conspicuous, until he got the
enemy's attention. There was a sizable gang of them. One
of them at least, he hoped, would be keeping an eye on
things out here, and would observe his behavior, read it as
a signal that he wanted to open communications, and come
out to talk. Of course, especially after what had happened
this morning, the Valentine vampires and their breathing
friends might have other ideas, like killing Joe on sight.
But now that the bloodshed had started, no course of
action could be described as safe.

Maybe his plan wasn't much good, maybe it was a
mistake, but it was the best he could come up with. Joe
stood around on the plaza, fighting the wind, watching
shoppers, office workers, wanderers come and go. North
Michigan was definitely an upscale neighborhood. There
were no police cars in sight, but that meant nothing. The
cops, on being summoned to the big building, would
doubtless pull into its indoor parking garage.

A Matter of Taste

Today the weather kept threatening to turn sunny, but as a veteran Chicagoan Joe had no faith that it was really going to come out that way. With a cop's acquired patience, he put in a couple of hours standing around on the street, watching and feeling the precious hours of daylight slide away. He broke his vigil once for a grilled cheese sandwich and hot coffee, in a coffee shop whose large front window allowed him to keep an eye on the plaza where he had been standing. Twice, at intervals, he stepped into a plaza phone booth to call Angie and John. They were glad to hear from him, as might be expected. Each time he talked with the frightened young people, he could hear them hesitating, sometimes in midsentence, as if there was something they wanted to tell him, but couldn't, keeping in mind the warning he had given them earlier. Joe in turn let them know openly what he was doing now and why—except of course that his main goal was stalling for time. If the enemy overheard that he wanted a conference, so much the better.

Whether the information was passed along through a phone tap or not, Joe's plan eventually succeeded. Shortly after three o'clock Valentine Kaiser's representative showed up to talk to Joe and see what was going on.

The emissary appeared in the shape of a breathing woman. Joe identified her while she was still fighting the wind halfway across the plaza, walking toward him through one of the temporary wooden pedestrian tunnels. Not a vampire. She was wearing the same army surplus field jacket she'd had on when he'd clubbed her down and stuffed her in a closet up in Valentine's high-altitude apartment.

She came walking right up to him; this time she had shoes on. Nothing coy in her approach. "You bastard.

You're Joe Keogh who used to be a cop?" Her voice sounded rusty, as if perhaps she had a sore throat, or maybe just didn't use it all that often.

"That's right." He watched her warily, planning what he would do if she suddenly produced a weapon. "Glad to see you're still alive. What's your name?"

No answer for that one. She was looking at him with what seemed curiosity, perhaps studying the miracle man who'd walked away from a vampire who'd wanted to keep him prisoner, and had somehow made the vampire vanish too. Her long dark hair kept blowing into her eyes. "Val Kaiser sent me. He wants to know what the fuck you're hanging around out here for."

Even now it still bothered Joe, on some level, when women used that kind of language. Not that he would react visibly. "I figured he'd get curious and send someone. You can tell Val Kaiser I'm here because I want to talk to him."

"You want to talk about what?"

"Several things. I think there's plenty of material. Tell him that if I knew what he wanted from the old man, or out of the old man's apartment, what he really had to have, maybe we could work something out. Whatever it is Kaiser wants, he doesn't seem to be getting anywhere the way things are going now."

"You'll have to talk to him yourself."

"That's what I'm trying to tell you." Joe looked at his wristwatch. "Within an hour from now, or else early tomorrow morning. The Art Institute—you know where that is?—right inside the Michigan entrance, by the main stairway. I'm heading there now, but I'm cutting out before it gets dark. If I don't see him today, I'll come back in the morning. If he absolutely can't make it either time, tell him to send someone with a message. If he wants to name another place and time, I'll consider it, provided it meets my conditions, broad daylight and very public."

She looked at him with narrowed eyes. She had come out here really hating him. "The old man send you to try to make a deal?"

"I'll talk to Kaiser about that."

"Wait here, I'll see what he says."

Joe waited where he was, stamping his feet in the chill wind, aware of how the dull daylight was sliding almost perceptibly away, while the emissary trotted across the street and ducked into another building. She might be going to phone from there, to pass along his message. Or Kaiser himself might be in there. It didn't matter; Joe could wait.

In less than five minutes the young woman was back. In the tones of a stern boss, she ordered him: "Be where you said, in the Art Institute, at the time you said."

"The time I said this afternoon, within an hour, or tomorrow?"

"He's going to try to make it this afternoon. If he doesn't, he'll be there in the morning. Val says he don't think you'll need any warnings, about certain things you shouldn't do."

"I'll be there, alone. I guess Val has some sense anyway."

The young woman glared at him, turned, and walked away. If his revolver barrel had left a wound, it was hidden beneath her dirty hair. Her fatigue jacket was rumpled in the back.

Joe looked at his watch, and decided to phone the apartment once more, tell them the time and place of the meeting he'd set up. Then he'd catch a cab, not wanting to waste any time. The Art Institute was a little over a mile south on Michigan, and there was an old German proverb the old man had once repeated for him, something about the dead traveling fast.

Joe reached the indoor spot he'd chosen for the meeting well ahead of time, and settled down to wait, finding a spot on a padded bench, amid a bustle of art enthusiasts passing to and fro. It was great to be out of the cold and wind, and he had a little time to prepare himself. Not that there was much to prepare. This time Kaiser would have to take him seriously; beyond that Joe could only estimate what might be going to happen.

He couldn't see a lot of art, just a handful of massive statues, from the spot he'd chosen. Some of this stuff around him was doubtless older than the man he was going to meet. Joe thought about that. He thought about a great many things that ordinarily he tried to avoid considering. He looked at his watch frequently. At four o'clock, no matter what, he was leaving. He'd take no chances on not being locked up safely, behind private doors and walls, before today's invisible sun went down. He might be a little stupid, setting up a conference with a murderous vampire, but he wasn't completely crazy.

At about a quarter to four Valentine Kaiser showed up. The vampire had changed his suit since this morning. He looked jaunty and very handsome this afternoon, extremely youthful in appearance. That was often a sign of recent heavy feeding, thought Joe, and felt an inward shudder. He hoped it didn't show.

He'd chosen his corner bench so he had a wall at his back, and whoever sat down to talk to him would be on his left. It would be easier that way for Joe to reach for the holster under his left arm, pull a gun and aim, or to shoot from the holster through his own coat if it came to that. The revolver snuggled against his ribs was vastly comforting, freshly reloaded now, all six rounds tipped with lead-cored lignum vitae bullets. Hard wood, so heavy that it wouldn't float in water. Someone—probably the old man himself—had told Joe that the Latin name of the stuff meant "wood of life." But he knew that it was far from certain protection.

And then suddenly the vampire had arrived, and with a nod and a smile was sitting down beside him. Sitting too close for comfort, considering how fast one of them could move.

Joe shifted openly away, positioning his body with his back against one wall, right shoulder against another. People observing his retreat might get the idea that Kaiser, for all his snappy clothes, didn't smell too good.

"What do you want?" Joe asked.

Kaiser smiled faintly at Joe's maneuvers to increase the distance between them. But when he spoke he sounded genuinely sympathetic. "Tell me, how's the old man doing?"

"Great. He was up early this morning and went out jogging."

The other nodded, almost as if he had taken the answer seriously and was considering the implications. "Good. I hope he did. And I hope you'll believe me when I say this is all very much a misunderstanding."

"There's already two people dead that I know about. If it's all a misunderstanding maybe we better stop it before it really turns serious."

Kaiser looked innocently hopeful. "You do count us as people, then. Even when you kill us."

"Oh, I know you're people. I know that. But I kill people when I have to."

The other looked at him as if he found it sad and disheartening that Joe could have such a reckless attitude.

"I was trying to frighten your two young friends, nothing more. We wouldn't have done them any harm if they'd let us in."

"What about Elizabeth Wiswell?"

The handsome, young-looking man frowned. "I didn't know she was a friend of yours. Actually I don't see how she could have been."

"I'm interested anyway."

Friendliness disappeared, as if a little switch had been turned off somewhere behind the vampire's dark eyes. "One of my friends was alive this morning but she isn't now. Lila was with you in my apartment when she was last seen alive. Do you want to make this a personal matter between the two of us, or shall we call it even?"

Joe's lips were very dry. He resisted the urge to lick them. "All right, let's call it even between us. I'm here trying to make peace."

The other looked off into the distance as if meditating. At length he sighed. As if he were the one who had a right to be doubtful of Joe's motives. Suddenly he asked: "Now are you willing to go back with me, and ask me in?"

"Back to the old man's place? He can ask you in there himself if he wants you in."

Kaiser looked sadly misunderstood. It was an attitude that he wore very well; perhaps he practiced it a lot.

When he spoke he sounded perfectly sincere. "We both know that the old man, as you call him, is in no shape to do that. I'm not going to rob him or kill him." His tone, his manner, assured Joe that that was the most preposterous idea anyone had ever heard of. "I just want to talk with him, to see him face-to-face. I'm really concerned about his welfare."

"He's doing fine."

"Then why doesn't he answer his door himself?" After allowing time for Joe to answer, Kaiser went on. "Probably you think you're protecting him. But have you considered that you might be putting him in danger, and your young friends also?"

"I don't think so."

Kaiser shook his head. "How many years have you known him?"

Joe was silent.

The vampire persisted. "How many? Ten years? Fifteen?"

Joe said: "About eleven." He realized that he was starting to respond, almost to cooperate, automatically. The feeling was almost one of relief.

Kaiser leaned just a little closer to him on the bench. Lowering his voice, he confided: "The old man—as you call him—and I go back almost five hundred years. Believe that?"

"It's possible."

"It's quite true. Now, my friends and I didn't murder that woman, Elizabeth Wiswell. We didn't harm her in the least. We were trying to help her, though she died when she was with us. What you saw, what horrified you so, was part of our effort to examine her dead body, to see if she had been somehow used as a tool to poison him. But there was no indication of that. The results of our tests, that you found so alarming, were negative."

"I don't believe she was quite dead when I first saw her."

Kaiser dismissed this idle notion with a small wave of his hand. "What really killed her was something that the old man did."

"No, I don't believe—"

"What's really happening now is that the old man is having one of his seizures. I don't suppose you've ever seen one of them before?"

"Seizures?" Joe cleared his throat. His own voice sounded terribly weak and ineffective. "What are they?" He couldn't help it, he felt like a kid trying to argue with a grown-up, gripped by the conviction that nothing he said was really going to count.

"His seizures, or call them fits, occur four or five times a century, fortunately no more often. As a rule they begin suddenly, with an attack of extreme lethargy. Unnatural sleep, unconsciousness—I mean of course unnatural by his, our, standards, not by yours. The lethargy is followed in a day or two by a fit of violent madness."

"Sounds pretty horrible."

"It is pretty horrible," Kaiser said simply. "Do those symptoms sound like anything that you've observed recently?"

Joe forced himself to break eye contact, to get up off the bench. He walked five paces away, in the process several times almost colliding with people in the ceaseless flow of visitors through the museum. Then he turned and came back and stood confronting Kaiser, who had remained seated.

Joe said: "Look—you people *poisoned* him, somehow. You drugged him, using that woman. Getting something into her blood."

"Bah. I hardly think such a thing is possible. Besides, why should we want to do that?"

"You did something like that. Yes."

The vampire gestured casually. His attitude said that Joe was proving impossible to talk to.

"You drugged him," persisted Joe. "And then you

tried everything to get into his apartment. To make sure he was dead, or to finish him off."

"Joe, Joe—it's all right if I call you Joe? You weren't there personally, last night, were you? Or early this morning?"

"I was in your apartment this morning. I saw that dead woman hanging over the bathtub."

A passerby looked at Joe Keogh curiously when he said that.

"I would suggest you lower your voice," said Kaiser. "Not that it will make any difference to me personally . . . but about last night. You weren't there. The truth is that when I came to the door, your young friends panicked, for no good reason—the young man in particular, John. He's had a bad experience, hasn't he, at some point? With one of us, *nosferatu?*"

"With more than one of you."

"Well, that's too bad. But everyone has bad experiences, and must learn to deal with them. Last night John panicked, as I say. Today I can only hope it's not too late to convince you that's the wrong response. I wish you could believe that my friends and I were really trying to save Elizabeth Wiswell's life. Regrettably we failed. But, as I said before, she died as a result of something the old man did to her."

"No."

Kaiser sighed. His attitude of trying to be helpful was so plausible that Joe had to fight more and more fiercely in his own mind to keep from believing it.

But he could not quite be convinced. The man talking to him seemed to slip away mentally now and then. Facts, comparatively minor points but meaningful, kept getting shunted aside. The aura of plausibility had nothing to support it but a fierce ego and an active brain. God, what a salesman. Charisma was the buzzword for it now. But all was not well, Joe thought, inside the handsome head that nodded and smiled at him and spoke such reasonable words.

With a freezing sensation, Joe realized just how close he had come to letting himself be convinced.

Joe moved away again. This time he leaned against the wall.

"Can we make a deal?" he asked abruptly. "Arrange some kind of temporary truce at least?"

The other blinked at him. Kaiser, as if sensing the shift in Joe's attitude, relaxed the sales pressure. "Why not?" he said in an ordinary voice. "Your people in the apartment can come and go freely. We'll give up badgering them to get in. Maybe the fit will pass over without going into the violent phase. I expect my old friend will live through it in any case. If in the meantime he should inadvertently harm someone he likes—well, I've tried. I've done about all that I can do. Meet me here again tomorrow? Say, ten in the morning? If you've decided you can trust me a little bit, there might still be time to help our mutual friend."

"Ten o'clock," said Joe. "Right here."

"Right." Kaiser stood up and put out his hand to shake, an honest and manly gesture. When Joe refused, shaking his head just slightly, he shrugged, smiled a faint but winning smile, and moved along, heading toward the Michigan Avenue exit.

Joe watched him out of sight, as far as the throng at the main door. Then he went to a public phone inside the museum and punched the number of Uncle Matthew's condo.

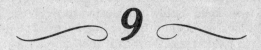

9

I have observed as I grow older that my chronic need for the home earth grows gradually less intense. In the year in which I electronically set down these words, standing in close sight of the end of the twentieth century, I find that I can ordinarily manage with a mere couple of kilograms of that dear crumbly soil, sealed sanitarily in a plastic bag beneath my bottom sheet or mattress.

Even in 1492, the year in which I at last managed to reenter Italy, this diminution of my dependence on the homeland had begun. Also by that time, to my considerable relief, I no longer found it necessary to sleep for years at a stretch. Even naps whose duration stretched into months were becoming increasingly rare.

As the time of my departure for Italy drew near, I had no very clear idea of where my two surviving assassins were likely to be found. About two years had passed since any intelligence regarding either Bogdan or Basarab had reached me. Given the perilous nature of their profession, I considered it very doubtful whether they were still alive. Therefore I decided that my first Italian destination should be Florence.

Roughly a quarter of a century earlier, at the time of my last visit to that intriguing, prosperous, often dangerous but never boring city, I had made some good friends as well as some fierce enemies among its citizens. I thought that some of those friends might be able to help me now, even if they could hardly be expected to recognize, in my youthful-looking, blood-drinking, and nocturnal figure, the breathing condottiere they had once known as Signor Ladislao.

From the beginning I had realized that to locate the objects of my vengeance would probably require my appearance in society, at any and all levels, listening everywhere, questioning discreetly. I had done my best to practice playing the role of a breathing man, first in the market towns of my homeland and then in Bucharest. That I had spent most of my life up until that time in such a state was of course a considerable advantage. By the last decade of the fifteenth century, I had no doubt of my ability to take my place in any company as a more or less ordinary breathing human—at least for a short time, when sunlight was not a problem, eating and drinking not absolute requirements. And now, at last, all was in readiness. My only real worry was that one or both of my intended victims might have gone to the grave before I had a chance to get my hands on them.

During my breathing years, traversing the Alps had invariably been something of an ordeal, and in the month of March it was often not possible at all. Now, traveling almost without baggage, alternately in wolf-form and mist-form, I found the cold and snow of spring—in the mountains, still late winter—almost no impediment. On the southern slopes, whose descent brought me down into Lombardy, I paused in man-form at an inn and rejoiced to find that the trunk deposited there the year before in the name of Ladislao was still safe, kept faithfully awaiting my arrival.

A Matter of Taste

From Lombardy, freshly equipped with money, clothing of Italian cut, and a small emergency supply of earth, I progressed by swift stages on to Florence, which city I found considerably transformed from the energetic metropolis I had known more than twenty years before. Now it seemed almost that a century of change had intervened; there was practically no one I knew left in the city. The people I did converse with were too distracted with their own problems to think about the Balkan mercenaries for whom I was so diligently searching.

Most disappointingly, I learned to my sorrow of the serious illness of Lorenzo the Magnificent, which was feared would be his last. Lorenzo had been a mere youth when I had seen him last, though already leader of the mercantile Medici clan, and more than anyone else the ruler of Florence. In the year of my return he was still only forty-one, and I had counted heavily on his friendship in my plan to obtain help.

Saddened to hear of Lorenzo's illness, I hastened on to seek him at his suburban villa at Careggi. It was early April when I arrived there, and the countryside in one of the seasons of its greatest beauty.

I had hoped to find the great man, if not recovering, at least not too ill to remember his former ally and friend, the ferocious mercenary Signor Ladislao, once sent here by the King of Hungary. Had Lorenzo been anything like his usual energetic self, with the unexcelled Medici intelligence network at his command, he could very likely have provided Ladislao's supposed son or nephew with vital information. But such, alas, was not to be.

I arrived at the villa about the time the Paduan doctors, at great expense, were feeding Lorenzo powdered pearls in wine, a concoction no more harmful, if considerably more expensive, than most of the other remedies of the time.

Not that I, a stranger to the attendants, was allowed in to see the sick man at once. While waiting in a shaded courtyard garden for my chance to speak to my old friend, I found a white-robed, black-cloaked friar tarrying somewhat impatiently, with the same expectation. We introduced ourselves, and thus I had the chance to converse briefly with the Dominican monk Girolamo Savonarola, who had dropped by in hopes of being able to hear the potentate's confession and give him absolution.

Savonarola was a small man, with a thick-lipped, worried-looking face; during our single brief meeting, I never saw him smile. His nose was huge enough to provoke taunts—had it been set upon another's face. I think everyone who ever met this man understood at first glance that he was to be taken seriously.

Around us in the flower garden, bees prospered among early blooms, and stone fountains splashed and played. What did we talk about? It is hard to remember a sermon after so many centuries. Savonarola was of course concerned for my immortal soul—he took that attitude with everyone he met. Also he was absolutely fearless regarding his own safety in this world. I do recall that when the subject of the upper hierarchy of the Church in Rome came up, the impetuous monk openly expressed his great contempt for all of them, the Pope included, condemning in the strongest terms the thousand corruptions that most of them practiced. Fortunately for the Dominican, Pope Innocent was soon to die, and Alexander, his successor, had at least one virtue—he was as thick-skinned as the bull that bestrode his family coat of arms, as far as personal insults or accusations were concerned.

My turn came first to see Lorenzo—most likely

because I had already hinted to the steward of a bribe. As soon as this potential offer had been discreetly realized, I was admitted for a brief visit to the dying man.

Lorenzo the Magnificent, pale and diminished as dying men are wont to be, showed little interest in my presence as he received me in his sunlit, ornate bedroom. Though still comparatively young, he was much changed from the robust youth of more than twenty years ago that I remembered. No one at the villa except Lorenzo himself was at all familiar to me, and apparently none of them remembered Signor Ladislao. Even Lorenzo's memory, as he lay dying, was certainly imperfect, and I was not sure whether he truly grasped my identity or not. We each had something to say about art, and toward the last he looked at me as if he did remember me.

And perhaps he did. For on turning over the name of Ladislao, he did finally recall that the man had come from far-off Wallachia. And, this leader of the Medici, dying as he was, beginning to perceive everything from the viewpoint of eternity, was not greatly impressed by the fact that I had not aged in more than twenty years.

Lorenzo, speaking automatically as it were, the mercantile instincts of the Medici still in control, asked me a question or two on politics, having to do with who was ruling in my homeland now, and I gave him such answers as I could. Political ambition had become the least of my concerns. I suppose I must have realized that I, in my present mode of mainly dusk-to-dawn existence, punctuated by trancelike sleeps sometimes extending over weeks or months, was in no condition to rule anything. However, my ignorance of current events in Wallachia was of little moment, for Lorenzo's gaze remained for the most part fixed upon eternity and he paid scant attention to my answers.

Even from the viewpoint of eternity, I was accepted as a man, and this was pleasing. Ever since the beginning of my trans-Alpine journey, my confidence in my ability to appear among breathing humans and be accepted as one of themselves had grown almost daily. So far I had confined my appearances in society mainly to the hours of darkness, though for some time now—as at Careggi—I had been able to demonstrate to my own satisfaction that daylight, at least of the dim and indirect variety, was not necessarily unbearable to my kind.

Only now and then, as I had moved across the Alps and into Italy, did I encounter anyone who appeared to suspect that there was something *really* extraordinary about me. No one in the suburban villa, with the possible exception of the Dominican, fit into this category; and the worthy Savonarola had much else on his mind.

I was still at Careggi when Lorenzo the Magnificent died, more peacefully than any great man has a right to expect, on the ninth of April, 1492.

As soon as the head of the House of Medici was dead, Savonarola hurried back to Florence to begin his campaign to take over and reform the city, and I moved on to Rome in search of the traitor Basarab, to whose whereabouts I thought I had received some clue.

But let Basarab go, for the moment. Ultimately he proves unimportant. It was in Rome, a city I had visited only briefly during my breathing days, that I had my first contact with the Borgias.

Lucrezia, whose illegitimate father Rodrigo Borgia was soon to become Pope Alexander VI, was in that year only twelve years old and living in a Roman household that also included one or two of her father's distant female relatives, and one of his mistresses, though not her mother.

Lucrezia's brother Cesare was just seventeen, and already had been consecrated—if that is the correct word—Bishop of Pamplona. In September of the following year, 1493, his father was to make him a Cardinal . . .

(The tape here contains a fairly lengthy pause.)

On thinking the matter over, it strikes me that the reader whose native habitat is the late twentieth century may require some preparation before being thrown into intimate association with the Borgia family. At the time when I set down these words, people have grown accustomed to an altogether different type of news emanating from the Vatican from that provided by jolly fat Rodrigo and his contemporaries. Here in the later nineteen hundreds we are accustomed to hear from Rome of stately ecumenical councils, of the celebration of religious feasts, of theological wrangles. An occasional canonization or—a serious matter—the solemn process by which some educator may be deprived of his full teaching authority. Now and then, every few years perhaps, a whiff of banking scandal, subtle and indirect. Once in a great while—no more often than that, the Lord be thanked!—someone takes a shot at the Pope.

I must warn the reader that, five centuries ago, matters were considerably different. The news from the heart of Rome often concerned questions rather—how shall I say it?—rather more *fundamental*. Moral issues were then more starkly drawn. The Popes of the Renaissance, trying to defend their lands and cities as energetically as any other temporal monarchs of the time, were, with occasional gentle exceptions, more likely to hire assassins than to suffer at their hands. Among the Sacred College of Cardinals, only a few men seemed capable of remembering the holy calling that must once have influenced them to become priests.

I was, as I have written elsewhere, quiescent in my tomb (or in a temporary sepulcher at least) at the time of the supposed transfusion of Pope Innocent VIII with the blood of several children, in an effort to keep life in his own aging, failing body. So I cannot comment intelligently on the truth of that most scandalous rumor. If true, it was an outrage, but hardly incredible given the morals prevailing at the time among the upper hierarchy in Rome— Savonarola, you did not exaggerate.

In any event, Innocent died in Rome on 25 July of 1492, and in early August, for various political and financial reasons the conclave elected as his successor in office a Spanish Cardinal, Rodrigo Borgia. This man, as I have already mentioned, was the illegitimate father of both Cesare and Lucrezia, along with half a dozen other off-spring of less historical importance. The new Pope, taking the name of Alexander VI, assumed the chair of St. Peter on 26 August; and whether the transfusion rumor involving his predecessor was true or not, Alexander was certainly no improvement. In Rodrigo Borgia, all authorities concur, the papacy attained its all-time nadir.

As long as I am setting the events of the Renaissance in perspective, there are a few other matters that should be mentioned. The selection of a new Pope was not the only momentous event of the month. On 3 August, half an hour before sunrise, all unbeknownst to me at the time, and unremarked by the vast majority of my contemporaries, an itinerant navigator named Christopher Columbus set sail from the port of Palos, Spain, on his first trans-Atlantic expedition in search of the lands of the Great Khan. The seventeen-year-old youth Cesare Borgia at about the same time quietly left his school in Perugia and made his way to

Rome to see what might happen to his father in the conclave. Also that year, in Spain, by order of the Inquisitor General Tomas Torquemada, all Jews were given three months either to accept Christianity or emigrate. Farther north, England's Henry VII, following in the footsteps of his illustrious grandfather, was first fighting and then making peace in France. At the University of Cracow, in Poland, a young student who would eventually be known to the world as Copernicus was hard at work. And near me in Italy, although I did not know it then, Leonardo da Vinci was making his first sketch of a flying machine.

However great a claim the doings of Popes and Cardinals might have had on the popular attention, they were but little on my mind when I arrived in Rome. My search for Basarab, and of course for Bogdan as well, still ruled my mind and soul. The dusty roads and the clerical conflicts of Italy passed by me almost unobserved, except as they might lead me to a likely gathering place for foreign mercenaries.

I rode alone, and traveled most of the time at night, having decided that any human attendants were almost certain to be more trouble than they were worth. Some of my devoted band of followers in Romania had volunteered to come with me, but I had discouraged them. Could you have met them, good reader, you would understand why.

Having been only once molested by bandits—the encounter, at dusk, was brief indeed, and afterward I recovered a purse that one of the highwaymen had dropped—I reached Rome in due course. The Eternal City, then excited as it always was by papal turnover, was at least as much transformed as Florence had been since I had seen it last. A new bridge had quite recently been thrown across the Tiber, and the municipal water supply

Fred Saberhagen

had been restored to a level of quality unknown since the time of the Caesars. Much of this civic improvement was the work of Sixtus IV, one of those Popes who had come and gone whilst I lay sleeping; the same man who in his spare time had once tried to arrange the murder of Lorenzo de' Medici, as a means of settling some political dispute.

I approached Rome in an optimistic state of mind. By this time my Italian had regained some fluency, and I had achieved, as I thought, a fair amount of skill in asking questions. Alas, the answers were no better than before. The clue I had picked up at Careggi seemed worthless. No one with whom I spoke had heard of Bogdan, at least for the past several years; and at first no one had heard of Basarab, either.

And then, someone had. The first clue came by chance, in a conversation I overheard in a tavern frequented by soldiers. What they were saying confirmed what I had heard at the villa of Lorenzo, and put me definitely on what I thought was the right track.

My search led me first near the Vatican, and then directly into it. Understand that I am not speaking of the great church-and-single-palace complex that we see today; in 1492 Michelangelo and others had not yet begun the great rebuilding of St. Peter's and its hundred corollary projects of renewal. Nor—let me emphasize again—were the Pope's temporal domains limited to the miniature quaint city-state, a few scant acres in extent, familiar to the twentieth century. Rather all of Rome, and a large part of central Italy besides, more or less acknowledged His Holiness as temporal as well as spiritual ruler. More presently about that "more or less."

The area of Rome closely surrounding the Vatican complex was thick with private palaces, elaborate houses and gardens, many of them belonging to Cardinals. The clues that I had hoped would set me properly on Basarab's trail soon led me in among these mansions.

But the trail was cold, and I began to realize the fact; and on one summer night I allowed myself to be temporarily distracted from my fruitless search by the voice of a young woman, singing with beautiful sadness beyond a garden wall.

Silently crossing over the high stone wall and prowling through the gardens that it enclosed, I soon encountered a pretty maid standing utterly alone, leaning with her back against a tree and singing softly to herself. Judging from the girl's clothing she was a servant of some kind, perhaps a slave—oh, yes, Rome tolerated chattel slavery at the time. And there was something odd in the girl's behavior, as if she might be under the influence of drink.

Whatever the cause of her being here, at this hour, alone, I considered the situation my good fortune. Appearing at a little distance before her in the moonlight, I greeted her in my kindliest and most reassuring manner— ah, I can do such things more smoothly now, but I did not do them too clumsily, even then. Of course I was lusting for the girl's blood, and the fact that she seemed somewhat the worse for wine meant little to me one way or the other.

I spare you the details of the conquest; but it will come as no surprise to you to hear that I was soon able to taste what I desired, there in that fragrant midnight garden. This maid's blood had a certain tang, a surprising flavor, that was then completely new to me. Perhaps I should add here, parenthetically, that drug-laden gore is ordinarily a matter of indifference to even the most discriminating vampire. On imbibing it for the first time, he or she will very likely realize that a new and special flavor has been encountered. But to the trained palate there is already an almost infinite variety of human tastes. These depend of course upon the variations in individual body chemistry, as well as upon what the breathing partner has recently had to eat or drink.

Certain substances in particular convey their own strong flavors to the blood, and to the one who tastes it. Yes, as you might imagine, garlic is one of them. Of course if some more subtle substance is ingested by the breather along with one of these, then the taste of the more subtle substance, be it drug or whatever, is almost certain to be well disguised.

Almost none of these various flavors, or substances, make much difference one way or another to most vampires. They will not, as a rule, affect the blood's palatability. The spirochetes of syphilis, brought back from the New World by the intrepid explorers on the ships of Columbus, are of no more concern to the blood-drinker than the molecules of alcohol or the harsh dissonance of cocaine. We are immune to all these substances. They are not going to do us any substantial harm, or, for that matter, bestow upon us any particular pleasure, any more than merely leaden bullets are going to rend our flesh. For us, usually, the flavors in the blood alone are there, often interesting, sometimes mildly attractive.

However, we are not entirely beyond the reach of chemistry. And much in my story depends upon that fact.

But to return to that first of my nights in the gardens of Rome. To my chagrin, the somewhat tipsy maid and I were interrupted in our dalliance before we were quite finished. The light of distant torches played upon my face, and youthful voices, secure in the certainty of power and position, were raised in merriment. The voices approached, beginning to call a woman's name; and she who still lay in my arms stirred half-consciously at the sound.

Presently, through the darkened garden, which had

seemed such a secure setting for romance at this time of night, there approached a sturdy, stalwart youth of seventeen or so. Dressed in black velvet, he was handsome and strong as a young Greek god, already with a good start on his beard. Accompanying him was a girl no older than twelve, also wearing the garments and speaking in the accents of the upper classes. From the familiar and demanding way in which she addressed the young man I was certain that she could only be his sister.

They called each other Cesare and Lucrezia, names that meant nothing to me then; but the name they called out loudly and most often was that of the maid I had just embraced.

They saw her at last, now lying alone, stretched out wantonly upon the grass. And they saw me as well, though I had already started to retire from the scene.

Now it may sometimes be unsafe to interrupt a gentleman of passionate nature in the midst of his amorous endeavors. The danger is compounded when the gentleman happens to be a vampire. But on this occasion I was willing to beat a meek retreat.

The truth was that, very suddenly, and almost for the first time since the wounds of my assassination had finally healed, I did not feel at all well. The onset of the malaise had been so abrupt that I could only suppose it must be connected in some way with the blood I had just taken.

One of my most immediate problems was that I found myself frozen in man-form, almost as if the sun had suddenly arisen. Therefore the two adolescents were able to see me in the moonlight as I went over the wall, and they were impressed with my agility. The boy was armed with a sword, and after briefly examining the maid they decided to follow me. A nearby tree, next to the wall, made the job easier.

From what I could overhear of the remarks that passed between my reckless pursuers, as I staggered toward the horse I had left tethered nearby, I deduced that Lucrezia must have been carrying out some kind of a devilish medical or chemical experiment, and that the maid had been its subject. But my head was spinning; science did not interest me particularly—it would not, for many years—and I did not pay close attention.

Besides, though daybreak was still far off, my illness had been suddenly compounded by an overwhelming urge to sleep. All I could think of was my nearest earth. Remounting my horse and clinging with some difficulty to his back, I turned him in the direction of the nearest of my earth boxes. Naturally I had memorized the locations of all such deposits put into place during the decades of my preparation.

The particular box I was now seeking had been concealed, if the reports brought back by my most trust-worthy lieutenants were to be credited, deep in a subterranean Etruscan ruin that lay then on the outskirts of Rome, and for all I know lies there still, now buried beneath the city itself.

My goal was not far away in ordinary reckoning, but it made for a long ride that night in my condition, and attaining it was one of the most difficult experiences of a busy and interesting life. All my will and determination were required simply to stay awake. I was forced to ride slowly to keep myself from being thrown out of the saddle. At some point during the ride I became aware that the two young people had somehow obtained mounts and were still following me.

I was too sick, too weary unto death, to fight or even to run from them. At long last I realized, by certain landmarks, that my desired earth, or the place where my earth should be, was close ahead. It was all that I could do to dismount without falling, drive my horse away, and drag myself into the cavity in the ground.

A natural crevice in the earth, somewhat wider than a human body, emitted a faint smell of sulphur. The appearance of this crevice, from the vantage point of its grassy lip, suggested a bottomless abyss. In the minds of imaginative people of the time, hell might well lie at the bottom of such a hole, and none of the shepherds who were wont to tend their flocks nearby were likely to explore it. But twenty feet or so was the extreme depth to which the man-sized passageway descended. There was an enlarged chamber at that level, containing an Etruscan sarcophagus, some ancient, broken pottery, and very little else—except my precious trove of Transylvanian soil, spread out on a kind of earthen shelf.

I dragged myself to the place where I could obtain rest, and there collapsed. I had just time, before lapsing into unconsciousness, to overhear a few more words from my pursuers, who had reached the opening above.

Whoever the two precocious children were, if I correctly understood what they were saying, they had followed me deliberately, excited by the prospect of being able to see what secondary effect the poison in the young girl's blood would have upon a vampire.

Vampiro. That word, uttered in upper-class Italian, was the last I thought I heard, though of course in my drugged state I could hardly be sure. Fighting to the last to stay awake and on guard, I was nevertheless overcome.

10

I t was Angie who picked up the phone first when Joe called Maule's apartment to report the results of his talk with Kaiser. She was able to tell Joe, in turn, some interesting bits of information regarding blood chemistry in vampires, that she'd picked up from listening to the old man's tape. She and John had decided that Joe ought to be told, whatever the possible eavesdroppers might make of the information.

It was about four in the afternoon when that call was completed. Sunset was still more than an hour away, but the cloudy sky, its brightness very gradually diminishing, made nightfall seem imminent.

Joe on the phone had been modestly reassuring, but he had been as insistent as ever that they stay in the apartment and remain on guard, crushing any hope that their problems might be over.

Within two minutes after Angie hung up the phone, the front door chime sounded, for the first time in many hours.

John and Angie were both in the old man's room at the time, occupying chairs, one on each side of his bed, and exchanging hopeful comments to the effect that he might soon be able to talk to them. His appearance, they agreed, had continued to improve, gradually but definitely. But he hadn't yet managed to say anything intelligible.

When the door chime sounded, the old man grunted. Both John and Angie, after uttering quick reassurances to their host, hurried to look at the front-door viewer.

Angie frowned at the small, bright image. "It's the lady we ran into last night," she said. "Isn't it?"

"What lady?" John sounded lost.

"The heavyset one who was just getting out of the elevator when the three of us were going up to the restaurant. Remember?"

"Oh, yeah. Maybe it is her. What does she want?"

"Better find out."

He flipped on the speaker. "Hello?" he inquired cautiously.

"Mr. Maule? It's Mrs. Hassler from down the hall." The voice was bright as a robin's, cheerful and enthusiastic though somewhat distorted by the speaker. It seemed to have as little connection with vampires as any sound that Angie had ever heard.

She and John looked at each other doubtfully.

The screen image spoke again. "Mr. Maule? Are you all right? I wanted to make sure you remembered the Residents' Association meeting tonight."

An incoherent groan drifted into the living room, from the direction of Uncle Matthew's chamber.

John whispered: "I wonder if there's some way that she can tell he's home?"

Angie hissed back: "Search me. But you answered her, now she knows there's someone here."

Again there was a faint sound, this time as of an intelligible voice, from the old man's bedroom. His two guardians looked at each other wide-eyed. A moment later, they were bursting in on him again.

He was sitting bolt upright in his bed, glaring at them,

and to their great joy they heard him utter a few coherent words: ". . . admit . . . no one . . ."

"We won't!" Angie hastened to be reassuring. "We haven't let anyone in. No one but Joe. You know, Joe Keogh? He was here, but he's gone now to try to get help."

The old man nodded firmly. He was definitely coming around.

Now he pointed toward the living room. "Mrs.—Hassler."

"Yes, what about her?"

Maule enunciated carefully. "Genuinely . . . my neighbor. Try . . . keep her quiet. No police. Not yet."

"Yes, we understand about the police. No police yet. Angie, go back and talk to her. No, wait, you stay here. I'll go, just in case." And John went bounding out of the room again.

"Can I get you anything?" Angie asked the patient, joyfully.

"Tell me . . . what has happened?"

Angie did her best, pouring out the story in a jumble of words. She concluded: "If we could only phone Joe now and tell him you're coming out of it . . ."

The man sitting in the bed looked grimly worried. "Yes . . . wait. If this phone is tapped . . . try to use—Mrs. Hassler's. Safer than—trying to reach—public phone. We do not want—the enemy to know—I am recovering."

Angie ran into the front room to communicate this idea to John. He had the front door open on its security holders, and was conversing warily with Mrs. Hassler through the narrow gap.

Angie joined him, hanging on his shoulder and smiling brightly, while thinking she must look a ghastly mess.

Introductions were quickly, if somewhat awkwardly, performed. Then Angie said, as sweetly as possible: "The phone's out of order here, on top of everything else—Mrs. Hassler, do you suppose we could use yours?"

"Of course, dear." If the smiling woman in the corridor was bothered by not being asked to step in, she didn't show it.

John stared at Angie, then caught the idea. With a muttered excuse he ran back to confer briefly with the old man. Moments later he was back at the front door, and a moment after that he was gone. Angie stuck her head out and watched him safely into Mrs. Hassler's apartment just down the hall.

Then she locked and bolted up the door again, turned off the viewer, and walked slowly back to talk to Uncle Matthew.

She found him out of bed, standing erect though he looked a bit unsteady, and wrapping himself in a white robe. As soon as Angie entered the room he asked her: "Where is Joseph now?"

"I don't know. He didn't want to tell us where he'd be. But we can call his regular number and leave messages on his answering machine; he can call in from somewhere else and have them played back. Shouldn't you sit down and rest?"

The old man muttered something—Angie felt sure it was profanity—in some unknown tongue, which had a Latinesque sound to it. But he nodded weakly and sat down.

He and Angie were still in the master bedroom, talking, a couple of minutes later, when a loud splintering crash resounded through the apartment, followed in an instant by a mutter of voices, unfamiliar and triumphant. Angie sprang up. The image conveyed to her mind by that sound was that either the front or back door had just been violently broken in.

It seemed to Angie that she was on her feet at once, but Uncle Matthew, who had shaken off his unsteadiness to move with startling speed, was already closing and locking the bedroom door. Then he turned and stood in front of it with his finger to his lips, gesturing her to silence.

The unfamiliar male voices, somewhere out there in the apartment, sounded again, low but victorious. Someone was being invited to come in.

John, invited to make himself at home in Mrs. Hassler's pleasant but somewhat overdecorated apartment, did the best he could to fend off the lady's kind attentions and bottomless curiosity, while using her generously offered telephone. He realized at once that he was going to have to give up all hope of speaking privately with Joe Keogh.

He had only one number to call, that of Joe's regular home phone.

The machine answered, as John had expected. After the recorded message had had its say, he cleared his throat and spoke: "Joe, this is John. I'm calling from the apartment next door. The phone here seems to be working without that trouble we had with Uncle Matthew's. Uh, I wanted you to know Uncle Matthew's up and about now, though he's still very weak."

Looking over his shoulder, John saw Mrs. Hassler beaming at him from across the kitchen. He smiled at her and continued talking into the phone. "His, uh, laryngitis is much better. One of those twenty-four-hour viruses, I guess."

Mrs. Hassler made no pretense of absenting herself or her attention, but continued to look on with approval.

John thanked her and prepared to hurry back to Angie. As he stood on the point of opening the front door, he paused. "Mind if I take a look out there first?"

"No, of course not." His hostess seemed intrigued.

John flicked on the viewer beside Mrs. Hassler's front door.

Someone, an ominous male shape, was standing guard in the hallway, obviously keeping an eye on the front approach to Uncle Matthew's condo. At the distance John couldn't tell if it was Valentine Kaiser or not, a vampire or a breather.

Muttering some kind of feeble explanation to Mrs. Hassler, who appeared more intrigued than alarmed, he walked through her apartment to the back door, where he flicked another switch. The landing of the service stairs was also occupied by a male sentry. This man was closer, and John knew that he'd never seen him before. As for being *nosferatu*, well, that was still hard to tell on screen.

His hostess had followed him, and stood with her arms folded, watching for whatever entertaining trick he might do next.

John sighed. "Is that—do you know if that's the back door to Mr. Maule's apartment?" He gestured at the screen, which provided a great view of the closed door opposite.

"It certainly is."

"It looks like Uncle Matthew's place is being watched."

"It certainly does, doesn't it?"

"Would you mind—uh, would you mind if I waited here for a little while?"

"Of course not! Would you like some coffee?"

Angie, in an agony of fear, trying to recall the prayers that she'd been taught to say in childhood, had moved back into the corner of the bedroom farthest from the door. Her host, moving and working with amazing speed, though occasionally stumbling, had taken one of the dark glass jars out of the hidden compartment in the dresser. Now he was mixing some stuff—it looked a horrible brownish yellow— taken from the jar in a glass of water drawn in the bathroom. He hadn't explained to Angie what he was doing, nor dared she speak to ask.

Judging by what she could hear from beyond the door, in the outer reaches of the apartment, the people who had broken in the door were advancing only with extreme caution from room to room, as if they were wary of ambushes. As if they had an enormous respect for the one they were trying to find.

At last Angie thought she could hear one of them, perhaps two, closely approaching the bedroom door on the hallway side. Whoever it was stood there for a time, evidently listening, and being very quiet.

In another half minute, the doorknob was tried gently.

Then whoever was just outside the bedroom door moved quietly away. Angie had the impression of a general conference being held at some distance, in the living room perhaps.

Evidently now believing that he could move unheard by those outside, Matthew Maule glided across the room, silently closed the hidden cupboard, and lifted the dresser back against the wall. Then, to Angie's astonishment, he handed her the drink he had just finished mixing. He made an urgent pantomime for her to swallow it.

Having seen the mess from which the drink had been concocted, she held back. There was no particular odor rising from the glass she held, but the liquid in it looked like dirty dishwater. What was he planning for her, suicide? Death before dishonor? But the fierce liveliness of Maule's expression and his gestures, even weakened as he was, made that suspicion an absurdity.

The taste was not nearly as bad as she had expected. There were even pleasant overtones. Almost anything liquid would have felt good in her mouth dried out by fear.

The next effect followed almost immediately. Angie's senses reeled. "Now what?" she gasped.

With one hand her protector—she hoped—once more gestured eloquently for silence, even as he took the glass in the other fist and moved in a few long, silent dance steps back into the bathroom. The unrinsed glass was stuffed into the medicine cabinet beside the electronic mirror.

If his closing the medicine cabinet door made any sound at all, Angie only a few feet away was unable to detect it.

Then Uncle Matthew was at her side again. Putting his lips very close to her ear, he whispered: "I must leave you here. There is no help for it. But I swear I shall return."

Angie couldn't really understand. "Don't leave me," she pleaded. Her head was spinning with the drink, and she collapsed into a chair, on the brink of fainting. She murmured a protest against being poisoned, which he ignored.

The one who some called the old man was already at one of the bedroom's windows, where he was doing something to the metal frame. Angie in her dizzy astonishment saw the window turn, letting in a breath of chilly air—she had thought that in a high-rise like this one none of the windows could be opened.

Curtains swirled, and a moment later the old man was gone. Angie began to whimper. He had left her totally alone.

She gave a little cry. Something had just smashed, with tremendous violence, against the locked bedroom door from outside. It was a substantial door, but the one blow had started the wood splintering.

Angie screamed.

Clinging like a fly on the ledge outside the window, quivering under the malevolent influence of the sun beyond the clouds, shuddering in his feebleness from the small exertion he had made thus far, feeling weak as a small bat, he made no effort to close the window again behind him. Let the hunters discover at once which way he had gone. Let them pursue him, if they could be induced to do so, instead of . . .

Never mind, for now, the girl he was being forced to leave behind. He had to get away, to survive, if he was going to be of any help to anyone.

He had emerged on the north face of the building, well into the last daylight hour of a gray and misty, violently windy day. Steel and glass were slippery in their dampness, and the wind tugged at him erratically. He was going to need all of his diminished strength to keep himself from falling.

He started down, feeling his way from one infinitesimal toehold and handgrip to the next.

Tentatively he essayed a shape-change; but he could tell in an instant that it was not going to work. Daylight lingered still, and traces of the subtle drug persisted in his flesh. He was frozen in man-form. Well, then he would have to climb down in the shape of a man. He had managed more difficult feats in the past.

Not much more difficult, though. And not often.

The sides of the building, while extremely steep, yet deviated from the vertical by a few degrees, a deviation that very gradually increased toward the ground. Perhaps there were even a few breathing mountaineers who'd find the feat within the range of possibility. However that might be, a fearless though desperate vampire ought to be able to make the descent, clinging to damp and slippery glass and steel, where no merely breathing human would be likely to survive.

Back in Mrs. Hassler's apartment, John Southerland roamed from the front door to the rear, and back again. Both of the sentries were holding their positions. Something was up, something was going on over there at Uncle Matthew's. John couldn't actually see Uncle Matthew's front door from Mrs. Hassler's viewer; all the doors were slightly recessed from the corridor, which just cut off his view. He could see with certainty that Maule's door was being steadily watched, or guarded, and he was becoming more and more firmly convinced that the watcher was *nosferatu*. Probably it was the figure's abnormal stillness most of the time.

Could it be the police? John doubted it. At this stage he had to assume that such continuous surveillance must be hostile.

Minutes passed that seemed like hours. To his dismay, the unfamiliar vampires—the more John looked, the more certain he was of the classification of the watchers, front and back—maintained their vigil with perfect patience.

John fretted, and thought, but he considered he had

no choice but to stay where he was for a time. If these newcomers were friendly—that was a possibility, if Joe had ever gotten through to Mina Harker—then someone ought to be coming along soon to let him know what was going on. The chance that they were friendly did not seem great enough to require serious consideration.

Should he try to call Joe again, leave another message to bring him up-to-date? Not yet, not with Mrs. Hassler listening. Maybe in a little while.

Mrs. Hassler, quietly but thoroughly enjoying the excitement, had a suggestion.

"Tell you what, young man. I'm planning to go down for my daily swim shortly—did you know we have a pool on the forty-fourth floor?—and I'll look over the man in the front hall as I go. You know, casually. If I discover anything about him that I think you should know, I'll call you from down there at poolside. So if my phone rings, answer it."

"Thanks. I'll do that."

John hesitated, wanting to warn his helpful hostess to be careful. But at the same time he was desperate for information. In the terse bits of conversation he'd shared with Mrs. Hassler, he'd been gradually elaborating somewhat on his and Angie's original story. The scenario as it now stood was based on certain unwelcome relatives of Mr. Maule having chosen this awkward time—awkward for unspecified reasons—to pay him a visit. Whether Mrs. Hassler believed this half explanation or not, she obviously loved the accompanying intrigue.

John's hostess retired into her bedroom, to emerge some five minutes later wearing a one-piece swimsuit half-covered by a kind of cape or robe, modestly concealing most of her heavy legs.

"Ta ta, young man. See you soon!" And with an

almost flirtatious wink she was gone, fearlessly out the front door. John, holding his breath at the viewer, nerving himself to rush out and try to help her if need be, saw her exchange brief neighborly smiles with the vampire sentry and march briskly on, her gay cape swaying.

Angie, alone and terrified in Uncle Matthew's bedroom, could feel her brain whirling giddily from the unknown dose he had prescribed and administered.

Another hard blow came at the bedroom door, and she cried out in a low voice, knowing that with the next impact the lock was going to give way.

11

My revival in the deepest habitable level of that Italian earth-crevice, amid the ruins of that ancient Etruscan burial vault, was a slow process. Stubbornly my dazed senses refused to focus upon the problems at hand. My hands and knees trembled, and my brain and body ached until I was reminded of the mornings following the worst drinking bouts of my breathing days.

And my memories on awakening, memories of those hours just before I had lost consciousness, were bizarre indeed—even for a vampire. What had that incredible, devilish, half-grown girl really said about me to her brother? If her remarks had indeed included the words I seemed to remember, then the children of Rome must be vastly more sophisticated than any I had encountered elsewhere.

Well, I was still relatively new to the vampire profession. In the process of becoming accustomed to my new lifestyle, I had begun to believe that we *nosferatu* possessed complete immunity to such attacks. But the latest evidence showed that to be a dangerously optimistic view.

Whatever the cause of my helpless lapse into unconsciousness, one thing was certain, that my sleep had not been a normal one. Looking back from the century in which I write, I suspect that I may have spent a full day, or even several, struggling in my borrowed tomb, between the moment when I first began to regain my senses, and the time when I could begin to function with reasonable dependability.

When at last I had regained strength and sense enough to turn my aching head toward the source of daylight—just then extremely irritating even if quite indirect—and squint up from the depths of my refuge, I found myself regarding a patch of blue Italian sky, with one small cloud of bloodless white just visible.

As usual, the first question to occupy my mind upon becoming fully awake was whether there was some immediate cause—some visitor, perhaps, already present in my sanctuary or on the verge of intruding? Discovering nothing of the kind, I immediately interested myself in the usual second question: For how long a period, this time, had I lain comatose?

Ominous signs were not wanting that this latest and most mysterious lapse had been a lengthy one—a small shrub, growing at the very entrance of my sunken grotto, was noticeably bigger than I remembered it. Perhaps, I thought optimistically, there is a spring and the plant is especially well watered there. For a time, at least, I could still hope that only months and not whole years had elapsed.

Sitting up on the earthen ledge where I had slept, averting my gaze from the bothersome pressure of daylight, I took an inventory of my person. I had, of course, acquired no Rip Van Winkle beard—whatever the length of my stay out of the world, I am generally spared that. My limbs were as supple as ever. As a rule most of my biological processes seem to come to a complete halt as long as I am tranced. But on this occasion some drastic changes for the worse in the state of my clothing argued for a long interregnum.

Fortunately, I had a spare garment or two on hand.

Well, whatever the interval had been, there was nothing to be done about it now. Still feeling strangely light-headed, I declared myself fully awake at last, arose from my hard couch, and bade a silent farewell to my perpetually silent host in his sarcophagus, whose slumbers had already endured much longer than the entire period of my life.

I was ravenously hungry.

Fortunately for my hunger and my impatience, the afternoon was already far advanced, and within an hour after arising I was crouched by the upper orifice of the cave, ready to face the dawning night. Emerging promptly at sunset, I soon disposed of a goat that had been grazing on the barren hillside nearby. It had the look of a semidomesticated creature, and I took care to leave a coin beside the bloodless carcass to reimburse its owners for my nourishment.

Even as I completed this gesture of payment, I became aware that I was no longer alone.

Turning to look in the direction of my sunken grotto, I saw a slender shadow detach itself from the greater darkness of a looming boulder; and for the first time since I had risen from my grave I recognized the presence of another of my kind. How I accomplished this so swiftly I cannot readily explain.

In the same instant that I comprehended the newcomer's vampire status, I understood that I was in the presence of a woman. And only a moment later I realized that I knew her—nay, our relationship went deeper than that. We had once been of considerable importance to each other.

I took a step toward her, blinking in my surprise. "Constantia?"

"I am pleased that you remember me, Prince Drakulya." The mockery in the little gypsy's voice was light.

"How could I ever forget? —But I see that you are greatly changed." In another sense, of course, the woman before me was hardly changed at all, for she appeared as young and comely as on that night many years earlier when she had violated my grave.

"Indeed I have. As none should know better than you, Prince Drakulya."

I doubted then, and still doubt, whether my embraces had been the sole or even the chief cause of her conversion. But if I had had a successor, or a rival, as Constantia's vampire lover, I was never to find out his name.

Certainly my little gypsy appeared to me as beautiful as ever. But both of us understood, from the first moment of our first Italian encounter, that our relationship would necessarily be different from now on. Henceforward, as a vampire herself, she might be my *nosferatu* friend, in a sense my sister, or even daughter; but the love that passes between man and woman we could share no more.

How had Constantia been able to locate me? Echoing some of the conversation of our first meeting, she gave coy answers to that question and put me off. Probably, I decided, her magical arts were considerably advanced over what they had been at the time of our first encounter.

I had other questions that I thought just as important: Why had she tried to find me? And why was she in Italy?

"There are many interesting things in Italy these days, good prince." It pleased her, for the time being, to be no more specific than that, and it pleased me for the time being not to press the matter. There was much else I wanted to find out, having to do with local and world affairs—by world affairs I of course meant those of Europe and Asia Minor. On such matters Constantia provided information freely. High on my list of things to learn, naturally, was the matter of how and why and by whom I had been drugged, and how closely my shadowy memories on the subject corresponded with the truth.

Constantia might well have recognized the Borgia offspring from my description of the mysterious young Cesare and Lucrezia. But she swore that she knew nothing. Either she could not or would not help me speculate on the identity of my juvenile poisoners, and for the time being I was forced to allow that problem to wait.

The next few hours of that night I spent listening while Constantia brought me up-to-date on what we both considered important current events. I had been in the earth with the Etruscan for about eight years; this was the Jubilee Year of 1500, so proclaimed by the Pope.

Naturally the identity of the current Pope was among the things I was most eager to learn, in an effort to reorient myself to a changed world. Constantia quickly informed me that the Borgia, Alexander VI, still held his position as Vicar of Christ. This was of great importance to the political and military situation in general. Certainly I would not have been surprised to learn that he had already gone to his reward. Popes as a rule are elderly men when elected—Alexander, I knew, had been sixty-one when he assumed St. Peter's chair—and in that century the average length of a reign was less than a decade. Alas for Christendom, Cesare Borgia's father still sat there.

Constantia talked with me a little longer and then departed, having naturally, as she said, her own affairs to attend to. We made tentative arrangements to meet again.

The later part of that evening and much of the next I spent mingling with the breathers in several marketplaces of suburban Rome. In the first of these I obtained new clothing. In all of them I listened much and spoke little, only now and then engaging cautiously in conversation. I soon was able to confirm much of what my former lover had told me, of events that had transpired whilst I was underground. Quietly I raged within myself at my own weakness that had caused me to lose eight years in sleep—at the malignancy of that incredible girl-child who played so recklessly with poisons—at my own stupidity in falling prey to one of her concoctions—and at the thought of Bogdan and Basarab, who were now most likely gone out of my reach again, gone far if not forever.

Of course by this time my juvenile poisoner, whoever she was, would be a child no longer, if she still lived. She would be about twenty, as I calculated, and her brother some five years older—but I still had no idea of who they were, beyond the fact of their belonging to the privileged class. Had I not been devoted already to vengeance on others, I might have tried to seek them out. Alas, it proved unnecessary for me to do so.

Among other information I had gleaned from Constantia was that for several years during my latest nap the fanatical reformer Savonarola had been in virtual control of the city of Florence. Fra Girolamo had been bent on establishing a Florentine government that would serve the interest of God's poor as well as of the wealthy. Like most such plans, his miscarried. Eventually he had been betrayed to his enemies, arrested, publicly strangled, and his body burnt upon the scaffold—so much for reform. In general, the leaders of church and state alike had been pleased to see their last in this world of that pesky monk. The Medici family were now once more in control of Florence, though from things I overheard I deduced that their rule was neither so firm nor so beneficial as it once had been.

On the next night—which I, to be on the safe side, planned to spend in a different earth—Constantia kept her appointment for our meeting, and we were able to have a second conversation.

This time it pleased her to speak of Bogdan and Basarab, or, more accurately, to inform me that since her arrival in Italy she had heard nothing of them.

"But, my prince, if they have indeed become condottieri here, then I should think that the place to seek them would be with Cesare Borgia."

There were a number of men named Cesare around, and at first I saw no reason to establish a connection with my little poisoner's escort. "Ah, yes. The Pope's son. What is he doing now?"

Constantia related the young man's accomplishments to me at some length—indeed, everyone in Italy was now interested in the career of Cesare Borgia, who had recently been appointed captain general of the papal army.

Always one to enjoy a juicy bit of gossip, Constantia informed me that in June of 1497, Cesare's older brother, Juan, until then their father's favorite choice for a military leader, had been murdered under most mysterious circumstances in the streets of Rome.

"Murdered by whom?"

No one knew, but during the years following many had come to blame Cesare.

By 1498, at the age of twenty-three, Cesare had with Alexander's blessing resigned his appointment as Cardinal, and had been dispatched upon an important diplomatic expedition, carrying an immense treasure—which included silver urinals, among other improbabilities—to the court of the French king at Chinon.

Alexander's most ambitious and dangerous child had remained in France until 1499, when he had ridden south of the Alps with Louis XII, monarch of France, on his famed and ultimately ill-fated expedition to Naples.

I frowned at Constantia. "Are you telling me that the French invaded Italy in force?"

"You might say that, I suppose. Well, yes, they certainly did, but in the end it came to nothing, and the only battle they really fought was when they were trying to get home again."

I had already missed the peak of the Jubilee Year in Rome. The month of February had been carnival, when pilgrims thronged in from all across Europe, seeking special indulgences. In that month Cesare had arrived in the city in considerable state, bringing with him prisoners from his most recent military expeditions. The purpose of these campaigns had been the subjugation of some of the petty lords of the Papal Territories, who had been minded to remove themselves from under the temporal authority of Christ's Vicar. Evidently Cesare, despite his youth, was already a most effective leader, in war and politics as well. According to Constantia he, with his doting father's blessing, was beginning to give himself almost royal airs.

Aut Caesar, aut nihil. Caesar or nothing. That was his motto, and he devoted himself to trying to live up to it.

I pressed my friend's hand thankfully. "If what you are telling me is accurate, then you are right, this Borgia is the one I must seek out. Mercenaries and war are going to follow him like soldiers after a prostitute."

Constantia soon took her leave. As for me, I had much to do before dawn.

Once more, as the evening deepened, I roamed the marketplaces of suburban Rome. No one I spoke to there, of course, had ever heard of two condottieri with outlandish names, Bogdan and Basarab. Many people were talking of Cristoforo Colombo, whose name had also been mentioned by Constantia. A daring but controversial navigator, it seemed, who had recently completed his second or perhaps his third round-trip voyage westward to the Indies.

A corollary of these explorations, though it was not perceived as such at the time, had followed. Immediately after the return of Colombo's crews from the New World, a new venereal infection, called the French disease by Italians, and the Neapolitan pox by the French, had begun to radiate rapidly from certain seaports, and was now well on its way to establishing a broad foothold in Europe. The modern name for this disease is syphilis.

Seeking news, suggestions, any hint at all that might lead me to the wretched pair Basarab and Bogdan, I continued to move among the markets and the taverns of the great city, keeping my ears open. As part of my general vampirish transformation, my hearing had become preternaturally acute, but of the men I sought I still heard nothing. Of the Pope, still hale and hearty at the age of sixty-nine, and of two of his children, I learned a great deal.

Lucrezia had recently been married for the second time—her father had annulled the first union. In the summer of 1500 her second husband was murdered. This time no one really doubted that Cesare was responsible, and that Alexander had given at least tacit approval to the act. Somehow I just managed to miss out on being on hand for that.

Everyone was talking of Cesare, in particular.

It is hard to remember now at exactly what point it dawned on me that the Cesare Borgia of whom I heard so much and his younger sister Lucrezia could conceivably be the pair of adolescents who had once sent me to my grave—at least to one of my borrowed graves—and followed me there, in a spirit of scientific curiosity. When the rumors linking the Pope's offspring with poison began to reach my ears, I could hardly have failed to make the connection.

Italy in that age was not yet, as France and Spain and England had already become, a united power. Rather it was the most chronic of Europe's chronic battlefields. Well, I thought, if I can find out nothing directly regarding the men I want, I can at least discover where fighting and campaigning are currently in progress, or where they are most likely in the immediate future. Those would be the best places to seek out enterprising condottieri; if not to meet them, at least to hear word of them.

But currently, as I came to understand more thoroughly with every hour I spent in learning more about events, there was no better place to seek for mercenaries than in the train of Duke Valentino, as Cesare had come to be known since the King of France had bestowed certain lands and titles on him.

In the summer of 1500, whatever spiritual influence the Pope's proclaimed Jubilee might have had in heaven, His Holiness barely escaped death from a falling ceiling and roof in one of his Roman apartments.

And at about the same time, Cesare, preparing to campaign again in the Romagna, where certain papal vassals were still showing too much independence, was signing contracts with a number of leading condottieri. Basarab, I considered, might well be among them.

But no one to whom I spoke there knew his name. He might, of course, have changed it. But if he had not done so early in his mercenary career, why do it now?

Prowling Rome by night and sometimes by day, concentrating particularly upon the area near the papal palace, I still failed to locate either of my old enemies. Military men were coming and going continually, however, and I still could not think of any better place to search. I decided to remain near Cesare Borgia, and search some more.

Given my permanent aversion to sunlight, and certain other peculiarities of my new mode of life, I considered myself as ill-suited for the life of a mercenary, or of any kind of regular soldier, as I was for that of a ruler. There were of course other ways to make oneself valuable to a great prince or general, and attach oneself to his staff. Of these, the intelligence service seemed the best suited to my training and talents. Indeed, I considered myself uniquely qualified for such a career.

I had other reasons for seeking a position. My modest stock of gold was running low, and I foresaw that I was likely to need more in the future. Food I obtained in my own way, but sometimes it would be necessary for me to purchase clothing, help, or information. Theft was of course not to be considered, nor had I any intention of allowing myself to be reduced to beggary. Honorable service seemed the only logical alternative. Therefore I met, or determined to meet, Cesare.

For both of us, it proved to be a memorable encounter. It took place in a military encampment on the edge of Rome.

I recognized him at once. If I had not previously suspected he was the youth who had once followed me to my burrow, I knew it now.

Duke Valentino was now twenty-five or twenty-six years old. He was darkly bearded, a tall man for his time, very powerfully built, and much matured from the seventeen-year-old who had accompanied his lethal little sister to what they must have thought was my final resting place.

He was sitting before a folding table, inside a tent, when I saw him for the first time. He turned his dark and piercing eyes on me, and I thought at first my image struck a spark of recognition in them somewhere. But all he said was: "Ladislao of Hungary? I am pleased to meet you, but alas, I have never heard of you before."

"Sir, I was formerly married to a sister of King Matthias. I have fought the Turks and other enemies of the Holy Father—I will serve you capably as a bodyguard, or in many discreet ways." I might have said that in my own land I had commanded armies, but I might not have been believed, and in any case that was not the job for which I was applying.

The man who was standing beside the Duke stirred when I mentioned my capabilities as bodyguard. This infamous henchman was informally known to most people at the time as Michelotto—his real name was Miguel da Corella, meaning that he came from Corella, in the then half-independent kingdom of Navarre.

"Who sent you?" he demanded of me harshly.

I looked him in the eye and decided to speak him fairly, though I made my tone only a little softer than his own. "No one sent me, sir. I make this application on my own decision."

Corella shook his head. "I don't like the look of you."

Cesare was watching us in amused silence; obviously, as I thought, testing my mettle.

I said to Michelotto: "Nor do I care a great deal for your appearance, if it comes to that." He was indeed a swarthy, ugly wretch. "But I will try to put up with you, provided you are good at your job."

The Duke was laughing now, almost silently but with evidence of real enjoyment. I did not know it at the time—nor would I have cared particularly if I had known —but it would have been hard to find another man in Italy, excepting the Pope's son himself, who would speak to Michelotto in such a way.

Things might well have come to violence between us on the spot, giving me a chance to demonstrate the skills of which I had just boasted, and at the same time creating an opening on Duke Valentino's staff. But, somewhat to my disappointment, Cesare, laughing, spoke to us both in soothing words.

"Michelotto, good friend—do me a favor and leave me alone with this hot-tempered visitor. I shall be quite safe, I promise you."

"My lord duke—!"

"Leave us." And on hearing the tone of that command, and seeing with what alacrity it was obeyed, I knew that this Pope's son might indeed one day accomplish all the marvels that others were predicting for him.

In another moment he and I were alone—though Corella had favored me with his foulest look before departing, and I felt certain, even if I could not hear his breathing, that he was watching the tent protectively from outside.

Borgia glanced at me, fearlessly, and then away. He stretched out a powerful hand—it was said that he could straighten horseshoes in his grip—and smoothed down the sketch of fortifications that was spread out on the table. "I think I know you after all," he said. "Though not by the name you gave just now. And I shall be happy to take you into my service."

His eyes came back to mine, and he must have read my surprise at this quick acceptance.

"Why am I so quick to hire you?" he added. "Because I need good men, men who can get things done." He lowered his voice a notch. "And most particularly I have need of a vampire."

12

As the wood shattered around the lock on the bedroom door, Angie shrank back as far as she could, cowering behind the old man's bed. Knowing what the sheer drop was like outside the window, she couldn't even think of trying to follow him that way. In the next moment the door burst open inward—a final blow had torn it from its lock and hinges alike—and monsters appeared.

The pair of them looked like men, dressed in ordinary casual clothing, men who might pass by on the street at any time. But Angie knew them for monsters nonetheless. Their actions, and the way they smiled at her, betrayed the fact. Both, judging by appearance, were in their thirties. One was tall, one short, the tall one black, the short one white. Neither, in a written description, would show any resemblance to Valentine Kaiser or Matthew Maule. But there was something, an attitude, a presence, an essence, that all four men had in common.

The two invaders advanced slowly, silently, warily into the room, looking around them at every step.

Despite her drugged state Angie was completely terrified, too much afraid to make a noise. Now, following the first two men, another couple of the enemy, this pair a man and a woman, stepped cautiously into the doorway of Uncle Matthew's bedroom. Angie felt sure, somehow, with

174

her first look at them, that these two were breathers.

The first of the enemy to reach Angie was the taller, black vampire. Hands of incredible power seized her and secured her, binding her hand and foot with strips quickly torn from the old man's rumpled sheets and expensive coverlet.

"Don't make no noise," her captor said, and threw her carelessly on the bed. But still she had no more than a small part of his attention, or his partner's. It was the hidden corners of the closet and the bathroom, and the space under the bed, that drew their primary interest.

Plainly they were looking for the old man. The plastic bags of earth, and the spilled earth on the carpet, were important finds.

The vampires talked between themselves. "This is definitely his room, then."

"Looks like it. But where is he?"

Angie trembled, fearing interrogation. But at the moment the enemy were relying on what they could discover for themselves.

They searched the bathroom, warily, a second time.

"Look at this." The white vampire paused in front of the video screen, as if he had not seen his own face for a long time. He did not look entirely happy with what he saw.

The other joined him in the bathroom to check out the electronic mirror. He too seemed briefly fascinated with his own image, but fought free of the distraction. "Yes, this must be his room. *But where is he?*"

At last their attention came back to Angie.

The short man demanded of her: "Where is he, the old one?"

The tall one echoed: "Where is he?"

Her head was spinning. She mumbled something.

Weren't they capable of discovering the open window for themselves?

It was one of their breathing attendants who called their attention to it.

The vampires themselves had seen and disregarded it. The tall, dark-skinned one said: "Bah, he left that open to mislead us."

The short one said: "It's still daylight, he can't change shapes and fly."

Angie, still too high on the old man's drink to feel the full measure of terror she should have felt, kept looking toward the doorway. She was starting to wonder where Valentine Kaiser was.

Now panic was starting to set in among the invaders. Enlisting the breathers' help, the two vampires launched a frantic, though still cautious, search for the old man, which swept once more through the whole apartment. The intruders grew more frantic rather than less with their continued failure to locate their quarry.

Angie, her mind drifting off in an amazing way, thought that perhaps Uncle Matthew should have hidden himself in the secret little cabinet, inside the back of the bedroom dresser. He might have done it, made himself small enough to fit in there, if he'd really tried. She almost giggled aloud, because the ones who were looking for him so frantically never thought that there might be such a secret place inside a piece of furniture. They never came close to discovering it.

When they had gone over the entire apartment again, they came back to the bedroom and looked at her. Now they were having to face the fact that they weren't going to find the old man in any of the rooms or closets, or under any of the furniture. He simply wasn't in the apartment any longer.

One of the vampires looked at his fellow. *"Can* he be out of man-shape?"

The other snarled back: "Not so soon after he was drugged. It's just not possible." Then the same man looked at Angie, and demanded: "Where is he?"

Automatically she looked toward the window, reacting to the question without thought.

Silently, warily, suspiciously—*we want none of your tricks!*—they all four of them, breathers and vampires together, went to look at the window again, and out of it.

Meanwhile Angie, hands bound behind her, ankles tied, lay helplessly on the old man's rumpled bed, and could feel herself continuing to get higher and higher. Brandy was like milk compared to the loathsome yellowish brown powder in that little jar of odd-shaped glass. Angie giggled again, finding her situation hopelessly amusing. But her captors, clustered at the open window, being forced to the realization that that was where the old man had gone, failed to pay any attention to the oddities of her behavior.

"How long," one of the vampires asked the other, "until the Duke gets up here?"

The other shook his head. "He didn't know, he wasn't sure. He wanted to stay with the breather who uses wooden bullets, until he had a chance to finish him."

Listening, Angie understood vaguely that Valentine Kaiser must be the Duke, and that for some reason he had left the storming of the apartment to these people. But it hadn't gone as expected, and now they didn't quite know what to do, and they were afraid of doing the wrong thing.

One of the vampires picked up Uncle Matthew's phone, listened to it, shook his head, and put the instrument down again. "It's dead now," he complained. "Now that we might have got some use out of it."

At the same time the other vampire ordered the two breathers to commence an immediate hunt for Dracula.

"Look upstairs, look in Val's place. Get everyone down on the street and look for him. Got your wooden knives?"

The breathing woman murmured a timid protest.

"Don't be afraid, he'll be very weak if he's lying down there somewhere. Take the people who're standing guard in the hallways. We don't need them here anymore."

As soon as the breathing couple had gone, the two *nosferatu* took turns leaning out of the window, gazing alternately upward and downward. Angie had looked out earlier, and she knew what there was to see, and could imagine how it appeared now with darkness falling: The surrealistic, slightly concave plain of steel and glass stretching away to right and left and up and down, vanishing indeterminately behind wreaths of darkening fog before the end of it became visible in any direction.

One of the vampires said at last: "Well, he's not hanging on a ledge out here. There really aren't any ledges to speak of."

"I don't expect he's hanging on to anything. I expect he's lying dead or crippled down there on the plaza." Evidently even vampire eyes could not see that distance clearly in this fog. "Even this length of fall upon concrete would probably not completely kill him—on wood, of course, it would have been a different matter."

"We've got to find him, finish him off—"

"He might have crawled into an alley somewhere—"

"He might have tried to climb up, instead of down. But I don't see how he could have gotten far—"

Angie was now experiencing a wave of nausea; but this reaction, like her others, passed unnoticed.

The two vampires were trying to think of everything important.

"Did someone block up the door? We don't want people just wandering in."

"I put it back in place again, just now when I let the breathers out. From out in the corridor you can hardly tell that it was broken in."

"What else should we do?"

"You and I wait here for Val. He should be coming soon."

"Meanwhile—"

The two of them had the same idea simultaneously. They turned their faces toward Angie and began looking at her hungrily.

The shorter man said: "*He* said we could have the blood, if there was any here."

The other was already on the bed, snapping off the strips of cloth with which he'd tied her. And now her clothes were going.

Angie screamed, once, and then a hand came smothering over her nose and mouth.

Before Mrs. Hassler had started down to the pool for her swim, she'd urged John to make himself at home. So far he'd poured himself a glass of low-fat milk from her refrigerator, and was nervously eyeing the bananas on the table. The last time he'd checked on the sentinels in the hallway, they were still there.

When the phone rang he jumped to answer it, hoping it was his helpful hostess, calling to report on what she had observed of the watcher in the hallway.

His hopes were realized. Mrs. Hassler's voice, sounding indignant, commented: "The one in the front hall, at least, seems a really *unpleasant* type of person—are the two of them still there?"

"I'm afraid so. At least they were the last time I looked." John took another gulp of milk.

Sounds of tsk-tsking came over the wire. "Isn't it a shame?" his confederate sympathized. "Not that it's any of my business, of course, but—"

"Not at all," John reassured her hastily. "We're grateful for your help."

The inane conversation went on. John accepted, for the moment anyway, the urgings of his absentee hostess to help himself to some health food from the pantry and refrigerator. He urged her in turn to enjoy her swim.

"I'm going to do just that, John—may I call you John?—thank you."

As soon as she was off the phone he hung up and ran again to look out. He chose the back-door viewer this time, but he saw the same thing as before.

He still couldn't be sure, with only electronic images to look at, whether the watchers were vampires or not.

He paced.

Worry about Angie threatened to overwhelm him from time to time, but in his cooler moments he saw no reason to doubt that she would be okay if she just sat tight in the apartment. The old man, recovering, was with her. And it might be important to keep the enemy from discovering that he, John, had slipped out.

Several times John considered trying to phone Uncle Matthew's apartment. But in doing so he might be passing more useful information to the enemy than to Angie.

Would Angie understand why he wasn't coming back? Of course, as soon as she looked into the hallway. But she would be worrying about him. Well, for the moment it couldn't be helped.

Once, John's restless pacing took him into Mrs. Hassler's bedroom, where she had star charts, zodiacs, the tools of astrology taped up on her walls. Small fireplace, with a sealed vase centered on the mantel. Some husband's ashes, maybe? She had seemed to have no qualms about leaving this nice young man alone in her apartment. Perhaps she had been reassured by her stars or oracles.

John paced from room to room, wondering what he was going to do next.

And the next time he looked out the front-door viewer, the sentry who had been there was gone.

The old man had endured a long, tryingly difficult climb down the slippery, all-but-vertical north face of the great building. The range of his descent had so far been something like forty stories, approximately four hundred feet, and in his present condition this journey had taken him the better part of an hour.

When he had swung himself out of his bedroom window, he had had basically two choices of direction open to him—up or down. But he had not hesitated for a moment. The various points of entry to the building, those accessible to a vampire who found himself locked temporarily into human shape, had all been charted by him years ago. Over the centuries, advance preparation for emergencies had become an ingrained habit.

Fortunately—and not entirely by accident, for the old man had a certain knack for influencing the weather—the fog had come back thicker than ever, deep and high and solid enough to protect him from any but the most unlucky observation by the mundane on the street below or in some other building.

To keep his mind off his exhaustion and other difficulties as he went down, he allowed himself to wonder whether anyone inside the windows he was passing might be able to catch a glimpse of his wiry figure, swathed in a white bathrobe, slipping by. A lot of curtains were open, here on the residential levels. But it would not be a particularly scenic day for looking out. People who caught sight of him would rub their eyes, and blink, and decide they could not have seen what their eyes reported. Office workers, like schoolchildren, tended to gaze out the windows of their daily prisons whenever they had the chance. But in this building most of the office space lay below the level of the swimming pool and health club.

For a time the descending vampire set his course along one of the huge external cross-braces that went diagonally down across the building's flank. The giant girder screened him partially from inside observation, and provided something large and relatively easy to hold on to in his weakness. The chief disadvantage of this route was that the total distance to be covered rather alarmingly increased.

On reaching the corner of the building, he switched back to the next diagonal cross-brace, angling down in the opposite direction, remaining on the north side of the building, where fortunately he was shadowed from the day's last traces of sunlight. Today's sun in any case was so muffled by fog that it presented only a minor danger, aside from preventing any change of shape that he might contemplate. Having followed this second girder for some distance, at the proper moment he slid off, and carefully resumed his progress straight down, window ledge by window ledge, supporting his weight by toes and fingertips. He knew precisely which window he was aiming for.

Methodically he had been counting floors during the whole descent, and he was below the fiftieth level now.

Shortly after resuming his straight-down descent he

was able to hear, faintly, unfamiliar voices above him. Someone was leaning out of his window and speculating audibly on where he might have gone. Knowing he was down too deep in fog for them to see him now, the old man grinned mirthlessly and did not bother to look up.

The street, now not much more than four hundred feet below him, had grown much easier to hear, and the conglomerate glow of headlights was beginning to be visible.

Far enough. He reached the window that he wanted, on the forty-fourth floor. The broad, high inside surface of its double glazing was faintly steamed by warmth and moisture, and beyond that heavily screened by live plants, growing in a kind of artificial ditch stuffed deeply with loam and neatly drained. It was unlikely that anyone inside was going to observe his entrance. In a moment his fingers had found the concealed catch whose installation, along with the necessary hinges, had taken him so much time and effort to arrange; and in another moment one vertical edge of the aluminum frame had silently swung out.

The climber listened carefully, then eased the weak, weighty, and comparatively fragile solidity of his body in through the narrow gap. Once inside, he pulled the window shut again immediately, then took the opportunity to rest his trembling arms. He was standing in the men's locker room, at the end farthest from the doors that led out to what they called the health facilities, on the right to the pool, on the left to something known as the fitness room, a chamber filled with exercise machines that impressed the old man as depressingly grotesque and ugly.

At the moment Fate was smiling upon him, and he had the locker room, or this aisle of it anyway, entirely to himself. Safely indoors, standing on a firm floor again, even swaying a little as he was with weakness, he felt that the most difficult part of his escape had been accomplished.

All around him, occupying more than half of the forty-fourth floor, were locker rooms, exercise facilities, showers, and toilets, and his senses informed him that at this predinner hour they were all practically unoccupied. Those among the building's tenants who enjoyed daytime leisure and cared to exercise, or most of them, had been here in the morning; the folk who toiled from nine to five in offices were not here yet, though their vanguard ought to be hitting the locker rooms at any minute now. He had no time to waste.

In another moment he was swiftly dialing the combination on his own locker, seldom visited but well stocked for emergencies.

The locker provided several items of which he stood in immediate need—swimming trunks to go on under his bathrobe, shower clogs, and so on. It held a full set of street clothes also, but for the moment they could wait.

Small change, also, of course. A public phone was available nearby and he made some calls. His first was to Joe Keogh, but he had to be content with leaving a message on the answering machine in Joseph's house. The second call went to Mrs. Hassler's apartment—fortunately her number was available in the public directory beside the phone. But, ominously enough, this effort went unanswered.

Where was John? Matthew Maule considered phoning his own apartment; if he got through, he'd give whatever villain might answer something to think about. But his phone had been dead, and he saw no reason to think service might have been restored.

Wasting no time, he hung up the receiver and moved on with unhurried speed, down the corridor in the direction of the pool. He had avoided the blow struck by his enemies, and now he would strike back—as soon as he was strong enough.

To accomplish that, there was one more thing he needed, the most vital resource, which neither his carefully prepared locker nor the telephone had been able to provide him. One thing he required, above all, to cure his trembling weakness. Forcing his legs to carry him with long, firm strides, he walked on toward the source of small watery sounds. Deliberately he inhaled, treating himself to the smell of dampness.

On entering the natatorium, he was not surprised to behold Mrs. Hassler alone in the pool at this off-hour. Several times she had, all unbidden, described her daily habits to him.

Smiling, he approached.

He remained unobserved until he reached the actual water's edge, because the lady was not dallying idly in the pool, but doing laps with her goggles and noseclip on, her face submerged. When she became aware of his presence she ceased this drill at once, made for the side, and pulled herself out lithely—displaying an energy, if not a shape, that would have been admirable in a woman half her age. Sitting on the damp rim, she caught the towel the visitor had just picked up from one of the nearby lawn chairs, and began to dab her shoulders with it.

She was disturbed by his unexpected presence, delighted, almost frightened. "Mr. Maule! I had almost despaired of ever persuading you to join me."

He smiled. He actually bowed. "And I, dear lady, of ever finding the right opportunity to do so."

She kicked at the water, demonstrating energy, struggling almost like a child to repress excitement.

Suddenly he could find her attitude endearing.

Worriedly she asked him: "But are you quite well enough to swim? Your nephew gave me to understand that the flu, or something like it, had—"

"My nephew?"

"When he came to use the phone in my apartment— because there was something wrong with your phone, you know—?"

"Yes, of course. Many thanks. If there is ever anything I can do for you—but you were kind enough to ask about my health. I fear I am not as strong as I might be. But so far, strong enough." He smiled. "And not at all contagious."

"I was just speaking to your nephew again on the phone a couple of minutes ago—he's a very nervous young man, isn't he?"

"Poor John. I'm afraid he has been going through a great deal of personal stress lately. May I ask the subject of this recent phone conversation?" Here he tossed his robe casually aside and sat down on the edge of the pool beside her.

"It was about those men—those people in the hall-way. The ones who were watching your apartment. But you must have seen them when you came out."

"Ah yes, of course. And did John have success with the other phone calls you so kindly allowed him to make—?"

"I'm afraid there was no one at the number he really wanted to reach, and all he could do was leave a message."

"Too bad." The vampire dabbled his pale feet in the water, beside those of his new companion. Making strate-gic plans had never been his strong point, but with half a millennium of experience to draw upon, one became adept in some things at least.

Drawing a breath with which to sigh, he said: "I suppose John explained to you something of our difficulties. Surely we owe you an explanation, at least, in return for your kind assistance."

"He said your phone wasn't working . . ."

"Yes, of course. That complicated matters inordinately. But I meant—the other, more basic difficulty?"

"Yes, well, I can understand. I've had some relatives myself that I spent a good deal of time trying to avoid—they were my first husband's, mostly. Yes, of course, I understand very well, and it's really none of my business."

He smiled, taking her right hand, gently but firmly, and raised it toward his lips for a symbolic kiss. He said, with heartfelt gratitude: "The perfect neighbor. One who helps one through one's difficulties, even when it must be quite impossible to understand them." His smile was sad, warm, appreciative, all at the same time.

The lady, for the moment, could not find a word to say. But her pulse, in the hand that he still held, had quickened quite remarkably.

As a rule this courteous vampire preferred to seek his nourishment, not to mention romance, at a much greater distance from where he slept. The waitress had represented something of a major exception in that regard; I am old enough to know better, he chided himself in bitter silence. Well, I did know better. And he had made the blunder anyway, and now he had paid for it.

It was of no comfort to the vampire's feelings to reflect that another exception was about to be made. Well, in this case there was no help for it. Others, to whom he owed a great responsibility, were depending on him for their very lives, and he must waste no time in regaining his strength. If the estimate he had now formed of the nature of his enemy was correct, all the strength that he could summon up was going to be needed.

"Mr. Maule—it's Matthew, isn't it?"

"It is indeed." Both of their apartments were for the moment unavailable. He looked thoughtfully about the natatorium.

In a voice still fluttered by that Continental hand-kiss, the dear lady asked him: "If I wouldn't be taking you away from your swim, or exercise—well, would you like to come up to my place for a bite of lunch? You and your nephew both, of course. Or a drink? Or is it too early in the day for that?"

"Dear Margot—it is not at all too early in my day to have a drink. But by the way, have you seen the moon tonight?"

"The moon?" She was almost whispering, ready for a revelation.

Which he thought he was certainly going to provide. "Ah yes, despite the fog, and all the many lights of the great city. Here." He extended a hand and she took it, and a moment later she was standing beside him, dripping, on the slippery tile. "If we could step over to the windows here—behind the tall plants, where the glass is somewhat shadowed—"

13

*B*y the end of the year 1501, Cesare Borgia was not only Duke Valentino, but Duke of the Romagna as well—feudal overlord of the central Italian territory, composed largely of papal states that he hoped someday to make the nucleus of an actual kingdom. He could claim impressive achievements in his role as Captain General, Gonfalonier, of his father's armies. The young man's actual experience in battle was still quite small—he threatened so skillfully with his army that he seldom needed to use it—but he possessed the essentials of leadership, the qualities that can hardly be taught, including the most important—the ability to inspire fear or loyalty almost at will.

I can testify from personal experience that in those days the life of a secret agent in the employ of Cesare Borgia offered enough excitement for any breathing man or vampire. My own actual duties, at least at first, were almost exclusively those of a messenger. By night I could traverse the countryside at high speed, by air as well as by land. I could pass in or out of any castle, any town or army camp, no matter how formidable the walls might be, or how well they were guarded. The messages that I conveyed in secrecy, to prospective traitors, loyal supporters, churchmen, or merchants, were seldom written down. Frequently they were in code, so that I had no way of guessing at their import, save by the looks of the men who sent or received them.

That I was not wholly trusted as yet by my new employer did not offend me; such minimal prudence was only common sense on Borgia's part. I, in turn, wondered at first why he had been so willing to hire on the spot a stranger of whom he knew nothing save that he was a vampire. But I had not long to wait before I found out.

On the day after I had formally joined the Duke's staff, I had an opportunity to speak to him alone. "There is one thing that puzzles me, Captain General."

"Speak."

"How did you know, at first glance, what I am?"

"You are not the first of your race I have encountered."

Something, a tone of amusement perhaps, in young Borgia's voice, a barely perceptible twinkle in his eye, made it impossible for me to resist questioning him further. "And did another of my race tell you that I was about to seek service with you?"

"I do not as a rule encourage questions about what my other advisers may have told me."

"My apologies."

"Accepted." He looked at me thoughtfully. We were quite alone. I could see him come to a decision. He said positively: "I know who you are, Drakulya, as well as what. And I know, among other things, that you were in Italy once before, as an agent of King Matthias of Hungary. It was some thirty years ago, and you were not *nosferatu* then."

Naturally I was curious to discover what else my new employer might know about me, and how he had learned so much. When I made my curiosity plain, Borgia shook his head. Then he ordered briskly: "Come to my tent this evening," and we went on to other business.

When I returned at the appointed time, well after most honest folk had gone to their beds, I found the Duke alone except for one other visitor—Constantia.

My old friend and I embraced, as brother and sister might; and I was soon given to understand that she had been for some time Duke Cesare's lover. It was obvious now that it was she who had told him of my presence in Italy—he knew from other sources that Prince Drakulya of Wallachia had once been here as Matthias' agent.

It was during the last half of that midnight conference that I met Lucrezia for the second time.

On the last day of the year 1501, Lucrezia had married for the third—and as events proved, the last—time. The bridegroom, Don Alfonso d'Este, heir apparent to the dukedom of Ferrara, was not personally present at the elaborate ceremony in the Vatican, his brother standing in for him as proxy. It was about six months later when I met Lucrezia in her brother's tent.

At the time I attached myself to Cesare Borgia, the dynamic, open, hearty young man who commanded the papal armies seemed to me no more violent or treacherous than any of his ambitious contemporaries (I suppose I must include myself). Originally I thought it very unlikely that he was really behind as many underhanded murders as he was given credit for. The lengthy list was highlighted not only by Lucrezia's second husband, but Cesare's and Lucrezia's own elder brother Juan, whose butchered body had been dredged from the Tiber in 1497.

Alas, experienced warrior and ruler though I was, I still had much to learn about the ways of princes, and about the Borgias in particular.

In any event, Lucrezia was much changed from the

twelve-year-old that I had seen in 1492, so briefly and under such unlikely and difficult conditions. She had blossomed into a sweet-looking and attractive young woman—not breathtakingly beautiful, but quite charming —still very little more than twenty years of age. I noted thoughtfully that she did not appear to hold a grudge against her brother over the matter of her second husband's violent death—he had been stabbed in the street, and, when that failed to finish him, strangled in his bed by Michelotto.

It was, I suppose, inevitable that I should find Madonna Lucrezia devastatingly attractive—of course in my eyes almost any woman, of any age, in any age, is fascinating. But there was more than that to my fascination. The fact that she was a Pope's daughter, which was something like a princess—how can I explain it to a modern reader?—added to Madonna's charm. So did the fact that she had nearly killed me once. The aura of Borgia danger made her doubly alluring, and the aura of mystery triply so.

In fact it will probably not surprise the reader to learn that Madonna Lucrezia and I were mutually drawn to each other during this our second meeting, and that we started to have an affair very shortly afterward. She was greatly intrigued by the thought of a vampire lover, in part perhaps of her brother's affair with the vampire Constantia; and like her brother she was clever enough, and capable of enough self-control, to avoid being converted. (Let me assure the reader that such restraint is quite possible, though perhaps hardly common.)

But to return to our meeting in the tent. Brother and sister acted in concert to put me at my ease, and soon we three were conversing quite informally. Duke Valentino took the opportunity to express his regret for any inconvenience I might have suffered on the occasion of our first, quite accidental, encounter years ago. "As must surely be obvious to you, Don Ladislao," (mindful of my rank in my own land, he was promoting me over the "Signor" by which I had generally been addressed in Italy) "your regrettable involvement on that occasion was purely fortuitous. We had no means of knowing that you, or any of the *nosferatu,* were nearby."

And Cesare, with Lucrezia chiming in quite charmingly, went on to offer an explanation of what the real goal of their researches had been—an improved kind of aphrodisiac. To their regret, they had not succeeded.

As for the lovely, dissolute maid whose acquaintance I had made so intimately just before my most recent extended sleep, when I asked what had become of her, the Borgias told me that she still lived, long since fully recovered from the poison, as a servant in the Pope's palace. That particular drug, it seemed, had little or no lasting effect upon breathing folk.

You might think it quite natural for me to hold a grudge against Madonna Lucrezia. Well, in the circumstances that would have been hard to do, and I had little enough inclination to try. Fighting with a woman, of whatever age or condition of life, is generally a matter of monumental futility. And what warrior will devote his time and energy to planning vengeance on a child of twelve, my lady's age when she committed the offense—quite accidentally?

As I have indicated, it did not take me long to banish entirely any lingering resentment. At the same time, I reminded myself to be extremely cautious from now on, to be ever on the alert for signs of unwonted gaiety or intoxication in anyone whose veins I tapped whenever I

was in the vicinity of Lucrezia or her most active brother—
or, for that matter, if I should ever be a guest at the table of
the Pope their sire.

I took considerable reassurance from the fact that—
as I thought—I would never forget the taste of that fair
maid's oh-so-subtly poisoned blood. I have said that
matters of taste are, as a rule, unimportant to us vampires.
The sugar of the Borgias, if I may so call Madonna
Lucrezia's discovery, is something of an exception.

I can personally testify to the fact that, on tasting for
the first time blood carrying the unshielded, undisguised
flavor of the Borgia vampire-drug, one of my kind will
notice a taste entirely unexpected, piquant, mysterious in
origin—and very pleasant.

Yes, very pleasant, despite the horrible way in which
the stuff was actually concocted—more on that later.

It was shortly after this midnight meeting in a
military encampment that Cesare, doubtless already aware
that his beloved sister and I had become lovers, confided to
me that he was considering the option of someday becoming a vampire himself.

I was casting about to find some appropriate words of
congratulation on this progressive attitude, when he raised
a languid hand, forestalling me. "But not just yet. Nor for
many years to come. You, Drakulya, who were a prince, will
understand. How can a man be *nosferatu* and at the same
time a prince, ruler of a daylight people? You must be at
least as well aware as I am of the immense difficulties."

I could not argue with that.

It was shortly after my first meeting with the mature
Lucrezia—I believe it was the second or third time that I
saw her after that—that I finally had definite word of
Basarab.

A Matter of Taste

In fact it was Madonna Lucrezia who gave me that word herself. Or her brother did. The truth was, they acted so in concert on this as on other occasions, that it was difficult to tell.

Definite traces of repressed amusement were apparent in the young Borgias' manner as they passed along to me the information that the aging traitor had been located. With their next breaths they warned me I might be surprised when I had found my victim.

"Surprised in what way, my lord?"

Cesare only smiled.

"My lady?"

"Nay, my lord Drakulya, if we were to tell you that, it would be a surprise no longer." And sister and brother laughed together.

"And where am I to find him? When?"

"As to when, it may be today, this afternoon, if you wish. Dear brother, have you any duties for our friend today?"

"None that cannot wait. Perhaps after sunset there will be something."

As to where I would be likely to find Basarab, my lady named a certain street corner in Rome.

That was all. I hesitated, sensing that there was something pertinent that I had not been told. No doubt it constituted the surprise.

Wary of my lord's and lady's humor, I ventured: "Basarab has been informed, then, that someone is to meet him there? And whom is he expecting?"

"He is expecting nothing—as far as I know. Who can say what expectations men will have? But he will be there all the same." And my informants, exchanging warm looks between themselves as they so often did, enjoying some secret joke, refused to elaborate.

Taking my leave from them as swiftly as I could, I armed myself—belting on only a common sword and dagger, nothing out of the ordinary—and found my way to the street corner that my lady had named. It was a warm day, though by good fortune cloudy, near the middle of the afternoon. The neighborhood, being a poor one, stank, enough more than the average of the city that I took note of the fact.

I stood on the street corner for some time, leaning as inconspicuously as I could against a building, that my enemy might not see me first and take alarm. It was a poor neighborhood indeed, though a cut above the worst of the slums, and not too poor to attract some beggars.

Ordinary buildings, some apartment tenements that looked as old as Rome itself, and for the most part ordinary folk. Some time passed before my attention was caught by one of the beggars, an especially loathsome cripple, who pushed himself about on a little cart. Boys of the neighborhood, ragged and barefoot, had taken to taunting him, pulling at his hair and at his rags, trying to snatch away the little purse he was trying to conceal. One of the urchins, approaching with great stealth, got close enough to urinate upon him before being discovered.

Choking out curses and lamentations, the beggar pushed himself laboriously across the muddy street upon his little cart—he lacked a leg, and his remaining lower limb appeared not capable of holding up his weight. Fortunately for him his tormentors were distracted at this point by some proposal put forward by one of their number. They gave up the game and ran off in pursuit of some new devilry.

Something about the hideous figure of the beggar caught my attention, and eventually I left my inconspicuous position and approached him. It was only when I stood close in front of this loathsome creature on his little cart that I was certain he was Basarab, and realized that he was not only crippled but almost completely blind.

Even at close range some time was necessary to convince myself entirely of my enemy's identity. The blindness and the disfigurement of his face were most likely due, I now suppose, to syphilis; at the time I hardly wondered about the cause. Basarab's missing leg, which could well have been the immediate cause of his retirement from military service, most likely had been lost to some spear thrust or cannonball.

"Alms, sir? Alms?" The voice was that of a beaten man, changed to the point where I should hardly have recognized it. The hand that held up a cup in my direction was shrunken and palsied. I found it hard to believe that I indeed beheld, in this cripple, this ruined husk of a man, who trembled with fear and rage at the jibes of the street urchins, the fierce soldier I remembered.

Because I wanted to hear him talk again, I pressed a coin into his hand, the smallest coin I had, thinking that I might snatch it away again before I left. He grunted something unintelligible, and hastened to thrust the coin away amid his stinking rags.

Not enough. I wanted to hear more. I spoke to him in Italian, asking sharply if he was not grateful. This time he responded with quavering thanks; oh, yes, I recognized his voice.

And I was sure, from the way he cocked his head, and squinted as if to make his blind eyes work, that he thought that he ought to know my voice, but could not place it.

"Do you know the name of Bogdan, my good man?" I demanded of him at last.

"Hey?" He quivered. I think the name meant nothing to him at the moment.

"Bogdan." I bent closer, and spoke softly, so that the beggar alone could hear my words. "He came to Italy from a far land. He came here to get away from one who would have killed him, otherwise."

And the blind old man shrank back in silence. Perhaps he recognized me then.

I considered taking back my coin, but it had vanished into some repository within his unspeakable rags, on which I had no wish to soil my fingers. I stood back a step, briefly fingering the hilt of my sword; I remember now that the wood and metal felt awkward in my grip and almost unfamiliar.

And then I turned on my heel and took myself away, stopping at the first respectable tavern that I came to, to wash the stench of that street corner from my throat, expel its traces from my unbreathing nostrils.

That evening, when I reported back to Cesare Borgia to discover what duties he might have for me next, he was eager to know whether I had finally attained my revenge.

"I tried, my lord duke. But others, as perhaps you already knew, had been there before me."

He considered my words, and understood them, and nodded, with a twinkle in his eye. "Ah, Drakulya." When we were alone, he—like his sister—often called me by my true name. "You are, as I suspected, a true connoisseur of requital. As I like to think I am. You have no plans to kill him, then?"

"My lord, I could not bring myself to do such a great favor for the man I saw today."

And Cesare, laughing, applauded my fine sensibilities in the art of vengeance.

Sometime later, when Madonna Lucrezia, in one of her gentle moods, heard my same confession of an act of superficial mercy, it earned from her a wistful commendation. Sometimes I could not for the life of me be sure when the lady was serious and when she mocked.

Such triumph as I felt, in reflecting upon my old enemy's downfall, was brief. And whatever satisfaction his fate afforded me was overshadowed by a certain emptiness, a sense of loss almost like that which must follow an amputation, in realizing that I had no need to think of Basarab anymore. But then I had already known for a long time that one must expect one unsatisfactory outcome or another when one pursues revenge.

14

When Angie came to her senses she was lying sprawled across the old man's bed, still physically in the grip of both of the vampires who had attacked her.

Their jaws had released their grip, one from her throat and one from her right thigh. But their four hands were still fastened on her arms and legs like handcuffs, like frozen claws, like the grip of long-dead skeletons. The sharp-boned fingers still wore their flesh, but the flesh of them now felt as cold and impersonal and stiff as plastic. On waking she could detect no signs of life in either of her assailants.

What she could feel—and see, and smell, almost to the exclusion of everything else—was blood.

Her own blood, cooling and sticky, seemed to be everywhere in the bed, and on the bodies lying in it. Angie's naked skin was smeared with the red stuff, as were the clothing and the waxen faces of her attackers.

Moving feebly at first, she tried to roll over in the bed, and was prevented by the clutch of those corpselike hands. Beginning to sob, she struggled more and more strongly to free herself from the bondage of those bony fingers. The men who held her did not move, and had she not known them to be vampires she would have been certain that they were dead.

Tugging at one alien finger after another, she straightened out enough of them to gain release. Breaking free at last, Angie staggered to her feet. The room was dim around her. All along the windows the curtains were still drawn shut, except for one side where a window still stood open narrowly, letting in a whiff of chilly dampness. Outside, full darkness had overtaken the city. Angie's gaze fell on the bedside clock. The time was only a little after five, which meant she couldn't have been unconscious long. A fifth of a mile away, just below the windows of this room, the evening rush hour would be approaching its peak.

Not until Angie had taken her first steps away from the bed did she realize that she was completely naked. Every piece of her clothing had been ripped off and lay about the room in shreds and little rags. Her attackers, both fully clothed, were still lying motionless upon the bed, their frozen claw hands stiffly clutching empty air, their faces smeared with blood. At the moment she could almost believe, she was at least able to hope, that both of them were dead. Certainly both of them were unconscious.

—and it was her own blood. Her own blood everywhere, although the bleeding had stopped now. In the first moments of full horror after she gained her feet, she had the impression that vast quantities must have been drawn from her body, enough to drown the whole room in gore, crimsoning sheets and carpets, smearing her skin and the clothing and faces of the creatures who had bitten her.

But she was still alive, and not too weak to move. Dizzily Angie put her hands up to her own throat. Yes, the stickiness felt freshest there, where one vampire's fangs had only recently released their grip. Another fresh wound, like a double pinprick, showed on her right thigh. In both places there was pain, sharp, awkward, and occasional; but it was bearable and therefore the least of her concerns right now. Worse was the fact that behind the pain and shock there still lay, lingering and insidious, remnants of an exquisite pleasure. Faintly her nerves still throbbed with an alien joy.

Beyond those sensations, something still persisted of the giddy drug-high Angie had been experiencing just before the attack. Dimly she understood that the potion administered by Uncle Matthew was still shielding her, to some extent, from what otherwise would have been the full extent of terror.

Dazedly, stumbling, she began to move toward the bathroom. There she could find water—thirst was suddenly very strong. There she could find a mirrorlike image of her own ravaged body that would let her begin to understand this disaster, this horror that had overtaken her. In a moment she was staring at her electronic reflection, pale to the lips underneath the smears of gore. In the next moment she was drinking hungrily from the faucet at the bathroom sink, then splashing water on her face, her throat, her breasts, her bitten leg. With a towel she wiped off as much bloodstain as she could.

Moving dazedly back into the bedroom, acting without a conscious plan, Angie groped in the closet for one of Uncle Matthew's robes, and put it on to cover her nakedness.

As she turned away from the closet, she saw movement on the bed. One of the vampires, the smaller one, was stirring, was pushing himself up slowly, first sitting, then sliding to his feet. His pale face still looked blind, looked dead. His figure moved uncertainly. It tottered and almost fell, groping outward with both arms like a blind man trying to achieve balance. The vampire showed no awareness of Angie's presence.

Pulling the skirts of the robe close to her legs, Angie

sidled toward the bedroom door, which stood half open, showing part of the hallway beyond.

Whether the pale-faced thing was able to see her or not, it suddenly knew that she was in the room. Perhaps it heard her movement. Eyes turning uncertainly toward her, feet shuffling unsteadily, it was just barely quick enough to block her path, before she could dash past it to escape the bedroom.

Rage exploded in Angie's abused mind, and simultaneously in her muscles. Screaming, this time more in rage than fear, she charged with shoulder and elbow straight into the unsteady thing, broke its balance and sent it sprawling.

Dashing past it, eluding hands that swept toward her ankles, she fled the room. A second later, in the bedroom hallway, she collided with a figure that blocked her path. An eternal moment passed before she realized that this was John. John was shouting at her, and gripping in both hands an object Angie could dimly recognize as one of the wooden spears that had decorated the living-room wall.

Disentangling himself from Angie, he stepped aside and thrust hard and desperately with the spear at the thing that had followed her out of the bedroom. She turned to see the vampire struggling on the impaling lance, pale face contorted, pale claws outspread and wrenching at the wood. The point of the spear had caught only grazingly in the vampire's ribs, and with an anguished grunt it seized the shaft. A moment later it had torn the weapon from John's hands and broken it in two.

Wood was what it took to hurt them, always wood. Angie had absorbed that lesson swiftly. Running into the living room, with frantic hands she swept bric-a-brac from a wall-mounted shelf, then grabbed from its supporting brackets the oaken weight and length of the shelf itself.

Turning quickly, she swung her weapon awkwardly, beating the pale-faced vampire across the forehead as it came running after her. At almost the same instant John came at it from behind and stabbed it with the broken lance.

It staggered but did not fall. It turned on John.

"Angie—honey—Angie—" Calling her name as if he couldn't see her, John drew back what was left of his spear and tried again. The splintered end tore flesh from his opponent's face before a powerful arm once more knocked it away.

John renewed the attack, calling to Angie meanwhile. His voice sounded inarticulate and almost crazy.

Angie uttered strange noises and strange words. She stepped forward, pounding away with her shelf at the damned thing, hitting it again and again; the blows from the inch-thick plank sounded dully on the creature's skull, heavy and hollow on its back.

The thing turned around, showing a red ruin of a face, all torn by John's spear. Fumblingly, but still capable of terrible quickness, it caught her by the left wrist. Her club almost fell from her right hand as it began to drag her back toward the bedrooms.

John returned to the attack. The fight moved down the hallway. Two sets of lungs were laboring, gasping for the air to drive exhausted muscles into new exertions. But Angie could not break the terrible grip that threatened to crush her wrist. With her free hand she still held her oaken board, and swung it, jabbed with it, when she could.

Now she could see into Uncle Matthew's bedroom once again. See that the taller vampire, who had been lying inertly on the bed, was now stirring, trying to get to his feet.

The mouth of its more active colleague opened, the creature drew in breath and uttered a cry for help. John jabbed his broken spear into its groin. The vampire beleaguered in the hallway gasped again, and giggled air out through its bloodstained mouth. The lips were bleeding, and some of the teeth were broken from the last time that Angie had hit it with the bookshelf plank.

Angie managed to wrench her left wrist free. She drew back her weapon now and swung two-handed, hitting the enemy again, with all her strength.

But now its colleague came lurching, staggering quickly out of the bedroom and into the hall. In desperation John grappled with it, tripped it with a wrestler's move and knocked it down. Still its hands flailed at him numbly. The poison it had drunk from Angie's veins would not allow it to get a grip or maintain balance.

The body of the shorter vampire dripped and oozed with its own blood, more driven from its veins every time John struck it with his splintered spear. Seeming to ignore his blows, it moved again toward Angie, to catch up with her as she retreated toward the living room once more. The one on the floor was crawling after her too, and the eyes of both vampires were locked on her. Both of them made odd, drugged sounds, like the sounds Uncle Matthew had made when he was trying to wake up.

Gripping her shelf with both hands once again, she swung and hit her standing opponent a blow, glancing from its shoulder to the side of its head, that would have broken the thickest bones of a breathing man. And then she drew back her weapon and swung and struck it yet again, upon its warding elbow. And then the shelf was knocked out of her grip.

The vampire who had fallen in the hallway was clawing itself erect again, leaning against the wall, unable to advance as yet.

John had come from behind the active one to grapple

with it for the second, third, or fourth time. This time John tried to strangle it from behind, pulling the shaft of his broken spear hard back against its throat. Trying to cut off its breath was a useless effort, and in a moment John was once more thrown aside.

This time he reacted differently. Crying out something, words she could not distinguish, he went scrambling past Angie, running back toward the living room.

Clear in John's mind was a vision of the other, unbroken spear, still on the wall. In his hectic passage he stumbled against the machine the enemy breathers had used to break in the apartment door. He fell, picked himself up, and with a desperate lunge at last got his hands on the remaining spear.

Running back down the hallway, newly armed, he heard a scream from Angie. She was between two standing monsters now. John could see the drooling mouth of the farthest enemy, open as if it meant to drive its broken fangs into her flesh again.

John skewered the nearer enemy from the rear with the new spear, the point going in just below the ribs on the right side, at the proper angle to nail a kidney. The creature screamed, a hideous, bellowing noise. It fell back. Angie came crawling past it, getting behind John, getting away. Inhuman noises came from her mouth too.

By now the second vampire was lurching into action.

John thrust his weapon into its body. The point hit bone, was turned away from vital organs. The second spear failed to do fatal damage before it was caught in a fumbling grip of inhuman strength and broken, like the first.

The fight lurched and bounced out into the living room. Angie had picked up a light wooden chair, and out here she had room to swing it.

Eventually a turning point was passed, in some way

that John was not aware of when it happened. A time arrived when both of his opponents were on the floor, and he was crouching over them, soaked in their blood, stabbing and stabbing with wearied arms, sinking a sharply splintered spear shaft again and again into their flesh. Angie, swaying with weakness, still hovered beside him in a blood-soaked robe, clubbing at the enemy with one wooden weapon after another. The struggle had ceased to be a fight, it had become a slaughter, a process of finishing off the wounded.

The deadly dangerous wounded. Both vampires were incredibly strong, even in the half-dead state brought on by the poison, and incredibly hard to kill. Their bodies gave forth ugly sounds, meaty and yet drumlike, when beaten with a solid wooden club. With each new injury they howled again, the sounds a blend of rage and terror, like some mockery of Angie's own cries when they had seized her. They bled, as if their reservoirs were inexhaustible, their bright-red vampire blood.

The limbs of even a dying vampire, flailing about without coordination, still could deal powerful blows, and John and Angie were each knocked once more off their feet.

And then, at last, the ghastly things were dead.

There could be no mistake. Angie, with John at her side, watched the corpse of the last one dissolve in mist, mist that curled away across the floor, pushed back by the dank breeze still drifting in through the open window.

The victors both slumped in exhaustion. Angie fell into a chair, in an exhausted near faint, as soon as the fight was won. Under the fresh stains of vampire blood, her face was hideously pale.

John slowly sank down beside her.

The whole apartment, or every part of it that they could see, was a ruin of bloodstained carpets, broken and disordered furniture.

There was a sound from the direction of the front door. The door after being broken in had been propped back into place by the invaders, then pushed halfway aside again by John in his hasty return.

Too late Angie and John reacted, stumbling to their feet.

Someone was stepping in through the space that John had made. A man whom Angie could not recognize at first. The man gaped at John and Angie for a moment in astonishment, then drew a pistol and aimed it at them.

With his free hand, working behind him, he started tugging the broken door back into a more completely closed position. And now Angie could recognize the breather who had come with Kaiser on his first visit.

"Sorry for not knocking," Mr. Stewart said, and smiled. "The door was open."

15

*T*hus two of my trio of old and bitter enemies had been
disposed of. In the days that followed, I could not
help reflecting grimly on the fact that, despite my years of
unrelenting hatred, of intense and bitter planning, Basarab
had been destroyed by forces having nothing to do with
me—call those forces Fate, Chance, or what you will.

Struggling against the feeling that much of my life
over the last few decades had been completely wasted, I
somewhat gloomily resumed my duties in the service of
Duke Valentino. Privately, my first concern, of course,
continued to be the still-surviving traitor Bogdan.

For years I had been able to hope that when I found
the first of the pair of surviving traitors that man would,
willingly or not, provide me with some clue to the location
of the second. But Basarab had been no help at all in that
regard. Bogdan might as well have vanished totally from
the face of the earth.

In the most recent year of my search, I had talked to
several informants who knew Bogdan or claimed to have
known him, but none of them had seen or heard of him for
many years. These informants were united in their opinion
that the man was dead. None of them, however, had seen
him fall, nor could any recall convincingly the specific
circumstances of his demise. Therefore I was skeptical of

the reports of his death and nursed my hopes of being able to catch him still alive.

Shortly after I saw Basarab, Cesare Borgia dispatched myself and Michelotto, together, on a type of mission that was new for me in the Duke's service, though familiar enough in my own land. We were placed in joint command of a handful of men and sent into the countryside to exterminate a nest of bandits. I should note here that in spite of his devotion to the arts of treachery, intrigue, and murder, Duke Valentino provided many of the Romagna towns the best government they had experienced in decades—not out of the goodness of his heart (if any such quality existed), but in accordance with a calculated policy to broaden his support as much as possible among the people. On this day Borgia had in mind another goal also: to test, in a comparatively minor matter, how well the pair of us, Corella and myself, could work together.

Informants had brought word of where the bandits could be found—if only a punitive force could approach their lair without alarming them. I argued for a night attack, and my colleague was willing to agree. With our squad of half a dozen chosen men, riding in full moonlight, we approached the rocky hilltop nest—I suppose the building had once been a farmhouse—where our prey, or so we hoped, awaited us.

We had timed our approach to bring us to the house at about an hour before dawn. At this time, we thought, any sentry that might have been posted was most likely to have succumbed to the lure of indoor warmth or sleep.

For me the situation was rendered more interesting by the fact that neither Corella nor any of the men with us knew I was a vampire. For all I knew, none of them were even aware that such creatures existed outside of the fearful minds of peasants. Among breathers at that time only Cesare and Lucrezia, and perhaps their father, shared my secret.

The former farmhouse was well situated to command the land around it and the winding road below. We established ourselves in the best available position to study the house, and Corella and I between us decided on our plan of attack.

I voted for posting our men to surround the house, with orders to catch the enemy as they fled or retreated, whilst my co-commander and myself alone broke in, through whatever doors or windows might offer us the opportunity. Once inside, we would deal with the bandits as we found them.

Michelotto studied me in silence for a moment or two. Estimates of our adversaries' strength ranged from six to sixteen, and although bandits were unlikely to stand and fight with the discipline and courage of well-trained soldiers, the odds were certainly enough to give a prudent commander pause. So my colleague blinked, and hesitated, but in the end he was not one to let a challenge of this type go unaccepted.

After dispatching our men as I had suggested, to take up their positions around the silent house, we two stealthily approached the building and decided on our points of entry. Each of us was carrying a short axe, as well as sword and dagger.

On the way we came upon the sentry we had been half expecting, just where we thought he should be, but asleep, wrapped in two blankets. Michelotto quietly and efficiently cut his throat. One down. Five to fifteen left.

Somewhere on the far side of the house, a dog stirred

in its slumber, senses tickled subliminally by the presence of hostile strangers. Just as the beast was about to give us away, I soothed it back to sleep, exerting a certain influence silently and at a distance, without my companion or anyone else being aware of the fact. My rapport with animals had been steadily developing since the beginning of my new life.

Under slightly different conditions we might have set fire to the nest and burned the rascals out. But much of the building was stone, and the weather had been wet for some time. Therefore, having chosen our respective points of entry, Corella and I broke in simultaneously—he through a shuttered window, whilst I smashed in a door—making our separate entrances on opposite sides of the house, which was basically only a one-room shelter.

Other dogs than the one I had soothed woke up to bark at the outrageous racket. Simultaneously human voices were raised in even greater panic.

On this chill night a fire still smoldered in the house, faint coals giving enough light for the adapted eyes of breathers, my companion and our victims, to see what was happening and about to happen to them.

Breathing bodies wrapped in blankets lay everywhere, on the floor and furniture. My entry, at least, had been so swift that some were only struggling to their feet whilst others had not yet stirred. The axe in my right hand did deadly execution, whilst with my left, picking up a chair, I fended off the first blade thrust at me.

Across the large room, Corella had got in through the window. Once well inside and on his feet, he slew and parried with remorseless goodwill, displaying a formidable aptitude for the job.

It was soon obvious that the true number of our foe lay

somewhere near the midrange of our intelligence estimates, and that their eagerness for combat was no greater than we had expected.

Soon the handful who had taken up arms against us were all cut down, and we changed our tactics to search-and-destroy, routing out thieves from under furniture and blankets and dispatching them on the spot. With all the doors and windows barricaded as they were for the night, escape from the house was no easy matter, requiring more time than our hosts had readily available. In the end only two or three of them got clear, to be picked off neatly by our efficient troops outside.

Of approximately a dozen occupants of the house, only a woman and a girl survived. I saw to it that they were left unmolested. Our men, when they had a chance to see the inside of the house, looked at Corella and myself in awe.

At dawn, when we were ready to leave the scene, Michelotto and I shook hands. Thus began our period of mutual respect.

By the middle of the year of Our Lord 1502, both Niccolo Machiavelli and Leonardo da Vinci had come, for different purposes, to spend considerable time in the company of Duke Valentino.

The writings of Machiavelli that were to make him famous were still in the future. At this time he was a rising Florentine politician in his early thirties. A sly, calculating man, yet filled with the desire to see his beloved Italy stand united and respected among the nations of the world. Physically he was thin and pale-faced, with high cheekbones and a piercing glance. He spoke little, but gave an impression of deep thought.

I suppose that for a time it seemed to Signore Niccolo

that the Borgias might accomplish a united Italy. In any event, Machiavelli attended Cesare in the capacity of an emissary from Florence; and he was a witness to the Duke's bloody vengeance on his mutinous captains at Sinigaglia, December 31, 1502.

Leonardo da Vinci was now a graybeard about fifty years of age, serving in Valentino's train in the capacity of an engineer, with his main or exclusive job the observation and development of military projects.

On several occasions during my attendance on the younger Borgia, I was able to converse with Machiavelli. In the course of our conversations, we frequently spoke on the future of Italy, and I heard Machiavelli's hopes expressed that Cesare might be the prince destined to create a real nation out of the squabbling principalities and towns of the peninsula, or out of the central Romagna, at least.

Everyone agreed that Cesare was going to need his father's continued help if he were to have any chance of succeeding in such a grand design. Father and son together made a truly formidable team. And fortunately for the son's ambitions, there was no sign that the father was going to do anything but keep spending, intriguing, and conniving furiously in an effort to insure the success of his favorite surviving child.

I also had, during that same epoch, more than one good talk with Leonardo. We two had met once before, when he was a twelve-year-old apprentice in the studio of Verrocchio in Florence. I thought it most unlikely that the successful artist and designer would remember me now. But he did—in a way. After all, he had once sketched my face.

I seriously doubt that Leonardo truly recalled the circumstances of our previous meeting. Rather, I think, he was puzzled, and thought he remembered me from somewhere, but could not place a man of my apparent youthfulness that far in the past.

The artist was chiefly occupied in the Duke's service with studying and designing fortifications. Cesare Borgia was unfailingly interested in the subject, though rarely if ever in his brief career did fortifications do him any good. He was several times faced with the problem of attacking them.

And then there arrived the day when, by sheerest accident, in the course of my duties in the service of Duke Valentino, fate brought me face-to-face with Bogdan.

The scene, improbably enough, was a simple country road, not far from a Franciscan monastery. On that day I chanced to be engaged with Michelotto in another honorable skirmish, part of our ongoing effort in the cause of good government, suppressing bandits within the towns and territories now accepting papal rule.

Michelotto and myself, in the guise of two portly graybeard merchants—someday I must compose a treatise on disguises—had achieved the little ambush that we sought, and engaged four robbers in a spirited debate at twilight, exerting our greatest eloquence to persuade them to give up their evil trade forever. In the course of our discussions I had been clubbed from behind with a broken spear shaft, and this wooden weapon had had effect. Not too seriously, but seriously enough to cause a Franciscan monk, who I heard called Fra Francisco by one of his companions, to come to me to inspect my wound. By this time those of the enemy who were still on the field required only spiritual help.

Corella, when he saw that I had been hurt, looked first

surprised, then somewhat concerned, and then relieved, to see this proof that I was not, after all—as he must have begun to think—some kind of superhuman immortal. He took a seat on the far side of the road and began to refresh himself with wine.

The hands of the elderly monk were gentle as he probed the back of my head, sponging away a minimal amount of blood, checking the swelling. I did not see his face clearly until my treatment was concluded. Then, to my amazement, I was able to recognize, despite the changes wrought by age, the countenance of Bogdan.

The remainder of my disguise was wiped away, and the murderous traitor saw my face clearly at the same time that I saw his. I saw the color drain from his cheeks and he took a step or two backward. A moment more and he sat down, upon a roadside stone, as if afflicted by a sudden attack of dizziness. The companion who had come with him, another monk, expressed concern.

"Brother Francis? What is wrong?"

The monk who was sitting on the stone only shook his head. Brother Francis.

Almost thirty years had passed since Bogdan and I had last looked upon each other, and he, at least, had undergone great visible alterations. Not that he had degenerated into a human wreck like Basarab—on the contrary, this greatest and bitterest enemy of mine looked hale and well for a man of his present age, somewhere around fifty.

My former comrade and deadly, sadistic enemy. There was nothing really so strange in my running into Bogdan by accident, after I had searched for him so many years.

The last survivor of the trio of my enemies sat for a time at the roadside as if stunned. Then he closed his eyes, bowed his head, and prayed aloud.

When he had concluded his prayers and looked up

again, he saw me standing over him. He spoke to me, his hoarse voice lapsing into the language of our homeland.

"You are Drakulya—and yet you cannot be. Vlad Drakul has been in his grave for more than twenty years."

I nodded slowly. "He has been there, in his grave. He has been in many graves, but never yet to stay."

His eyes, in horror and disbelief, probed mine. "What are you saying?"

"Only what you already know, but do not wish to believe. That I am Drakulya, and you are Bogdan. Once—is it possible?—you were my trusted comrade. Then you became Bogdan, the traitor, who took great pleasure in my slow death. Bogdan, who thought he had sold the head of Drakulya to the Sultan. But that was not to be. For a quarter of a century you have escaped my vengeance. But no more."

Bogdan could only stare at me, shaking his head. It was obvious that, although he now recognized me, still he did not believe. He was searching for an explanation.

"You are Bogdan," I said to him remorselessly. "And I know, we both know, what manner of filth you are. What is this pretense of robe and tonsure?"

"I was that man, Bogdan, once," he admitted, after a long pause. Still he maintained his unbroken stare at me. "That unspeakable traitor, murderer, thief, and lecher. But Christ had mercy upon that man, mercy even in the uttermost depths of his sin and degradation. And now, for fifteen years, through the Lord's mercy, that wretched Bogdan has been no more."

My voice was as quiet and monotonous as his. No one else could hear what either of us was saying. "Say rather, that soon he will be no more upon this earth. Soon he will have been sent to hell."

Once more my enemy bowed his head and prayed.

217

Perhaps his prayers gave him strength, for when he raised his head and looked at me again, his gaze was less obscured with fear.

"I see who you are now," he said at last, speaking with the relief of a man who has solved a mystery. "I begin to understand. There is indeed a great resemblance, and you, young man, must be Drakulya's bastard. Perhaps you were born only after he died; in any event you must have been so young that you can never really have known your father Vlad Drakul. He can scarcely be a real memory to you at all. Others must have brought you up, taught you to spend your life in vengeance—why have you come to Italy?"

"To find you. And now I have succeeded."

My enemy, sitting on his rock, took thought. Now it seemed that he was more concerned for me than frightened for himself. "I must tell you that your father was a man who worked much evil in the world. Well, he paid for his sins heavily in this world, and it is not for us to judge his condition in the next. Daily I pray for his soul."

"You—" In my outrage, I could not speak.

"I pray daily for your father's soul," my enemy repeated simply. "He had great faults. Yet he also did much that was right and good—he could inspire such loyalty—"

The treacherous monster seemed much moved. To my great confusion and anger, I found myself increasingly at a loss for what I should say to him. This monk who sat before me was not at all the Bogdan I remembered. And yet at the same time I knew him for the same man. When he spoke the same voice sounded in my ears, only the words were different.

Now he was asking me in kindly tones: "How much of your young life have you already wasted, seeking revenge?"

"Tracking down Ronay took me only a matter of hours, once I put my mind to it. Basarab took a great deal longer, but I found him as well. You have taken a very long time to find, but you are the last, and you are still alive, and I am not too late."

He shook his head. "Ronay died almost at the same time as your father. I think someone—"

I stepped forward and seized him by the shoulders of his robe and pulled him to his feet. "Fool! Fool! Imbecile, utter and contemptible! I say to you that I am Drakulya!" I fear that at this point I must have grown somewhat incoherent, beginning to snarl and rage at my defenseless adversary, accusing him of a whole list of monstrous crimes. Perhaps he was not even guilty of them all.

By this time Michelotto had moved closer, and was watching and listening with ever greater curiosity, despite the fact that most of our argument was in a language alien to him. Obviously he was beginning to enjoy the scene hugely.

Once again Bogdan grew troubled by my behavior, but this time in a sad and thoughtful way.

Half turning his back on me, he started to pack away his medical kit, meanwhile addressing me over his shoulder. "All that you say of the fool and traitor Bogdan is true enough. He was a mighty sinner, committing all the unspeakable crimes of which you accuse him, and more. He lied, he stole, he devoted himself to piling up earthly treasures. Worse, he murdered and tortured and raped— worst of all, he forgot God.

"But for all those crimes our Heavenly Father has granted him forgiveness. Not because he possessed the least merit of his own. Rather the One who takes all sins on Himself has granted him new life, as Brother Francis."

"Hypocrite! Brother Rat! Brother Shit! *I* have granted you no forgiveness!"

Now my victim, alarmed, cast down his pack and

turned to face me once more. "My son, in Our Savior's name I beg of you to overcome this obsession with vengeance. Not for my sake, but for your own. It is your own soul that you are now placing in great peril. Someday you too will perish."

I beg that the reader will understand me. Had this been unctuous hypocrisy on Bogdan's part, it would not have stung me so. I would have taken him in my grasp on the spot, and enjoyed his slow dismemberment. But despite the names I called him in my anger, I could not escape the conviction that the aged, gentle Brother Francis who stood before me was perfectly sincere—or as sincere as any mortal man can be. In fact, Bogdan existed no more, and this was someone else who tried to save my soul. My greatest enemy had escaped my vengeance after all, and it was that I found unbearable.

In my most monumental angers I am often quiet.

"You say that someday I will perish?" I asked him softly. "Nay, that I have already done, as thou must know."

A moment later, in the grip of uncontrollable rage, I struck him down without a moment's warning. Have I spoken yet of the augmented strength I possessed in my new life? Yes, but perhaps I have not made the matter sufficiently clear. I was a strong man in my breathing days, and my body had grown twenty times as powerful since the lust for life and vengeance had brought me back from death.

Under the impetus of a blow from my right arm, the body of Brother Francis flew tumbling into the air, came down at some distance, and only ceased to roll ten paces from where he had been standing. The Franciscan cowl, falling over the crushed skull, was already soaking red when the body came to rest. There was not, could not be, any need to strike again.

A Matter of Taste

Michelotto in the background grunted his awe and admiration. This he followed with a similar sound, softer and more thoughtful, but just as easy to interpret; definitely a criticism. He had understood a few words of the argument, and if this killing was for the purpose of revenge, over some ancient wrong, it certainly lacked artistry.

But I had little thought for Michelotto then. Slowly I went to the fallen body in the monk's habit and stood over it. Bogdan's arms and legs were twitching still, but that meant nothing. Certainly he was dead. Quickly and all but painlessly. All my plans—for how many years had I been dreaming of revenge?—all gone for nothing.

The truth, and I could not escape it, was that Bogdan had escaped me many years ago. This meddling elder, who had counseled me so sincerely regarding the welfare of my soul, was someone else.

Brother Francis.

Now, when it was too late, I could think of a thousand more cunning ways in which I might have proceeded once I had found my enemy. I might have tried to find a way to revive the soul of Bogdan in my foe, and then to ensure his speedy and direct passage to hell. I might have been inspired—no doubt it would have been by the devil—to work some trick, such as a sudden disappearance, to make my enemy think that I was indeed an evil spirit.

But—to meet him, to encounter him at last, and in that moment to realize that I had no plan ready! No plan ready, of all the hundreds, thousands of revengeful schemes, each more painful than the last, that I had dreamt of through the years . . .

What had I really been thinking of all that time?

I could have improvised. I might have assured the traitor that I had been sent from hell to collect his soul, that he was not forgiven after all, that Brother Francis was a fraud, that he was Bogdan still, and Bogdan, after all, was going with me down to hell. I might have . . .

But as matters stood, I had simply killed him. I, Drakulya, legendary even in my breathing days for the symphonic fury of retaliation with which I responded to all wrongs—

And every day, for fifteen years, he had prayed for my soul.

I had my full revenge at last. All the revenge on the three traitors that I was ever going to get.

And small satisfaction have I ever had from it.

16

The man who sometimes used the name of Matthew Maule picked up one of the lightweight poolside chairs, a folding construction of thin tubular metal and plastic webbing, and carried it back with him into the sheltered aisle behind the row of tall live plants. Carefully he positioned the chair to face the early night's magnificent play of high fog and distant lights outside the forty-fourth-floor windows. "Sit down and rest for a time, Margot." His tone was all tender consideration. "Presently the giddiness will pass."

Mrs. Hassler's response could have been described as a moan, were it not so filled with the tones of contentment and satisfaction. Obediently and rather gracefully she settled her considerable weight into the chair—the chairs looked very comfortable, her companion thought, given the materials of their construction. Next she allowed him to tuck robe and dry towel around her; her face now looked a trifle pale. The air in the natatorium, even here close to the windows, was comfortably warm, and he saw no cause for concern.

"I feel fine," she remarked, as if she found the fact somewhat surprising. "I don't understand what—what happened just now, but I do feel fine." Then, with a note of faint alarm: "Where are you going? Must you go?"

Standing behind the chair, he patted her shoulders and stroked her hair, with very genuine regard and tenderness. "Alas, I must go. And you must stay here for a time and rest. A restful time." His voice was growing rhythmic, soft, hypnotic. "Sleep now for a time, my love. Stay away from your apartment, and from mine, for an hour at least—there." With a final careful glance at the throat of the already sleeping woman—really nothing to be seen there, at least not without a close examination—the gentleman took his silent, swift departure.

His strength had been restored by feeding, and the last traces of the drug were fading from his circulation. With the onset of night, he was no longer restricted to man-form. In order to avoid being seen by several approaching exercise enthusiasts—the fewer people who saw him anywhere tonight the better—he chose to drift in mist-form to a stairway. Then, leaping on four wolfish feet, he darted upstairs to the level of his own apartment.

Clothed in his native shape of humanity once more, he stalked a corridor. The startling sight of the battered front door of his apartment, which obviously had been broken in, then rather clumsily propped back into place, elicited a silent curse. A moment later he was inside, and a moment after that he had materialized just behind the back of an armed breather, who stood holding John and Angie at gunpoint.

The grip of his two hands, left and right, fell on the gunman's elbows. Bones snapped and crumbled with the pressure. It was done quite silently, and with a minimum of fuss, though so painfully that the breather lost consciousness on the spot.

A moment later, the young couple who had been facing the wrong end of the gun collapsed upon a blood-spattered sofa in relief.

A Matter of Taste

Mr. Maule surveyed them with concern—the ruin that surrounded them could wait. Angie was wearing one of his robes and, to judge from the way she clutched the garment together in the front, most likely nothing else. Both she and John were spattered and stained from head to foot with blood, most of it surely not their own. John was dressed as Maule had seen him last, but he had obviously been through a lot since then.

Maule approached Angie. Her eyes closed and she slumped. Gently he examined her, opening her robe with a physician's brisk impersonality, observing the wounds on throat and thigh. To John, who hovered anxiously, he spoke reassuring words in answer to an unspoken question: "She is in no danger of being changed. Not unless she should be bitten again."

Maule closed the robe with the tenderness of a mother caring for a child. Then he laid his pale hand on Angie's forehead. A moment later her eyes opened wide.

"What's happening?" she asked, and sat up, almost energetically.

Mr. Maule spoke to her, and to her lover, words of further reassurance. Then he listened with sparkling-eyed approval to the tale they stammered out, about their fight with two drugged vampire rapists.

After that he had a couple of gentle questions for his young allies, following which he left the invader's gun with them in the living room, and chose to spare their tender sensibilities by carrying his prize catch, the still-breathing gunman—whose name they said was Stewart—into his bedroom, behind a closed door, for interrogation. In Maule's bedroom the signs of violent disturbance were as bad as in the living room and hall, a discovery that did not soothe his temper in the least.

When he emerged from the bedroom ten minutes

later, leaving the door open, he was alone, once more neatly garbed in fresh street clothes, and looking thoughtful. Angie and John, both somewhat recovered by now, met him in the living room, where they had been examining the machine that the attackers had used to break in the front door.

The appearance of this device now suggested to the old man some abandoned relic of the fitness room downstairs. Essentially it was a long lever, which when braced firmly on the floor outside a door could exert terrific force, over a short distance, to force the barrier in. Maule had heard of police, firemen, and several enterprising bandits who used very similar devices.

Maule advised his allies to barricade the door as firmly as possible after he was gone, using whatever furniture they could move. Then they were to rest, and eat. He spoke with peculiar emphasis to Angie, looking steadily into her eyes, once more touching her forehead with his fingers. Under his influence she brightened visibly. A touch of color came to her cheeks, and more life into her voice.

Stony-faced, the old man laconically assured them both that the atrocity of rape was going to be avenged.

They accepted whatever he said, nodding in agreement, not saying much. He could see that they were both almost worn out.

He asked them: "Have you heard from Joseph?"

Angie cleared her throat. "Not since—since before the vampires came in."

"I am concerned about him, and I am going out now to look for him. Where is this Southerland condominium that has been mentioned?"

John told him and handed over a key. "What about you? You're recovered completely?"

"I am."

"Thank God!" said John fervently. Then he looked as if he wanted to ask for details; but in a moment he had thought better of the impulse.

In any event, Mr. Maule, a gentleman to his fingertips, would not have dreamt of revealing his liaison with Mrs. Hassler. Briskly he changed the subject.

"If I understand the position correctly, the only *nosferatu* allies of Kaiser who have ever been invited into this apartment are now dead. If the breathers should assault your door again, have no hesitation in using the gun you now possess. Or in calling the police. Otherwise—I would prefer they not be called. Not yet, at least."

"We won't call them, then. Unless we have to. Where are you going now?"

"Out. To look for Joseph, to help him if he needs help. It is hard to be more specific."

John nodded as if he understood. "What about—?" He jerked his head in the direction of the bedroom hallway.

"My prisoner? Gone, completely gone. There is no need to concern yourself." And Maule, after pausing to provide himself with a trench coat from the front closet, moved on. Angie saw him, with a sense of wonder that would never be quite the same again, exit by the half-inch gap at the side of the propped-in-place front door.

Well, Maule thought as he progressed in man-form down the corridor, passing his neighbor's door, he would deal with the situation regarding Mrs. Hassler when the time came. Selling his condominium and moving elsewhere was about the least of the problems he could foresee in an interestingly crowded future.

* * *

Angie, a little pale and weak now that the first effects of Mr. Maule's bracing counseling were wearing off, and the last of the draught reasserting itself, thought she could feel herself developing an alarming tendency to faint. Against this she struggled bravely.

"God, I need a bath. But I'll fall asleep in the tub." She giggled lightly, a faint echo of hysteria.

"Try a shower, then. I'll fix you some soup."

"That sounds good. It sounds great. Oh, John? Uncle Matthew recommended iron tablets. He said there're some in our room's medicine cabinet."

On emerging from her shower Angie explored, on a hunch, the farther recesses of the guest bedroom's closet, which was deeper than she had thought at first. The effort turned up a modest collection of women's clothing, all new and discreetly packaged in protective garment bags. Angie found jeans and a pullover that fit.

Then she went to the kitchen, sat down, and ate some soup. John, sitting across from her, related how he had spent some of her shower time fortifying the apartment against a repeat invasion, wrestling and wedging some heavy furniture in place against the broken door. The enemy had left their door-breaking gadget in the living room, so John felt reasonably confident that they were not going to come smashing in quite so suddenly a second time.

Moving in a form invisible to almost everyone he passed, Maule ventured forth to meet the deepening night, night as always in the city slashed with a million wounds of electricity.

Five hundred years of experience as hunter and as hunted assured him that Kaiser's plan was working, up to now, even though Kaiser had decided not to take part in the actual break-in of Maule's apartment. Something else had been important enough to claim his attention instead. But what?

Before saying good-bye to Mr. Stewart, the breather with the mangled elbows, Maule had extracted from him words that tended to confirm his own suspicions—Joseph Keogh had suddenly become a most important target for the enemy.

Certainly Joseph, with his knowledge of vampires, and his wooden bullets, would be a dangerous opponent. But there had to be more to it than that, the old man thought. A matter of revenge, perhaps? A turning aside from the main goal, whose attainment had been and very likely would continue to be frustrated, to catch and crush an impertinent mere breather . . . or was there more to his opponent's plan than that?

Given the nature of the drug with which he, Maule, had been paralyzed and his young friends' description of the man calling himself Valentine Kaiser, Maule had little doubt what his chief opponent's true name must be. Valentine Kaiser—the name in itself was a kind of pun on the truth, which tended to confirm his insight.

So far, he had communicated his theory of the foe's identity to no one. It could not make any difference to the young couple heroically defending themselves in his apartment. But he intended to tell Joseph when he found him.

If he should not be too late to find him . . .

Descending from the remoter heights of the skyscraper with the nocturnal rush of an owl or a bat, moving swiftly and all but invisibly, Maule made good time, traveling airborne over a mile or so of city, to the Southerland condominium.

The building was a modern high-rise not unlike his own except for being much smaller. He arrived at the

condominium in less than a minute and tapped at the door.
A moment later Joseph Keogh, exhibiting great relief,
undid the bolts and locks and let him in.

"Man, am I glad to see you!"

"And I to see you alive and well, Joseph, I assure you.
Have you been besieged?"

"Since I holed up here? No. Nothing."

"Welcome news, on the face of it. Yet somehow I find
it ominous."

"What's going on?"

Maule brought him up-to-date as completely as possible in a few sentences. "And now I think we had better
return, swiftly, to my apartment."

Joe was ready in a minute. "What about John and
Angie? Are they still coping with all this?"

"As well as can be expected."

"And where the hell is this Valentine Kaiser now?"

"That is what I am trying to find out."

In another minute they had descended to an underground level of the building, a buried garage where a car,
belonging to the Southerland company, was available to
Joe. Maule, to be on the safe side, conducted a swift search
for bombs and other unpleasant surprises before allowing
Joe to touch the vehicle.

Then they were on their way. As Joe drove, the two
men continued to compare notes.

Joe explained the course of evasive action he'd em-
ployed, using taxis and the subway briefly, to get from the
Art Institute to the Southerland condominium before
nightfall. Since he'd been holed up he'd called the overseas
phone numbers that could have put him in contact with
Mina Harker, but so far he'd only been able to leave
messages.

Maule nodded in approval. In turn he explained to Joe

some of the essential facts about the drug with which he and now two other vampires had recently been poisoned: What happened to breathing people when they swallowed the stuff, what happened to vampires when they bit those breathing people, and how he himself had been able to recognize the taste, although it was disguised by garlic, before he had taken enough to disable him for a long time. Luckily he had been able to regurgitate some of the blood he had already swallowed.

Then Maule related how he had induced Angie to take a dose of the same drug when it looked like she was going to be captured.

"Clever move," Joe admitted.

"Yes—because it worked. I myself have tasted the Borgia sugar at least once before, in the year 1492. I must tell you about that sometime. It will be in the next book."

"I'm looking forward," said Joe absently.

"I wonder," Maule murmured thoughtfully, "where the man now calling himself Kaiser obtained his supply? The question opens interesting possibilities, but for the time being we can leave them open."

"You know him under some other name?"

"Indeed I do. As Cesare Borgia. When there is time for leisurely discussion I will speak to you about him."

Vaguely Joe thought he could remember hearing the name of Borgia somewhere. Something in history, something villainous. "I don't suppose it makes any difference to the present situation."

"No, I think not."

Discussion moved on to the enemy's general strength and capabilities. Of course one always had to allow for possible miscalculation in such matters; but by now Maule thought he could be fairly sure that the ranks of Borgia's auxiliaries had been drastically depleted. One vampire woman dead, fallen this morning to Joseph's wooden bullets. Two more *nosferatu* gallantly eliminated by John and Angie in Maule's apartment. One breather, Mr. Stewart, even more recently departed. There was at least one more vampire woman remaining, besides Valentine himself, the lady Joe had seen up on the maintenance floor. And an indeterminate number of breathers also; but Maule thought those would pose no problem once their master had been rendered inactive.

Maule came back to the remaining enemy vampire woman. "From your description, Joseph, I think I know her. There are not that many vampires currently in the world, you know, and most of them I think are known to me in one way or another. I expect she will pose no danger, once her leader has been rendered harmless."

"And how are we going to do that?"

"I am not yet sure. What apartment number is he in?"

Joe provided the information.

They drove into the tall building's underground parking facility, fortunately now emptied of most of its daytime users. Joe had no difficulty in finding a space.

"I must say, Joseph, that the absence of the man you know as Kaiser seems to me increasingly ominous. We had better first look in on John and Angie before we set out to attack the enemy."

"Sounds like a smart idea to me."

Mr. Maule felt a special responsibility for those two young breathers. They had been his guests when hell began to envelop them, and he had plans to hold a strict accounting with the man responsible for that onslaught. Of course, if the villain was who Maule thought he was, that accounting could hardly be as strict as it really ought to be . . .

They reached Maule's battered door, and Joe tapped on it and called. To his relief, and Maule's, Angie and John were still snugly and safely fortified within. They reported having seen nothing of the enemy since Maule's departure only minutes ago. The hunters urged the breathing couple to stay where they were and hold the fort.

John, when he heard of Maule's and Joe's planned expedition, volunteered at once to come with them.

"You think you're going to leave me here alone?" Angie snapped at him. Red spots showed in her anemic cheeks.

Maule regretfully refused John's request, with an appreciation of what it took to make it.

"You have borne quite enough of the burden of combat, so far." He smiled faintly. "I should feel deprived if I were not allowed to have a turn."

Then Maule and Joe Keogh proceeded to the eighty-ninth floor, the level of Kaiser's apartment.

"I take it you are still suitably armed, Joseph?"

"You waited until now to ask? Damned right I am."

A few moments later, Joe was ringing Kaiser's doorbell, standing squarely in what ought to be the viewer's field of view.

"Who is it?" The suspicious voice on the speaker sounded like that of the young woman in the surplus field jacket.

"Me. Take a look."

"What the fuck d'you want?" Now she sounded outraged.

"Let me in and find out." He could only hope they didn't realize the old man was up and running at full strength again.

A moment later, bolts and locks were being undone.

As soon as the door began to open Joe stepped in and called out in a loud voice words in Latin, words that he'd burned into his memory years ago.

Confronting him in the sparsely furnished living room, gaping at the way he'd yelled, were the young field-jacket woman and an overweight, hairy man, a breather too, who held an automatic weapon ready in both hands.

"What'd you say?" the man with the gun demanded sharply. "Was that a name?"

"It was," said the old man, coming out of thin air to stand some six or eight feet to Joe's right. He ignored the Uzi now suddenly leveled at him and in polite tones posed a couple of questions for the youth who aimed it. "Where is Valentine Kaiser? What orders has he given you?"

The potbellied one stood playing with his weapon, a finger on the trigger. "Up my ass. Ya wanna look?"

As far as Joe could tell, he himself was the first one in the room to start moving. He jumped before anyone else, as soon as the contemptuous vulgarity had registered. Because no one was going to get away with talking like that to the old man, not in this kind of a situation. It just wouldn't work. A photofinish camera would have caught Joe somewhere between a standing position and the floor, just at the moment when the old man, having taken time to think things over, started moving too. But still Joe's reaction, like those of the other breathers in the room, came much too late and in fact he needn't have bothered.

The Uzi, finger on the trigger or not, never fired. Instead it was wrenched out of its owner's hands with a force that might have harvested a finger or two with it and should have produced a yell of pain.

But the potential yell never had time to get started. The automatic weapon came right back to the man who'd lost it, the curved steel bar that formed the stock driving right into his face, thrust at him by the old man's one-handed grip on the barrel. Why bother to use two hands to swat a fly? The sound of the impact, metal gunstock crunching flesh and bone, was to stay with Joe for a long time. The man who had once owned the Uzi went down in his tracks. There would be no need to worry about his getting up.

By now Joe, lying prone, had his own pistol out of the shoulder holster. But he saw no evidence that it was going to be needed.

Mr. Maule cast the Uzi aside disdainfully—when you needed a flyswatter you could always find something that would serve—and dusted the fingers of his right hand lightly against one another, demonstrating grace and distaste at the same time.

He smiled briefly in Joe's direction. Then, with an expression of sorrowful contempt, he turned to regard the young woman in a field jacket, who for the last ten seconds had not moved a muscle, but had turned quite pale.

"Valentine Kaiser?" Maule inquired gently. "His present whereabouts? His most recent orders?"

"I don't know," said the young woman, in equally polite tones. Then she collapsed to the floor in a dead faint.

By this time Joe was on his feet again. He put his gun away. Then he knelt beside the field-jacket lady and searched her for weapons.

The old man had started going through the place. Joe followed. He looked into the bathroom where Liz Wiswell had died, but her body had been removed. The tub and surrounding tile had been scrubbed clean. Only the bolts and fasteners driven into the walls above the tub remained to show that something strange had happened here.

He prowled on, cautiously, joining the old man in a

bedroom, where Maule had just discovered some of Valentine Kaiser's—or someone's—home earth.

The old man was murmuring thoughtfully to himself, ripping open plastic bags with fingernails suddenly grown talonlike, running the dried earth through his fingers onto the floor. Then he dropped the stuff, dusted his fingers again, and faced the bedroom windows. "This is on the north side of the building, like my own abode. Joseph, see if one of the windows opens."

Joe went to confirm the fact that here, as in Uncle Matthew's own place, one of the windows had been modified so that it could be opened. No doubt untrammeled access to the night air was a handy thing for any vampire to have. He asked: "How about getting rid of some of this dirt while we're here?"

"An excellent idea."

When Joe turned from emptying the last plastic bag outside, he saw that Maule had left the room. He was back in a moment, carrying one-handed the body of the man who had once owned an Uzi. Hauling the inert figure to the window, Maule pushed it out through the narrow opening, still supporting it in his grip. Then he maneuvered his own arms and shoulders out.

Joe saw Maule's body twist, and heard him grunt with a burst of explosive effort. Then he was standing still. Joe, pushing back a drape and looking down, could see nothing but some moving lights of traffic.

"There," Maule said. "A neat landing, atop the new construction. Beside his fellow, who went down some time ago, from my own window. On this foggy evening, it appears that no one struggling with the traffic in the streets below, or on the building's lower floors, has yet noted anything amiss."

Joe cleared his throat. "I see," he said.

Maule started briskly for the living room once more, this time with Joe right on his heels. They both checked out other rooms on the way. There was no one else in the apartment. When they reached the living room, Joe saw to his relief that the body of the young woman who had fainted was gone, and the front door was standing slightly open.

"I will not pursue her, Joseph." Maule was looking at him with a mixture of sympathy and amusement. "My mind is on bigger game."

17

Around the middle of August, in the year 1503, word reached me at the distance of a few days' ride from the Eternal City that on the twelfth of that month both Pope Alexander and Cesare had suddenly been stricken desperately ill. There was grave doubt of the father's survival, and the son was incapacitated, prognosis uncertain.

The message arrived near midnight. It was in fact my old friend and former lover Constantia, Cesare's sometime lover (and, I believe, quite possibly Alexander's too), who brought me this information, at a speed greater than that attainable by any breathing human of the time.

I was to tell no one, but proceed to Rome as rapidly as possible, dropping at once all other business on which I was engaged. This created some awkwardness, which I dealt with as best I could, leaving a note at midnight for my immediate subordinate and taking wing from the nearest window, in bat-form, very shortly thereafter.

The news of course perturbed me, but actually almost any interruption would have been welcome at the time. I was still brooding over the sour aftertaste of my revenge, such as it had been, on Bogdan and on his fellow traitors. Why had my efforts been so fundamentally unsuccessful?

But now, as Cesare's faithful agent, I had much more

pressing matters to consider. On hearing that the Borgias had been simultaneously stricken, the first thought that leaped to my mind—and to the minds of a great many of my contemporaries—was poison. One of their damned plots had somehow backfired on them; or Madonna Lucrezia, driven mad by their continued ill-usage of her as a political pawn, had finally struck back at her father and brother; or some rival faction had suddenly acquired a skill equal to theirs in the formulation and use of deadly potions.

Constantia on bringing me the news let me know that she favored this last opinion. She also voiced her sadness that her young and powerful lover had been so stricken.

So concerned was she for her lover's life, she informed me, that before leaving on her courier's mission she had once more pressed Cesare, this time urgently, to drink her blood and thereby become a vampire. But in his great stubbornness, his absolute determination to achieve political success, he had still refused.

That both father and son could have been felled by some ordinary illness was an explanation that no shrewd observer at the time was willing to believe. And yet with the benefit of hindsight such an accident seems the most likely cause. That was a bad summer for disease in Rome, in an era when all Roman summers were unhealthy; and in the perspective afforded by modern science, acute malaria seems the most likely diagnosis.

Constantia, after delivering her message to me and tarrying for the briefest of conversations, hastened on. There were still others to whom the alarming news must be conveyed.

Three or four days after the father and son had fallen ill, and while I was still hastening toward Rome, the Pope's life was already being despaired of. Important folk of every kind, Cardinals in particular, who had received the word as soon as I did or sooner, were rushing to be on hand when the end came, hoping thus to be best able to pursue their own advantage. At the same time others already on the scene, who had become closely associated with Alexander and had made enemies in the process, were moving prudently away from Rome, not liking what they foresaw as the aftermath of his demise.

Fortunately, once I got under way I was able to move faster than any breathing person, given the general state of transportation at the time. My actual journey to Rome took me less than a day.

On arriving at the papal palace I found everything in turmoil. Actually that word somewhat understates the degree of political, social, and religious confusion that obtained. At the time of my arrival the Pope was not yet dead, and I was pleased to hear that my employer Cesare still survived as well, though the condition of both men was still very grave. At once I started to make my way up to Cesare's apartments, which were directly above his father's.

But before I had taken half a dozen steps up the broad stairs, I was intercepted by a man I recognized as an agent of Lucrezia. He drew me aside and murmured privately that his mistress wished to see me immediately upon my arrival. The matter, she had said, was urgent.

I was startled. "Then she is here, in Rome?"

"Indeed she is, Don Ladislao." It appeared that Madonna had received the news of her brother's and father's sickness even before I did, and in response to an urgent plea from Cesare had hurried to the Eternal City from Ferrara, making the long ride disguised as a man. Her third and current husband, Alfonso d'Este, was no doubt as usual out in the countryside somewhere playing with his artillery, and largely indifferent as to whether his wife was home or not, so long as the appearances of propriety were preserved.

Duke Valentino, my informant confided to me, had summoned his sister, the family expert, to Rome because he wanted her to test him and their father for signs of poisoning.

"Aha. And have such signs been found?"

"You will have to speak to my mistress about that."

"Then conduct me to her instantly."

My guide led me away at once, out of the palace and into a nearby garden, where an uncomfortable-looking stone bench proved surprisingly movable. Inside the cavity thus disclosed, stairs went steeply down below ground level.

"Where is she hiding, then? In a catacomb?"

"Something very like it, Captain. If you will please follow me."

We went down, and down, and down again, with intervals of lateral progression through thin tunnels. At one point I believe we were actually in a subbasement of the palace. Some of the stonework around me was indeed as old as the catacombs, but other parts were new. The Vatican, I realized, was changing rapidly, almost before the eyes of one who visited the area as often as I did. Alexander on becoming Pope had hurried into construction of an addition, called the *Torre Borgia*, to the papal palace. His addition, I thought, must be the part above me now. In succeeding years he had ordered additional remodeling. Probably his experience with the falling roof remained much in his mind.

I had not been entirely serious when I spoke of catacombs, those vaults and passages whose walls were lined with the bones of Christians, the majority of them interred more than a thousand years before my time. But now here we were among them, for a brief distance anyway. Then out again, into a passage of much more recent creation.

The air was close and dank. The way for a long time had been completely dark, at least to breathers' limited perceptions, except for the torch my guide was carrying.

And now a peculiar smell, even worse and stranger than those to be expected in a cave beneath a city, began to tease my nostrils. I became more and more convinced as we proceeded, that I smelled, of all unlikely things—a bear.

People I knew still spoke of how a whole bear, roasted in its hide, had been among the dishes served at a papal feast once given for the King of Naples. So the thing was not utterly impossible. Still, unwilling to sound foolish if I should be mistaken, I said nothing to my guide.

At last we emerged from the confusing series of tunnels into a surprisingly roomy chamber that I assumed to be our final goal. Sconces mounted high on the curved walls held torches that both stimulated and tested the circulation of the buried air, and gave light enough for even a breather's eyes to take in a scene of fantasy.

I blinked, and came near rubbing my own eyes. In the middle of the high chamber a large bear, one of the species then much favored by traveling entertainers, hung head down from the ceiling, suspended in an elaborate network of chains and ropes. I could hear the animal's wheezing, labored breathing. The beast hung almost motionless in its bizarre suspension, too nearly dead to struggle or make any other sound. A dozen feet below it, tubs and basins on the chamber floor caught what liquids dripped or trickled from its shaggy, slowly dying body. Around those receptacles, workers were busy with chemical and alchemical apparatus

—in those days the difference was lost on most of us, including me. These toilers looked up at our entrance, then went back to whatever it was that they were doing.

With a total lack of comprehension I studied the animal's dark fur, the yellow teeth, black open lips still trickling slime. Since my transformation I had gained a certain empathy with the lower orders of creation, and I could share, through channels other than those of the common senses, the sensations of the bear. Dim pain and outrage burned like banked-up fires, but they would not burn much longer.

Letting my gaze drift away from the bear, I surveyed the room in which we stood, which was strange and wonderful enough in itself. Roman portrait murals, their colors faded and encrusted with nitre through the centuries, looked down from the walls. For what purpose this room might have been constructed I had no hope of guessing. Ancient Rome, the city of the imperial Caesars, was of course never far away. On Palatine Hill the ruins of their palaces were grazed by sheep, overgrown with olive trees, and entwined in myrtle and rosemary.

"We wait here for a moment," said my guide, meaning that I should do so, while he went ahead to report my arrival. Waiting, I called to the technicians to ask them about the bear. One of them explained to me that the object of this exercise was to collect what the bear vomited, or voided by other means, and by judicious mixing, evaporation, and distillation create from those substances the finest poison.

Whilst I was pondering this, Madonna Lucrezia entered the room, beautifully dressed as she almost always was, and greeted me with her sweet smile, though with some restraint because of the others present. "Captain Ladislao, it is very good to see you."

"And for me to see you, my lady. More than good, it is essential." I kissed her hand. "I rushed to Rome as quickly as I could when the horrible news reached me. I have not yet seen either His Holiness or your esteemed brother. I trust they are—?"

"Still alive, dear friend. But I fear scarcely more than that." Lucrezia, looking uncharacteristically worried, gestured at the bear. "We are testing certain of their bodily discharges even now, having fed them to the animal. But so far there is no evidence of poison. So it appears that I will have no urgent mission for you today."

"One of your laboratory workers gave me rather a different explanation of this experiment."

"Ah, my workers. They show great devotion and are only doing their best to keep my little secrets." Excusing herself for a moment, Lucrezia began to talk to the chemical technicians, conferring on the progress of the experiment.

Once more I looked around the chamber in which we stood. The more details of the architecture and decoration I examined, the more I found myself gaping like the veriest tourist, marveling and blinking in amazement.

No doubt, I thought, one of the imperial Caesars had once inhabited this room. Such was the impression made by the high doorways, mostly blocked, the columns, some of them broken, and the few statues, battered but essentially intact, that still maintained their poses in the high niches of the wall. Except for the lamps brought by the latest generation of breathing occupants, the vast chamber was in darkness now, and its farther reaches were choked with rubbish. Once, I thought, this room must have stood much higher, resting freely upon the surface of the earth, while Caesar—Claudius, perhaps, or Caligula?—trod its marble floor. And somehow over the centuries it had been buried, encroached upon and covered by one generation after another of Roman buildings and pavements, litter and debris. How did such things happen? I began to have a sense of what a personal life of centuries might entail, besides the postponement of eternity.

Lucrezia had concluded her conference with her workmen. I returned my attention to the lovely woman who was concerning herself with bear vomit, and as courteously as possible expressed my curiosity as to how the Borgias, and she in particular, had happened to become so expert on the subject of poisons.

She laughed and said we had more urgent things to talk about, and I never received much of an explanation. But the opinion of my later years is that probably the first tendencies toward toxicity, when she and Cesare were mere children, had been cultivated by some old nurse. I wonder sometimes whether that nurse might have been a vampire too.

Lucrezia guided me out of the main chamber of the subterranean laboratory, and into another and more private room, where we might converse more freely. Harking back to our first meeting, Lucrezia went on to assure me, without my asking, that her and her brother's discovery of an anti-vampire venom had been purely serendipitous, and I their first subject only by sheer accident. Actually the two adolescents, as they then were, had been seeking a dependable aphrodisiac—a goal which, unhappily, had continued to elude her researches.

Lately her chemical researches had been allowed to lapse. With the added responsibilities of Lucrezia's new family in Ferrara—here she looked at me sharply, to make sure I understood she took those responsibilities seriously—she had little time and no longer much inclination for such pursuits. However, if it should turn out that her brother and her father had been poisoned—

I was glad, observing sweet-faced Lucrezia at this time, that I was not the one who had attempted to do her brother harm.

Taking advantage of the opportunity offered by the private room, we exchanged a kiss or two to cement our own relationship. This led to a more fervent exchange of endearments, and I fear I must now report that poor Cesare and Alexander had to wait.

While I am on the subject of the Borgia poison, the one so effective against the nonbreathing component of humanity, let me say here that I believe one of its vital components must be some compound of burnt and powdered wood. I have reason to believe that liqnum vitae might be particularly effective, but the final determination must await a new round of research.

Madonna Lucrezia and I both delighted in our subterranean meeting, but neither of us wanted to dally overlong. Within the hour I was hurrying aboveground to the Vatican, where I resumed my delayed efforts to get in to see Cesare.

The Pope on being stricken had taken to his bed in his usual apartments, and Cesare, likewise, in the rooms he normally used, which were just above those of his father. Both men were still in the chambers when I arrived.

I was told that the Pope, on the day before my arrival in Rome, had recovered enough to play cards; but then the indefatigable physicians had their way, and bled him once again. Still he lingered, but perhaps the bleeding was really the finishing stroke.

Cesare, when I was admitted to his room at last, still clung fiercely to life and swore even in a delirium of fever that he would recover. I offered what I could in the way of hearty encouragement, though silently I admitted to myself that he looked in a bad way. I wondered whether I should add my urgings to those of Constantia, advising my leader to save his life by becoming a vampire, even if that meant giving up his chances to be a king.

But I refrained—the choice was up to him, and if he wanted advice he would ask for it. Either Caesar or nothing—what a motto! What a man! Or so most of his friends and associates agreed. I could not fail to be impressed by the way he commanded fierce loyalty among them, a demonstration even more marked now in his time of helplessness.

On the night I have been describing, I arrived at Cesare's apartments, and argued and pushed my way in, just a few minutes before the time his physicians decided to stuff his delirious body, wracked with fever, into a bath of icy water in an effort to save his life.

Michelotto, who was now sitting in almost continuous attendance upon the sufferer, drew a blade and threatened these supposed healers—it was only with some difficulty that I and others persuaded Corella to sheathe his weapon again.

Looking closely at Valentino, I beheld certain lesions on his face that I did not remember seeing there before—of late he had affected to wear a mask much of the time—and seeing these eruptions made me think of certain other oddities I had observed during the last year or so. It came to me that in that period Cesare had started to display some signs of the infamous French pox.

Once I got a good look at the illness now threatening Cesare's life, it did look to me like malaria, with which everyone who then lived in southern Italy was more or less familiar. Many in Rome caught the disease in that unhappy summer.

Duke Valentino at the time of his icy bath was in no

shape to give coherent orders, to me or anyone else, so Michelotto and I simply stood by.

But the physicians' heroic measures succeeded, and the fever soon left the Duke. By the eighteenth of August, when word suddenly came from downstairs that his father the Pope was dead, Cesare himself was on the road to recovery, though still extremely weak.

His immediate reaction on hearing that his father was no more—the news certainly came as no surprise—was to call Michelotto and myself to him, and dispatch us with orders to accomplish the looting of the papal apartments located just beneath his own. There, in the Pope's own bedchamber, built into the wall directly behind his bed, was a vault in which Alexander had been wont to keep the bulk of the papal cash, jewels, and gold on hand.

Michelotto saluted and was ready to leap into action. He got as far as the door of the room, where he stopped, looking back impatiently.

I was still standing, frowning, beside Cesare's bed.

"Well?" the patient snapped at me in his exhausted voice.

"Captain General," I said, "you have just told me that the money and other valuables down there belong to the Church." It was no secret to anyone that Alexander had, all along, been squandering Church funds to further his son's career in any way he could. But that a Pope might choose to abuse his authority gave me no excuse to commit a robbery.

Cesare had no idea what I was talking about. "Yes, and what of that?"

"Sir, you are asking me to steal this money for you."

The glazed eyes of the sick man betrayed no hint of understanding. Feebly he endeavored to prop himself up in bed. At last he began to comprehend. Wearily he croaked: "What strange scruples are these? My father, while he breathed, *was* the Church, was he not? And so the money was his, and what was the father's passes on naturally to the son."

I considered this a childish attempt to twist the logic of morality. "Certainly, my lord, a father may pass on his own property at will, to his son or any other heir he chooses. But that scarcely has any application in the present case."

Borgia glared at me. I had seen strong men quail at far milder looks from him. But my own gaze was unblinking. Sternly confronting my bedridden commander, I demanded: "When Alexander died, did the Church die? No. And you, Duke Valentino, will surely not maintain that you have become the Church?" The jaw of Michelotto, who had now returned to his chief's bedside, dropped at that thought.

I doubt that the Duke and his chief lieutenant would have treated anyone else in the circumstances with the patience they accorded me. In words of one syllable, as though they thought my intellect deficient, they explained the vital necessity for the Duke to replenish his own treasury in anticipation of hard times, now that his father's support had been so suddenly removed.

I listened patiently to what were for me irrelevancies. Borgia had treated me fairly, as far as I knew, up to this point, and so I owed him a fair hearing. But their arguments left me unmoved. Thievery was thievery. To suggest that the honor of Drakulya might stretch so far as to accommodate theft, and sacrilegious theft at that, more than verged upon deadly insult. I bit my tongue, telling myself to make allowances for fever.

I was aware that Corella had for some time taken to

carrying a concealed wooden dagger. I watched him carefully lest he might go so far as to draw it.

I have no wish to dwell upon the scene. Vicious words
were exchanged; the sick man all but called me a traitor. Or
perhaps—certain words were said that I chose not to hear
quite clearly—he actually did so, and I swallowed the
insult because of his fevered illness and his fairness to me
in the past. But I resigned from his service on the spot and
stalked out. Rather, since I wished to remove myself from
the Borgia's presence with as little delay as possible, I flew
out, changing shape right in his bedroom, and departing in
bat-form through the window. The last sounds I heard
behind me were the scream of a terrified servant and the
shattering of a dropped chamber pot.

Cesare, as I learned later, wasted little time or energy
in hurling curses after me. He immediately dispatched his
favorite henchman Corella to do the looting job.
Michelotto took a few chosen fellows with him, and I have
heard that the task was carried out with remarkable
efficiency. Some two hundred thousand florins in coin,
silver, and gemstones, all legally the property of the
Church, were stolen that night to enrich Borgia's personal
coffers. During the coming weeks and months he was to
have need of all of it, and more, to feed and arm such
troops as he could raise, to pay bribes and buy support.

On that same night that I left Borgia's service
Constantia arrived back in Rome. As soon as I became
aware of her presence there was a miniature conclave,
consisting of Cesare's two closest female companions and
myself. The newly orphaned Lucrezia and Cesare's devoted
vampire lover listened sympathetically to my complaints
regarding his behavior. Both said they understood my
position, but still both remained angry with me for resign-

ing from his service now in his hour of need. They, of course, remained unquestioningly determined to do all they could to save their beloved Cesare.

I in turn listened sympathetically to the pleas of the two women and swore quite truthfully that I had no plans to become the enemy of Valentino, who from my first hour in his service, down to my last, had treated me well. I agreed never to play an active role against the Duke— unless, of course, he first should try to strike at me.

This last proviso unreasonably alarmed Borgia's tender sister, who, after all, had much to be alarmed about. Yielding at last to Lucrezia's tearful pleas, I took an oath that even in the event of Cesare's someday attacking me, I should never kill him, nor inflict injury upon him beyond the absolute requirements of self-defense. She wanted me to swear my devotion to his welfare in even stronger terms, but in the case of a man who had impugned my honor, I could not. No, not even for her.

Shortly after my departure from this meeting, as I was informed later, the women hastened to meet with Cesare himself, mainly to urge him yet again to consider becoming a vampire. But whatever pleas or arguments were pressed in favor of such a move on the Duke's part, they were urged in vain. Cesare, quite lucid now though still kittenishly feeble, swore that this illness, whatever its cause, was not going to kill him. Moreover he was still going to be the ruler of Italy, as his father had intended. Time was to prove the first claim quite correct, the second false.

As for myself, I returned to the palace on that same night. Belatedly it had occurred to me that I might remove some at least of the Pope's treasure to a safe place, and later see that it was handed over to some good bishop, far from Rome, or somehow to the poor. Alas, the brigands had been there in Alexander's rooms before me. Not only the treasure in the vault, but all else of value, down to the candlesticks and bed curtains, had been taken. Scavenging jackals had come through on the trail of the great predators.

The Pope's body, too, had already been removed, and this made me curious. Drifting silently through one hall and chamber after another, I sought to find him. Looking back, I think that it was also in my mind to see whether he, adopting the advice now being given to his son, had turned vampire at the last moment.

To me, Cesare's condition had suggested nothing more sinister than severe malaria. But when at last I beheld the body of the dead Pope, who had been stricken at the same time, I was suddenly not so sure.

A wax taper, stuck in a plain wooden holder, burned at the head of the ordinary table, and another at the foot, but otherwise this holy relic had been left completely ignored and unattended. In some neighboring room, guards were making a racket, quarreling about some minor piece of loot—from what they were shouting, I gathered that there were more valuable wax candles there.

Unobserved—not that anyone would have cared—I assumed the solidity of man-form and came closer to the rude catafalque. Perhaps the best thing most people could have found to say about the late Pope in his present condition was that he certainly was not a vampire.

I counted myself fortunate in not being required to breathe, and my stay beside the bier was brief. Alexander's body was blackening and rotting quickly, and swelling also, so that the clothing that had been put upon him when he died was stretched to bursting at the throat, as if his collar had been an instrument of strangulation. In the morning, as I was told much later by an eyewitness, the men who came to bury him could not force his distended carcass into the prepared coffin. They were unanimously drunk, for which I cannot blame them, and they chanted obscene songs as with a rope they dragged the villain's remains from his bier, through marble hallways and courtyards, to his hastily dug grave.

18

Shortly after the gavel went down to end the Residents' Association meeting, Mrs. Hassler emerged from the Boulevard Room on the fifteenth floor of the great building. As she turned toward the elevators, she found, with mixed emotions, that she was still accompanied by Mr. Kaiser, who had sat next to her part of the time tonight. He was a charming but somewhat diffident young man who had introduced himself during another meeting weeks ago.

"Have you seen our friend Mr. Maule during the last few days?" young Kaiser inquired now. He too, it seemed, was acquainted, though only slightly, with the somewhat reclusive Maule. And he too thought there might be some current reason for Maule's friends to be concerned about him.

Mrs. Hassler cleared her throat. "Only briefly," she temporized.

Her companion did not seem to be paying close attention to her answer. "You look a little pale yourself," he commented in a solicitous midwestern voice, continuing to walk right at her elbow. "If you don't mind my saying so. Are you all right?"

"Well"—she could feel herself blushing—"I did feel just a little under the weather earlier. But I've been looking forward to this meeting for some time, and I was just determined not to miss it."

Kaiser murmured sympathetically. They shared again their mutual dislike for the building's new owners, and particularly those owners' new architectural plans, which had caused the front of the plaza to be enveloped in ugly scaffolding, and as a byproduct had revived the otherwise moribund Residents' Association and brought about meetings like the one tonight, at which the possibilities of legal action and other alternatives to preserve the character of the plaza had been discussed.

On the way up in the elevator, Kaiser showed himself ready to listen to a little gossip about Mr. Maule's strange relatives, who lately had evidently been bothering the poor man without mercy.

He gave the impression of not having heard about that particular problem before. "Standing around out in the hall, you say? What sort of people were they?"

Feeling uncomfortable, Mrs. Hassler told a fib. "Goodness, I never really got a good look at any of them. It was just the—the *way* they stood there."

Her young companion frowned and seemed to be taking the matter rather seriously. "I wonder—should we just stop at his door, right now, and ring?"

"I don't like to bother him, if—"

"No, nonsense, if he sees us both at his door he'll let us in."

Mrs. Hassler, her worries again aroused, went along with the young man's suggestion.

In a few moments they were standing in front of Maule's apartment. Kaiser prodded the doorbell with an energetic finger.

"That's very strange," said Mrs. Hassler a second later. "I'm just now noticing it."

"What's that?"

"The door. Look. It's not really on the hinges any longer. You can see a crack of daylight all the way around."

"Why, so you can." Kaiser was standing right in the viewer's field of view, and making sure that his companion was in it also. His ears were quite good enough to bring him the faint sounds from beyond the door, of a pair of breathers who had begun to creep about again like frightened mice. Their little electronic screen would be showing him standing in the hall, and now when he silently raised his left hand they would be able to see it clearly, poised in the air a few inches from the back of Mrs. Hassler's neck.

"Push the bell again," said Mrs. Hassler. But before he could do so, his first attempt was at last answered.

"What do you want?" The breathing voice from inside came through the speaker as a tortured squeak.

"May we come in?" the man who called himself Valentine Kaiser responded politely. And his eyes twinkled.

Maule, arriving from the eighty-ninth floor with Joe, approached his own apartment very cautiously. While he was still ten paces down the corridor Maule sensed Kaiser's presence within, and himself promptly vanished into the air. Out of the air came a whisper in Joe's ear, instructing him to go on and tap at the front door.

Here we go again, thought Joe Keogh. He approached the door with no particular effort at stealth, doing his best to suggest to anyone who might be watching or listening that he had no suspicion that anything was wrong. He tapped the button briskly and called out in a low voice to identify himself, then stood where the viewer could pick him up.

In a moment there came the sound of shifting furniture; then the detached door was lifted partially aside by unseen hands. Joe took a deep breath and stepped in through the gap.

"Where's the old man?" he asked as innocently as he could, looking at John's and Angie's frightened faces. "Isn't he—"

A force that felt like the grip of an angry gorilla clamped down on Joe's shoulders—

—and in a moment was wrenched away. Before Joe had time to think about crying out, he was free again, uninjured. Two blurry and tremendous figures, looking somehow larger than life though both were in human-form, were spinning about the room, crashing into such furniture as had somehow survived the earlier struggle. Maule at last had come to grips with his chief opponent.

Angie was crawling into a corner behind a sofa; John appeared to be trying to find his wooden spear again. Joe caught sight of the woman he had seen briefly in the hallway earlier, Mrs. Hassler. She was stretched out, fully clothed, on another sofa at the far end of the room, and appeared to be peacefully asleep; as Joe watched, her lips puffed out in a gentle snore.

Dodging away from the two combatants as they crashed into the piano near the center of the room, Joe moved toward the far end where Mrs. Hassler lay. He'd drawn his gun now, but hadn't had the chance to get off a clean shot.

Before that chance came, the wrestling match was over.

It ended at one side of the room, with Kaiser—or Borgia—pinned facedown in a hammerlock, with his head and shoulders atop a sturdy wooden table that managed to support both his and his opponent's considerable weight.

Joe, sidestepping for a clear shot with his revolver at Kaiser's head, saw that there was to be no shape-changing in this spasmodic struggle between two powerful vampires. Borgia appeared to be trying something of the kind, for waves of liquid change distorted his face and body momentarily. But Maule, standing above and behind him, gripping him with immovable hands, cried out, in a language none of the breathers could understand, such words as seemed to prevent it.

John had located the broken shaft of a wooden spear, and was approaching with this weapon raised. Joe still aimed a liqnum vitae bullet. But Maule, raising his voice, forbade either of them to kill this man.

"I swear," said Borgia, sounding half-strangled, "on my sacred honor that I will honor a truce if you will grant me one."

The man who pinned him only laughed. It was a strange and unfamiliar sound.

"No killing, and no truce? Then what?" Borgia's choking laugh was even stranger. "Do you mean to grip me like this forever?"

"Until I have decided what to do next—why do you hunt me?"

"You know full well why, Prince."

"On my own honor, I do not."

"Then you can guess. Because of the four hundred years of torment I endured. Four centuries buried in alien soil, where I could neither rest, nor regain full consciousness, until at last the drug wore off—"

"That was not my fault," said Maule in slow, inexorable tones.

"Why shouldn't we finish him?" John demanded.

Maule did not answer.

"What are we going to do with him, then?" Joe wanted to know.

Angie, struggling against what felt like terminal exhaustion, had retreated to the only chair currently upright in the room, and let herself sink into it.

And then she realized that she could not really rest. Not yet.

Pulling herself slowly to her feet, she left the room, unnoticed by any of the men. Moving as in a daze, without much conscious emotion, she stooped in the bedroom hallway to pick up from the floor a large, sharp, convenient wooden splinter.

In Maule's bedroom she somehow found the strength to tug the dresser out a little distance from the wall. The secret compartment opened easily. There were the jars. She found the proper one. Not likely that she would forget what it looked like.

Back in the living room, the debate was still going on.

"Again you will spare my life, I suppose," said Borgia in a less strangled voice. He had been allowed to shift his position slightly, and was now lying more on his right side and shoulder than on his face. One arm was still bent up beside his back. "Because of your damned honor. I suppose you can discover some way to imprison me again. And then in two hundred years, or a hundred, or whenever I can, I will be coming after you again."

"Perhaps," said Maule.

"No perhaps. There is no doubt about it."

"I thought," said Maule, as though the words constituted some kind of explanation, "that Spain would be your native soil."

"At this date I am not likely to accept apologies."

"Nor am I likely to offer any."

None of the men were aware of Angie's immediate presence until she was very close. None of them paid much attention to her even then. Not until she had whipped out the long, poisoned splinter from behind her back and thrust it, hard, up under Borgia's ribs, aiming for his vampire's heart.

19

Feeling doubly repulsed by the behavior of Duke Cesare and the blackened and hideous spectacle of his father's body, I hastened to distance myself from the Vatican through which, for some eleven years, they had sought to dominate the world. Rome in general agreed with me in being ready to see the last of the Borgias; Alexander's death was celebrated in a general wave of rejoicing. At the same time, out in the farms and villages of the Romagna, many mourned the impending fall from power of his son, the young man who had given their towns the best government they could remember.

As for myself, I rejoiced in my new freedom. Indeed it was freedom in a degree that I had never yet experienced; that night marked the first time since the beginning of my life as a vampire that I felt myself under no obligation, either to the Borgias or to that even grimmer master called Revenge.

Of course my liberty was not perfect; I suppose that in this world no one's ever is. In my case the sharpest boundary was drawn by the beautiful Lucrezia, for whom my love was undiminished. She had not accepted my explanation as to why I had severed relations with her brother in his hour of great need; but I convinced myself that if I were to go about the matter properly, she could

eventually be made to understand. Though devoted to
Cesare, she understood as clearly as anyone that he really
was a treacherous scoundrel.

Before leaving Rome I had one more opportunity to
speak to Madonna in the underground complex where we
had met on my most recent return to Rome. The murdered
bear was gone now, but ropes and chains still hung from
the ceiling, as if in readiness for some other creature to
take its place.

At the time of our final meeting in that chamber, days
had passed since Alexander's death, but Lucrezia was
reluctant to start back for Ferrara as long as her beloved
brother's life, health, and fortune still hung so perilously in
the balance.

I presented myself before her, and we began a conversation that quickly turned into an argument. Madonna
Lucrezia declared, with great spirit and passion, that dear
Cesare at this moment needed all the help that everyone
could give him, and I was a scoundrel for choosing this
time to leave his service. I in turn described the way in
which her brother had mortally insulted me, and assured
the lady that if he were not her brother, he would even now
be sharing in the funeral rites, such as they were, of
Alexander.

To vindicate myself in Lucrezia's eyes, I justified, in
legalistic detail, my reasoned refusal to take part in the
ordered cleaning-out of her father's treasury, the thievery
of money that, as everyone admitted, belonged to the
Church. As far as I was concerned, their father might have
stolen freely from the Church he was sworn to protect, and
Cesare might continue to do so, if he considered such
actions compatible with the Borgia honor—but theft of
any kind has always been utterly repugnant to the honor of

Drakulya, and that the contemplated thievery was sacrilegious only made the matter considerably worse.

I asked Lucrezia whether she had never heard of my reputation as a ruler, of the thousands—the numbers grew with the stories, from year to year—of impaled bodies of bandits that lined my highways? Her reply—something to the effect that if I could impale all those people, why should I draw back at a little pilfering in a good cause?—showed her failure to grasp the true moral principles involved.

It argues much for the closeness of our relationship that, after we had such a discussion, we were still on speaking terms. I of course volunteered to escort Lucrezia safely home to Ferrara. Word had reached her in Rome that her husband had come home from one of his artillery outings rather sooner than expected, and was complaining of her absence. Or if she preferred, I was available to carry a message there for her.

But haughtily she said: "If you will not help me to save my brother, then I will accept no other gifts or favors from you." And as we parted matters between us were left in that unsatisfactory state.

I felt the need of rest, but at the same time I was troubled by a vague uneasiness—from my early youth (as I have explained elsewhere) I have been immune to fear, but no sane person made an enemy of Cesare without feeling some unease about it. Therefore I chose for my place of retirement the newest of my several Roman earths, one I felt confident the Borgias did not know about.

The location I had chosen for this facility was not far from dear Lucrezia's poison laboratory. Intrigued by the riches of ruins underground, I had spent some of my spare time in reconnoitering the vicinity and had in the process located another buried chamber that was eminently suited to my special needs.

The chamber in which I now established my new earth was another remnant of imperial Rome. Once it too must have been located on the surface of the ground. But now it formed a subterranean hideout, cut off virtually completely from the surface as far as access by breathers was concerned.

To this remote cavern I had managed to convey most of the Transylvanian soil from one of the caches that I now considered only doubtfully secure. Naturally I did this work at night, when the smallest crevice served as well as an open door to let me through. And in my new earth I was able to rest securely through the following day.

When night dawned again, I awoke feeling utterly tired of Rome, of Italy, of the entire situation in which I found myself. I felt convinced that the best thing to do was to put as much distance as I could between myself and the affairs of the Borgias as soon as possible. There was really nothing to hold me in the city any longer; nothing to keep me in Italy but my wavering affair with Lucrezia, and I foresaw no very smooth course for that in the immediate future. And there would of course be danger, subtle and miasmic, without any real prospect of anything in compensation. Borgia at the moment was too intensely concerned with his own survival to spend much time scheming for revenge, but with him one could never be too careful. I had no inclination to break my vow to Lucrezia with respect to her brother's safety, and certainly no positive wish to die.

(Here there follows a period of silence on the tape, broken occasionally by sighs and mutterings too faint for intelligibility.)

* * *

A Matter of Taste

There is a small narrative problem here, but I shall handle it this way: The following three or four years of my life, until approximately the end of 1506, constitute an interlude having little or nothing to do with the Borgias, belonging rather with a series of unrelated events that I may decide to chronicle at some time in the future. Therefore I shall now pass over this interlude in silence. Suffice it to say that I spent the bulk of those three or four years out of Italy, and most of the time away from my homeland also. Thus a considerable period elapsed in which I saw neither Lucrezia nor Cesare, though news of Duke Valentino did reach me on rare occasions.

It was in late 1506 that I began to interest myself closely in Borgia affairs once again. The proximate cause of this renewed concern was a message from Lucrezia brought to me, in a far land, by Constantia, who had committed it to memory, word for word. This was the first time in several years that I had seen my little gypsy friend, and her visit, apart from any news she brought, gladdened my heart.

In the interval since our last meeting, of course, the world had changed, though as so often happens the greatest changes were not immediately perceptible. Tomas de Torquemada, the Grand Inquisitor, had died in 1498, and Columbus in 1506. The newest Pope, Julius II, was directing his considerable fierce energies to the task of creating St. Peter's as we know it today, and to this end he had summoned to Rome a horde of artists and craftsmen, Michelangelo among them.

Lucrezia, at the time I received her urgent message, had already begun to be intensely on my mind. Ferrara would have been the natural place for me to seek her, and indeed I was considering such a pilgrimage when her communication arrived. Her situation in Ferrara had not changed drastically, except that her husband's father had died in the interval, and she was now the Duchess.

Her message began appealingly, telling me that I was the only one she considered strong and trustworthy enough to save her brother now, from whatever immediate danger was posed by his swarm of enemies and his own nature. She was not specific about the danger. None of this surprised me particularly; what did somewhat surprise me was that I was not urged to go immediately to Navarre, where Cesare was now, but summoned to Ferrara first.

I have said that it was not at all unexpected to hear that her brother was in trouble. I already knew that once the prop of his father's powerful support had been knocked from under him, his own career had gone downhill rapidly. He had careened briefly around Italy, surviving episodes of imprisonment, escape, and exile. He had confounded his enemies by recovering from his near-fatal illness of 1503, and then rebounding from one fresh political and personal setback after another, but in three years the total sum of his bad fortune had proved too much for him. As it would have done, I suppose, for any man.

Among his legion of enemies it was certainly necessary to number the new Pope, Julius II, a harsh autocrat who had long been a Borgia rival and was certainly no friend to Valentino now.

I found Madonna Lucrezia predictably in Ferrara, to all appearances happily and comfortably settled in there with her third husband, the fortunate Duke, and their several *bambini*. It was apparent to me at once that she had no wish ever again to play a role upon the world's stage, that great arena in which the power-hungry, vengeful, and materially ambitious act out their lives.

A Matter of Taste

Meanwhile, Lucrezia herself, in opting to remain in Ferrara, enjoying the consolations of religion, and sharing the life of the breathing man who had given her a decent life along with their children, had with clear eyes given up all thought of vampirism—for herself. She was not even tempted, finding the idea increasingly repulsive despite its promise of certain enhanced powers and a much extended life.

She was, however, even more concerned about her brother than her message had indicated. And she knew that her brother would never rest, in this world, until he could get back upon that stage himself.

Adding to Lucrezia's burden, so she informed me, was her increasing concern lest Cesare become a vampire, whether fully intending to do so or not; and she persisted in viewing this outcome as somehow bad for his soul. Madonna had some difficulty in expressing this latter objection in plain terms, at least to me, but eventually I managed to grasp her meaning.

"But that is not his main problem at the moment, dearest Vlad. He now serves King Jean of Navarre. At that court intrigue is rife." She nodded solemnly.

"Indeed?" And at what court, I wondered silently, was it not?

"Oh, you are right, perfectly right, to look at me with such cynicism. But my brother has repented his shameful treatment of you. The more he has seen of adversity, the more he has come to respect a man of honor like yourself. If you were only there to counsel him! I will be very grateful indeed—words alone will certainly not be able to express my gratitude—if you will help him now."

How could I refuse?

As I was on the point of leaving, Madonna Lucrezia

provided me with several small glass jars, cryptically labeled, each containing a different potion. Cesare would have need of these, she said, among such dangerous surroundings as the royal court of Navarre—as a matter of self-protection, of course. And as I was making the trip so speedily, I could bring them to him.

Before I left Lucrezia in Ferrara, I renewed in the most solemn terms my vow to her that, no matter what new disagreements might arise between us, I would never kill Cesare; nor would I ever do him any harm except when absolutely necessary to preserve my own honor or my life. She would have liked to extract an even stronger pledge, but beyond what I had already given I would not go.

And that, dear reader, was the last I ever saw of Lucrezia Borgia. It was at about this time, I believe, that she began her affair with a certain breathing poet, Pietro Bembo. Fortunately for Bembo, I was not in those days— in the case of Lucrezia, at least—a particularly jealous man.

Inhabitants of the late twentieth century know the district of Navarre, if they are aware of it at all, as one of the northern provinces of Spain. But at the time of which I write, it persisted as a rather more than semi-independent kingdom. The land was, and is, beautiful in its own way, delighting the traveler who is susceptible to such things with a great variety of scenery. As I made my way in that direction, as always keeping my eyes and ears open in inns, taverns, and along the roads, particularly as I approached my goal, I had little difficulty in gathering bits of information from which to piece together the latest adventures of Cesare.

* * *

A Matter of Taste

Viana, the town near which I was advised to look for Cesare, lay near the frontier between Navarre and Castile. A few months past, Borgia had taken service under Jean d'Albret, King of Navarre, who happened to be the brother of Cesare's long-suffering and almost forgotten wife. I have had no reason to mention the name of that unfortunate woman in these pages previously, and I see no reason to introduce it now.

The King of Navarre's chief problem was not very unusual. Don Juan, rebellious Count of Beaumont, held a nearby castle in defiance of his monarch, and Cesare Borgia, who had once threatened to make himself King of Italy, had been given the task of putting down this minor-league rebellion against his brother-in-law. It was almost as if the Pope himself, demoted to the office of priest in some obscure parish, were sent to a remote village to hear a few confessions and teach a class in catechism.

It caused me no surprise, on reaching the vicinity of Viana, to find that my old friend Constantia was there, keeping attendance on the man she loved. I talked with her briefly on the evening of my arrival, before I presented myself to Cesare, and expressed to her my doubts as to whether Lucrezia might have been over-optimistic about her brother's desire for a reconciliation with me.

My little gypsy vampire nervously twisted a strand of her long hair. "No—no, he wants you as his friend. I am sure of that."

I was surprised to hear her say that. Constantia's attitude toward me during this meeting was somewhat awkward and strained. But when I pressed her to tell me what was wrong, she assured me there was nothing. At one point I considered showing her the poison jars that had been entrusted to me by Lucrezia, but in the end I decided not to do so.

In the course of this encounter Constantia told me wistfully of her hope—it was scarcely any longer a plan— that she could someday convert Borgia to a vampire, perhaps even without his specific approval. Though this would necessarily mean the end of their passionate love, yet she thought it would save his life.

She had evolved a scheme, she told me, in which Cesare's death in a skirmish would be faked. He would then disappear and take up a new *nosferatu* life. All his breathing enemies would be convinced that he was indeed dead.

"But your lover, I suppose, will have none of this."

"No, he will not," Constantia admitted softly. Then she burst out: "Vlad, Vlad, will you help him?"

I thought. "I make no promises," I said at last. "At least I must speak to the man himself again before I can promise anything."

Half an hour later, arriving officially at Cesare's camp in the guise of a breathing messenger from his sister in Ferrara, I found him living in a military tent again. It was a scene somewhat reminiscent of our first meeting.

Michelotto, who had been with us then, was present once more, to improve the similarity. Corella from his first sight of me watched me warily, as I had known he must if ever we met again. But still he greeted me cordially enough and seemed ready to let bygones be bygones, to accept me once more as his comrade in arms if fate should so decree.

And Cesare himself was—penitent. There was really no other word. I was reminded of the repentant Bogdan.

As I entered the tent Duke Valentino rose from his folding camp chair, his dark eyes lighting up with joy at the sight of my face. "Drakulya! It has been many years—far too long a time! Not that I blame you—you have had good cause to turn away from me. But a man of your generous soul cannot forever hold against me what I said in fever, on the day of my father's death."

I grasped the hand that Borgia extended toward me. "My lord is gracious," I said, "to give me credit for a generous soul."

"But nonsense! Of course you have. Here, sit down. Michelotto, have them bring wine—but how foolish of me, I had forgotten."

"Drink your wine by all means, Captain General," I said. "If you are moved to celebration."

"I am moved to rejoicing that you have come—but tell me, what news of Lucrezia? You bring me a message from her?"

I handed over the sealed paper that I had brought, and sat silently watching Cesare as he broke the seal and perused the contents. I could well imagine that this man might have brooded long and darkly on what he perceived as my betrayal at a crucial moment. It was quite true that with a faithful vampire at his side, he might never have been brought to his present comparatively low condition. At the very least, he could have avoided his several bouts of imprisonment, or at least could have escaped from a certain castle without being forced to drop from a too-short rope, breaking several bones.

During my visit with his sister I had taken great pains to make it plain to her that, beyond the immediate aid that I would give for her sake, I had no intention of ever going back to work for Cesare. Nor did his warm welcome in Navarre change my mind. When he made the effort, he could be charm personified. Otherwise he was—to understate the case—a very difficult man to deal with, and sooner or later we would be bound to have another falling out.

* * *

Before we parted, on that first evening in Navarre, I handed over to him also the jars of drugs with which Lucrezia had entrusted me.

A moment later I wondered aloud whether one of the vessels contained the sweet-tasting drug so specific against vampires.

He shook his head lightly; the question seemed to have no impact on him. "No. Alas, if only I could get along with my fellow breathers as well as I do with the *nosferatu.*"

Dawn was not far off by that time. I was tired from my long journey, and it was time for me to seek my rest. I had had to carry my own earth with me on the trip, of course.

Constantia spoke with me again briefly before I retired. She was anxious to discover how my encounter with Cesare had gone.

"It went well enough," I told her. "He seems, as you say, quite willing to let bygones be bygones."

"And you, Vlad?" she burst out, obviously in the grip of some emotion she could no longer repress. "Are you not willing to do the same?"

"I have taken my solemn oath to Madonna Lucrezia," I assured her, "that I will not harm this man, unless under the most dire necessity of self-defense. I take the same oath now, again, to you."

"Vlad, if I could only believe you!"

I looked at her steadily for some moments. Then I said: "He has arranged with you to kill me, has he not? He has convinced you that I am planning to kill him?"

She could not utter a word, but the stricken look in her dark gypsy eyes was all the answer that I needed.

I gripped her hands, and was reminded of that first meeting, decades earlier, the young would-be witch and the apprentice vampire. I saw in Constantia's eyes that the same memory had come back to her.

"Go now," I said. "Tell him you have slain me, if you like. Tell him anything you choose. I am going to rest for the day, or through two days perhaps. After that I shall depart, and if the matter is left up to me, I shall never lay eyes again on Duke Valentino in this world. The oath that I have taken still binds me."

"Vlad!" And she kissed my hands before she hurried away.

"Guard yourself!" I called after her, softly. I was sure that she heard me, but she did not turn.

It was on the evening of the next day, in March in the year of Our Lord 1507, when Cesare Borgia, alone in his field tent, opened one of the small sealed jars that I had carried to him from Ferrara on the instructions of his beloved sister. He followed his sister's instructions, these printed in tiny coded symbols on the label, as he measured a small amount of the jar's contents into a cup of wine that stood on his small folding table. He put the jar, and the spoon he had used as a measure, carefully away, well out of sight. Then he blew out his light, as a signal to his troops that he did not wish to be disturbed, except for some grave emergency.

Around him the encampment of his modest army— no more than a couple of thousand men—was quiet.

Presently, Constantia, unseen and unheard by any of those other men, came to him, moving wraithlike through the tiny opening at the closed flap of his tent. In solid woman-form again, she cast aside her clothing and joined Cesare in his narrow military bed.

He had been lying very still, but he was not asleep.

"Tell me" were his first whispered words. "What of Drakulya?"

Constantia began weeping softly. "He is dead," she said.

"Staked properly through the heart, with wood? By your own hand?"

"Yes."

"You actually saw his body disappear?"

"Yes." She was weeping more hopelessly than ever now. "Yes, I have seen him disappear."

"My dearest love! I knew that I could count on you!" Cesare sat bolt upright in the narrow bed and reached for the cup of wine that until now had sat untasted on the nearby table. In a moment he had drained it to the dregs. Throwing the cup aside, he seized the woman who lay with him.

Borgia in his triumphant lust then knew her carnally, in the way of breathing man with breathing woman. Constantia wept on—for a little while—and yielded herself in silence to her deceived lover.

Presently, as he had on so many other nights, he pulled her mouth against his body, offering her his blood in return for further ecstasy. And then, drunken as he was with wine and Borgia drugs and revengeful triumph over a hated enemy, feeling invincibly secure in his good fortune, he tempted fate. Taking my little gypsy's unresisting hand, he used one of her own sharp nails to open the skin upon her breast. Then as a breather he enjoyed the final ecstasy, that of drinking vampire blood.

A little after that, as debauchees, like other folk, are wont to do, Cesare Borgia fell asleep.

And then, in the small hours of the morning, the gods of war threw dice and rolled a chance that altered all our lives. What actually occurred was some puny blunder of patrols in darkness, not a real attack on the camp—the rebellious Count Beaumont had neither the men or the nerve for any undertaking so bold as that. But the effect was disproportionate.

Roused before dawn while still under the influence of the drug, given confused misinformation by some frightened sentries, Cesare behaved quite uncharacteristically. He mounted quickly and went charging out recklessly toward the reported enemy position, accompanied only by a terrified squire. All who saw him said later that Valentino acted in a bellicose, drunken fashion, all but losing control of his horse, superb horseman that he had always been.

When he came upon a small squad of the enemy, he rode alone, rampaging in berserk fashion, right in among them—and was brutally butchered for his pains.

When this happened Michelotto was still back in camp, not dreaming that his master was reacting to a minor crisis in such a mad, seemingly suicidal way.

It was midmorning before Borgia's friends and attendants could locate the place where he had fallen and gather him up. And by that time Cesare's butchered body had long since ceased to breathe.

It was midafternoon of the same day before a haggard, grief-stricken Michelotto entered, alone, a certain crumbling mausoleum in a long-disused cemetery on the far side of Viana. He was carrying a carpenter's maul, and a long, thick, keenly sharpened wooden stake. Grunting, he dragged the heavy lid off the coffin on the right-hand side and stared down with hatred at the woman's form, young and attractive in appearance, that lay so peacefully within.

Corella raised his stake—and in an instant was seized

from behind, turned around, and thrown staggering across the little room. I had been waiting in ambush beside Constantia's still form, expecting that sometime during the daylight hours a would-be assassin would appear.

"Drakulya!"

"As you see—but I was expecting that your master would come to perform this task himself."

Michelotto's features worked. "My master is dead."

For once the man had surprised me. I knew that Cesare had gone to answer some military alarm during the hours of darkness, for he had not been in his tent when I found Constantia there before dawn, heavily drugged and almost totally unconscious. Under my ministrations she had regained her senses long enough to whisper, as I was conveying her safely to her earth, a few details of what had happened to her in Borgia's bed.

Now she slept on, unwaking and undead, in a slumber that for all I knew might endure for years. And Michelotto, a wooden stake securely through his own heart, was soon laid to rest on the floor of the mausoleum near her feet.

By the time I was able to rejoin the innocent breathing citizens who were mourning Borgia's fall, and had laid my hands on his fresh corpse, the time was after noon. At the first touch of his cooling, stiffening flesh, I could sense that Borgia had been changed. His last drunken session with the drugged Constantia had been too much for him. Until I learned of his death I had been in a quandary as to what to do next, having taken an oath not to kill this man; and now my position was complicated further.

For the time being, it was easy enough simply to let the breathing people of Navarre, soldiers, servants, and loyal citizens under good King Jean, bury the King's brother-in-law. Among a modest host of mourners I followed to his grave my quondam friend and former employer, more recently my enemy. Then I settled back to wait, prepared to allow nature to take its course.

I am reasonably sure that no one but myself among the crowd at his first interment—the breathers' ceremony —realized that we were burying a vampire—although some might have suspected. Cesare did start to come out of his death-sleep when being taken to the tomb—his original tomb, in the church. Those of his pallbearers with particularly keen senses might have been aware of him stirring lightly inside his coffin. At one point I even heard him giggling.

Whether he now comes back and walks or not, I told myself, the news of what has happened to him is going to come as a devastating shock to Lucrezia. Well, I was not going to be the one to carry it back to her. The more I thought the matter over, the more firmly I understood that she must be as guilty as her brother in their plot to use two vampires, an old enemy and an inconvenient lover, to remove each other from the scene.

It was while I was listening to the tombside prayers that another interesting point first struck me. It was highly unlikely that Cesare, determined to the end not to become a vampire, would have made provision to have on hand a supply of his native earth against that eventuality. I supposed Constantia in her earlier concern for his welfare might have considered the matter, might even have done something about it. But Constantia was beyond consultation now.

But as I thought the matter over I realized that there

really ought to be no problem at all. The Borgias, as everyone knew, were originally Spanish. Rodrigo, the patriarch, had brought his illegitimate family to Rome only when his climb to high church office compelled him to spend almost all his time in that city. Therefore the ground we trod on here in Navarre—or at least that just across the border in Castile—*was* Cesare's native earth.

Actually, of course, although I did not know it at the time, his birthplace had been Rome.

And now my enemy was dead—well, more or less—but certainly not by my hand or connivance. I considered that my vow to Lucrezia was still proudly intact.

The minor war between King Jean and the rebellious Count dragged on, as such things will. The world of breathers saw me as Lucrezia's emissary hanging around, doing such occasional intelligence service for the King of Navarre as made me for the time being a welcome guest. I made an earth for myself near Constantia's resting place, and rested there myself in daytime, slumbering lightly. I considered it my responsibility to be her guardian. Several times at dusk I allowed myself to be seen near the spot, in one impressive shape or another, by a few local inhabitants. After that I felt reasonably sure we were not going to be disturbed.

And each night, when the last worshipper had left the church in Viana, I stepped in to visit the tomb in which Lucrezia's brother had been laid to rest. Each night I expected that he would wake, and walk. But night after night went past, and there was no sign of Cesare. Could I have been mistaken? Had he not been made *nosferatu* after all?

And then, one night, he—stirred. I could hear him

scratching and twitching in his tomb, behind the modest depth of marble.

It took some maneuvering to get him out, even vampire as I was, without disturbing any of the pious stonework. But once I had him out, there was no possible doubt as to what had happened to Cesare. He was alive, but suffering grievously from want of his native earth. In the process of transformation he had gone from being a drugged breather to a drugged vampire. He could not come properly out of his dazed and dangerous condition: not totally unconscious, but totally helpless. As he lay sprawled on the stone floor of the church, his glazed eyes widened in astonishment to see me still alive, then fixed on me malignantly. But he could not speak.

I have never been one to agonize at length over any problem, moral or otherwise. By my lights, to stand by while Cesare died would have been a certain violation of my oath to Lucrezia, as much as directly killing him. I assumed that burying him in Castile would take care of his problem, but my current watch over Constantia took precedence. I considered myself fortunate in being able to enlist some local gypsies—relatives, in some degree, of those dwelling near my home castle, and no strangers to the ways of *nosferatu*—to take him over the border and plant him there, somewhere, wherever they could find a likely spot, in what was indubitably Castilian soil.

I should add here, parenthetically, that nearly two hundred years passed before a Spanish bishop, having studied Cesare's original grave marker in the Viana church and read his history, became incensed that such a scoundrel should lie in such a holy place, and ordered his bones removed. Those relics—or someone's—were dug up accordingly, and the pieces that did not crumble into dust were reburied under a nearby road. When, in a more scientific spirit, the supposed site of this second interment of Valentino was excavated in 1871, the bones unearthed on that occasion all disintegrated before anything of a scientific nature could be accomplished with them.

20

Mrs. Hassler had gone home around midnight, half-asleep, half-hypnotized, tenderly escorted by Mr. Maule. She was back, unexpectedly, at his front door around noon, where she stood tapping rather timidly on the doorbell, though the doorway at the moment was empty of any barrier. The workmen Maule had summoned to do repairs were already on the job.

She looked around the ruined room in wonder. She had had the strangest dreams, she told him when he appeared, and she just had to make sure that he was all right.

Her host, looking badly in need of rest, asked her forgiveness and wondered whether she could come back in the evening.

Around midnight John and Angie had gone to a nearby hotel, at Mr. Maule's expense, of course.

The TV and newspapers, Joe Keogh noted, on the afternoon following the discovery of a pair of bodies on the low roof, were already starting to talk about the affair as the Helicopter Murders. The battered corpses gave the appearance of having been dropped from a spot in the air eighty or a hundred stories above the new construction on the plaza. Or else they might have been thrown, catapulted outward from somewhere high on the central building; but it was difficult to see how that could have been accomplished.

Joe had just been called in by Captain Charley Snider for an informal talk. He hadn't been back to visit the Homicide Bureau for a considerable time, and it was interesting to see the changes.

Charley, large and black, was not as paunchy as he had begun to be a couple of years ago; dieting, Joe thought, was taking over everwhere. But the captain had a little more gray hair every time Joe ran into him.

As far as Joe knew, Liz Wiswell, the waitress, had not yet been reported missing, but of course it was necessary to anticipate that she would be. Well, he'd worry about that when the time came.

Charley was saying: "Neither member of this pair is anybody we really worried about losin'. Fact is, someone clean up a lot of old paperwork for us here." As usual, Charley's black dialect came and went, perhaps at will, perhaps randomly. Joe had frequently wondered about it, but he'd never asked.

Joe grunted something. Behind his desk Charley was making no effort to hide his satisfaction at having a couple of violent offenders taken off the streets.

"Know what this remind me of, Joe?"

"Should I try to guess?"

"I think you know damn well what it reminds me of. About eleven years ago, when you were just a poor-ass city cop on the pawn-shop detail. At that time we in this department observed a cluster of rather bizarre events."

"We did indeed. But they were not too much like these events."

"Well, yes and no. I seem to detect something of the

same—artistic touch?—in this affair today. Nobody report any helicopters flyin' around north Michigan last night. Anyway, I would like to consult with you today on just a couple things."

"Shoot."

"What about this Valentine Kaiser?"

Joe shook his head no. "I'm guessing again—only guessing—"

Charley was nodding. "I know you only guessing. Shoot."

"You're not going to find him."

"If we ever do find 'im, I s'pose he's dead?"

"Highly probable. Yes."

"We ever gonna find who killed him?"

"I doubt it."

"Uh huh. Well, that bring me to the second query. Concernin' these folk on whom the speculation is maybe they were dropped from a helicopter. Given your experience in similar matters, you think our chance of busting the dropper is very high?"

"*My* speculation is, no. I know you've got to at least make it look like a big effort, Charley, but my advice is that you'll get more out of your manpower working on some other case entirely."

"You offerin' me not much to hope for, man."

"Honey?"

"What?"

"We are still getting married, aren't we?"

Angie looked at John. He looked a great deal better now than he had about twenty hours ago, when they'd checked into the fancy hotel. She supposed her own appearance had improved also. She certainly felt much more human.

She said: "You're not trying to get out of it, are you? Have I scared you, more than the vampires?"

"Me? No!" He was properly outraged. "It's just that I didn't know whether—after everything you had to go through—"

"After I've gone through being attacked by vampires and all the rest—after I've done—what I had to do—well, I'm not going to let them win after all. They're not going to keep me from running the rest of my life the way I want to run it."

They were both thinking about that when the knock sounded on the door.

John looked, and then relaxed. "It's Uncle Matthew."

Dapper, well dressed, looking young, well rested, and healthy, he came in for once with the manner of one uncertain of his welcome.

"Uncle Matthew," said Angie immediately.

"Yes."

"Are you coming to our wedding? I know you said there was a problem about the date. But I really hope you can."

He came to her. Eyes sparkling, he bowed and kissed her hand.

"I shall be there. Somehow."

He was once called Dracula, but in Chicago
in our day he is known as Matthew Maule.
John Southerland, like the rest of the
Southerland family, calls him Uncle Matthew.
After all he's an Old Friend of the Family and
he has risked his un-life more than once to
protect the Southerlands. But with Matthew
rendered comatose by a fiendish plot from beyond time, the Southerlands must rise to *his*
defense—and battle five hundred years worth
of Dracula's enemies!

A MATTER OF TASTE

52575

0 37145 00399 3

ISBN 0-812-52575-2

A
Tom Doherty Associates, Inc.
Book
Printed in the USA